The Muck

JOHN RYLAND

This is a work of fiction. Names, characters, places, and incidents are products of the author's imagination or are used fictitiously and are not to be construed as real. Any resemblance to actual events, locations, organizations, or persons, living or dead, is entirely coincidental.

World Castle Publishing, LLC
Pensacola, Florida
Copyright © 2023 John Ryland
Hardback ISBN: 9781960076977
Paperback ISBN: 9781960076984
eBook ISBN: 9781960076991
First Edition World Castle Publishing, LLC, July 3, 2023
http://www.worldcastlepublishing.com

Licensing Notes

All rights reserved. No part of this book may be used or reproduced in any manner whatsoever without written permission, except in the case of brief quotations embodied in articles and reviews.
Cover: Karen Fuller
Editor: Karen Fuller

ONE

November 2019

Carrol Stivers opened the closet doors in the upstairs spare bedroom, sparing a peek over her shoulder at the closed door though she knew no one was around. Deeming the coast clear, she reached up and clutched a shoebox in the middle of the neat stack on the shelf. She knew exactly which one she wanted. The boxes were stacked in an alternating, brick-like pattern on purpose, so she could pull one out while leaving the rest of the stack in place. This wasn't her first visit to this particular box.

She looked at the square hole created by the box she'd just removed and smiled. There was something pleasurable about the geometry of the hole and the stack itself. Like the boxes, she, too, was good at hiding a secret.

Her eyes fell to the box she'd just removed, then the letter in her hand. She sighed with a mixture of emotions. She didn't like keeping secrets, but this one wasn't hers alone.

She went to the bed and sat down, holding them on her lap while she switched on the bedside lamp. She set the box aside and unfolded the letter again. She'd read it twice but couldn't believe it either time.

She looked at the paper in her hand, marveling over

the fantastic nature of the tale it covered. Elvey Stivers—her husband's mother—had gone into great detail about dark spirits and witches and the waters outside her house, leading Carrol to believe that her slow descent to senility was complete.

Named Elizabeth Gail, Elvey had lived in the old river house all eighty-two years of her life. It had belonged to her parents, and when they died, she stayed. When she married a poor man named L.C., he moved into the house with her. They'd had two children, both boys. Alvin was the oldest, but he'd died of a mysterious ailment at a young age. Years later, they'd had Barry, her husband.

Carrol ran a hand through her short, neatly styled brown hair and looked at the window, her attention captured by the rain. It fell from the cold winter sky and lashed against the pane with what she considered undue violence. The wind was up. It was going to be a long night.

She turned back to the letter. Shaking her head, she thumbed through the eight pages, torn from a wire-ringed notebook like the ones she'd used in high school. Her eyes fell on the closing line, written in the rough, uneven script she'd gotten used to. A chill ran through her as her eyes passed over the words.

"I beg you, please be careful and keep a sharp eye on your son. Stay away from this place. It's bad for you, for Barry, and especially for your son. This is no place for the innocent. Love, Elvey."

Her eyes narrowed as she drew in a deep breath. Over the years, she'd only met the woman twice, once at her wedding to Barry and once when her own son, Brandon, was five. Despite the lack of face-to-face meetings, she'd come to know the woman closely through the years.

By way of infrequent telephone calls sometimes necessitated by arthritis in Elvey's hands and a series of letters, she'd learned all about the woman as well as her own husband's troubled youth. At the request of the writer, she'd kept them from Barry all these years.

"His mind and heart have been touched in ways you can't imagine," Elvey said long ago. "I would prefer if you kept our correspondence our little secret."

Carrol's eyes fell to the shoebox. She set the pages aside and removed the cover, revealing a stack of letters, every one written by her mother-in-law. The early ones were light and didn't have much substance of note. She'd talked about the river flooding, her small garden, and new trinkets she'd picked up at flea markets. Especially garden gnomes. Elvey loved them. The weirder, the better.

As the years progressed, however, her letters slowly turned dark, bitter, and sometimes angry. Sometimes she called Brandon by the wrong name. Sometimes she rambled about "things that she could not control." She also talked about the garden gnomes she'd collected, saying they were good luck charms and "the bearer of truth."

The only constant was that she received them on Tuesdays. Elvey knew her son was a banker and that they occasionally took Mondays off and usually played golf on Wednesdays. Every banker, she insisted, worked on Tuesday. "That's when they really screw you over, on Tuesdays," she once said.

Mailing the letters so that they arrived on Tuesday made sure there was virtually no chance of Barry intercepting the mail. For her, it was vital that he not find out about the letters. There was a deep animosity between them that Carrol couldn't wrap her head around, but there was also a little fear too.

The old woman was undoubtedly lonely. Although she often expressed her joy that her son and his family never visited, Carrol thought there had to be pain as well. She thought it was a very strange family dynamic, being very close to her own parents. In the early days of their marriage, she'd made attempts to bridge the divide but gave up after years of disappointment.

The current situation did, however, make the holidays easier. They always went to her parents for Thanksgiving and Christmas, and she loved it. Brandon loved it. Barry liked her father's expensive booze.

Carrol pushed her hand through her hair again, sweeping a few loose strands from her face. Her hand went to the letter, picking it up as if it were an ancient parchment.

"This may be my last letter. I haven't felt well lately, and the cold has put a pain in my chest that won't go away."

Carrol shook her head. She hated it when old people predicted their own death, considering it a cry for attention. Her eyes darted back and forth across the lines, reading the letter for the third time and hoping to make sense of it.

When she finished, a hand went to her mouth, covering it as she stared at the pages in disbelief. It still sounded like the ramblings of a lonely, senile old woman. Witches and haunted mud and spirits that stirred the waters. It sounded like so much backwoods voodoo to her.

She'd read and heard about black magic practitioners in and around New Orleans and other places, but this was Alabama, and that sort of thing just didn't happen here. *Hell*, she thought, *even in the swamps of Louisiana, it was most likely all superstition or just plain old ignorance.*

Her shoulders slumped as she imagined the old woman sitting in her little shack alone, widowed many years ago, and then abandoned by her only living son. Carrol imagined her in a ratty housecoat, sitting beneath a lone lamp, scratching out the letters in the dead of night.

"Things move in the shadows, Carrol. They think I can't see them, but I can."

How could she not be bitter and angry? Especially with the long winter nights and the gloomy weather. An old woman, watching the ever-present threat of being flooded by an unchecked river, frail and alone. Scared.

"*The bastards hate me because I keep people away from the waters. Away from them.*"

Add in advanced age, and it was the perfect scenario for fantastic stories of ghosts and witches. Like forecasting her own death, it was all a cry for help from a desperate woman.

"*I hope you never find yourself in this situation. Fighting with every breath against a power stronger than you are.*"

Carrol sighed, shaking her head. She folded the letter and slipped it back into the envelope it came in, determined to respond quickly. She'd fill her letter with bright, happy news in hopes of lifting the old woman's spirits, asking again if she'd rather move in with them instead of staying way down there alone. Of course, she'd refuse, citing Barry's lack of desire to "look at my ugly face every day."

The two weren't close, to say the least. Elvey had written many times about the friction they'd endured in his teenage years. She'd even considered sending him to the military school over in Marion. Had the arrest of one of his girlfriends during his senior year not shaken him out of his rebellious stage, she would have.

The girl had been caught robbing a liquor store and charged with armed robbery. She'd gotten a lengthy sentence, and it shook Barry and his friends out of their raucous lifestyle.

In the end, he'd gone to community college up in Souls Harbor for two years before transferring to Mississippi State for his degree. As far as she knew, he hadn't been back home since and rarely talked to his mother.

Carrol put the envelope on top of the stack and closed the box. She put it back in its hiding place and straightened the boxes around it. Closing the doors with a sigh, she switched off the light before leaving the room.

"Putting the tree up already?" Barry asked, interrupting the soft sound of "White Christmas" coming from the Bose radio in the corner of the room.

Carrol turned and looked at her husband, standing in the doorway of their family room. His normally well-groomed dark hair was mussed slightly, and his suit coat hung open. His tie hung loosely around his neck, and a battered briefcase at the end of his right arm.

"Rough day?"

Barry grunted. "About the same. End of the year and whatnot."

"I'm sorry." Her eyes darted to the clock on the wall. It was well after seven.

"It's fine." He threw a hand at the tree. "Christmas already?"

"Uh-huh. We'll go to Mom and Dad's next week for Thanksgiving."

"It is that time of year again, I suppose." Barry crossed the room, depositing his briefcase on the mahogany buffet on the way. He went to the bar and dropped ice cubes into a crystal tumbler, pouring bourbon over them before turning back to his wife.

"Thanksgiving is late this year. Christmas is right around the corner, you know," she said as she placed another ornament on the tree.

Barry sipped the drink and grimaced. "I guess it is," he said, looking at his glass. "What do you want for Christmas?"

Carrol forced a smile. Her husband hadn't picked out a gift for her on his own in years. Although a part of her considered it sad, another part knew that she had more vacuum cleaners and sets of cookware than any woman needed.

"I've got a few things in mind. I'll text you some ideas."

Barry nodded, then sipped his drink again. He went to the sofa and sat down with a groan. "My mother called me today."

Carrol stiffened as she lifted an ornament from the box next to her. "Oh really?" she asked, forcing her hand to steady as she placed the glass ball on the tree's limb. She didn't look around, sure that he'd notice the apprehension on her face.

"Yeah." He shrugged the arm, not holding his drink. "She said she wasn't feeling well."

"What's wrong?" Carrol spared him a quick glance, glad to find his gaze on the drink in his hand. She turned back to the tree and placed another ornament. A part of her always worried that the old woman would forget about their secret letters and say something about them to Barry.

"Who the hell knows. She's probably fine. You know how old people are, always talking about dying and crap. I think she's fine. Probably just a cold. She just wants some attention."

"Maybe she's got the flu or something," Carrol said, remembering the letter. Elvey had mentioned a heavy chest. "It's been going around. That's rough for an older person."

"Not hardly. She never leaves the house. Where would she get the flu?"

Carrol shrugged as she adjusted the decorations on the tree. "I don't know. The weather's been bad. Maybe she's got something."

Barry shrugged and took another sip of his drink. "I told her to go to the doctor if she felt bad. I mean, what am I supposed to do?"

Carrol's shoulders dropped. "Barry, she's your mother. She might really be sick."

He stood abruptly. "And she might just be putting on to get attention. You don't know her like I do, Carrol."

"Maybe she's just lonely, with the holidays coming up and all."

"She's just being melodramatic. I've told you how she does."

"I know. It's just—"

"Just what?" Barry asked. "Do you want to forgo visiting your parents for Thanksgiving and go down there? We can eat cold turkey sandwiches, drink fruit punch from plastic cups, and listen to her complain about what a terrible kid I was."

"If you wanted to, I would." She leveled her gaze at him, standing her ground.

"Well, I don't want to. She's fine." Barry rounded the couch and went to the buffet. He finished his drink before sitting it down hard. Grabbing his briefcase, he turned back to her. "I don't have time for this right now, Carrol. My mother has been doing this kind of crap for years. She makes things up and runs with them. She's got issues." He tapped the side of his head with his fingertip. "Big issues."

"She is getting older, Barry. Old people get sick."

"The only place she's sick is in the head. I don't have time for this, Carrol."

She watched him storm from the room, wondering if there was any affection at all within him for his mother. She shook her head and turned back to the tree. Guilt swamped her when she considered they'd not spent one Christmas with the old woman their whole marriage. Seventeen Christmases and not one with Elvey Stivers.

Her mind returned to the last line of the letter she'd received in today's mail. *"Stay away from this place. It's bad for you, for Barry, and especially for your son. This is no place for the innocent."*

She shook her head, turning back to the tree. Her eyes fell on the small round cast of Brandon's hand that he'd made in preschool. The blue paint was cracked and faded but only served to testify to its durability. Her hand went to it, a finger gently lifting it from the branch to afford her a better view.

A sad smile slipped across her lips as she remembered the early years. Everything was perfect. He was a bright-eyed child with a warm smile and a loving heart. Back then, he was just like any other kid in his class, with the notable exception that he didn't talk.

She sighed and released the ornament, watching it swing back into place against the green plastic branch of the artificial Frasier Fir.

As the sounds of "Oh Holy Night" filled the room, Carrol closed her eyes and said a prayer. She prayed for Brandon, for her marriage, for her husband, and for Elvey Stivers. All of them presented their own challenges that left her sometimes feeling like she was herding cats.

Carrol opened her eyes as she turned back to the box of ornaments, intent on finishing the tree even though Barry had killed her Christmas Spirit. She was startled when she found her son, Brandon staring at her wide-eyed at her. His mouth was open in an excited, silent scream.

"You wanna help?" she asked, smiling. He would make the job more difficult, but his enthusiasm and joy would make her feel better after talking to Barry.

He nodded emphatically, clapping his hands as he came to her.

"I know you love decorating the tree," she said, handing him a glass ball. "Be careful. Okay?"

He nodded, flashing her an excited smile as he took the ornament carefully in his hands. His head tilted to one side as he examined the thin, golden glass of the ball.

Carrol watched him carefully. On more than one occasion, he'd dropped and broken one of the balls, once cutting himself. She watched as he scanned the tree for a few minutes before placing the ornament gingerly on one of the branches. He stepped back, smiling proudly.

She retrieved another ornament and handed it to him. His slow process would take hours to finish, but she didn't mind. His innocent joy was what the season was about. "You're doing great, kiddo."

Brandon smiled at her, then returned his attention to the tree. He held the ornament close to a limb, decided that it didn't look right, then repeated the process on another. He found the perfect limb on his third try, then stepped back and clapped again.

Physically, he was fifteen years old. Mentally, no one could definitively say. He was smart in some areas but struggled in others. There was more to him than the casual observer would notice and less when you got to know him.

Carrol sighed. He wasn't perfect, but he was her only child, and she'd do whatever it took to keep him safe. As she watched him, her mind retrieved Elvey Stivers' warning, and a shudder ran through her.

It's okay, she thought. *They are safe. Brandon is safe.* They were miles from Elvey's place, and apparently, there was no plan to go. She didn't believe the stuff in the letters, but there was no sense in taking chances.

Pulled from her thoughts by Brandon's gentle clapping, she smiled at her son. "It looks awesome. Good job, sweetheart."

TWO

The collective voices of a hundred or so mourners singing "May the Circle be Unbroken" filled Mount Zion Freewill Baptist church, drowning all but the loudest traffic that passed by on County Road 117 in extreme southern Hillburn County. Their motley collection of voices echoed back down from the wooden cathedral ceiling to Carrol Stivers, sitting with her family in the front row.

The people in the small unincorporated community that Elvey Stivers called home for over eighty years were simple people living simple lives, and from the looks of the crowd, every one of them turned out to see her off. The group of mourners that had packed themselves into the church, many wearing clean overalls and white shirts, shared the collective warmth on a cold winter day. Most days in January in central Alabama were wet, cloudy, and cold. Today was no exception.

Carrol patted her son's hand as it picked at a small tear in the well-worn red fabric of their pew. When he looked up, she offered a smile, and his hand went limp beneath hers.

Although she felt every squirm, every tug at the tie around his neck, she thought he was doing well. He was uncomfortable and had looked at everything in the church except the casket in front of them. Part of her awaited a meltdown, almost hoping for one. At least that way, she could take him outside and wouldn't have to face the guilt of never visiting the old woman who lay dead before them.

She hadn't settled on her feelings yet. Of course, part of her was sad for the woman. She was her husband's mother, and she'd seemed nice enough though she was a bit eccentric. They'd only visited twice, so there was no real emotional connection.

Another part of her was relieved. Surely Barry would sell the old place, thus ending the need to worry about keeping Brandon away. Although she didn't believe a word of the old woman's warnings, she wasn't keen on taking chances either. There must have been something. Why else would she repeatedly beg her to keep them away?

Carrol sighed, casually scratching her head while she scanned the crowd over her shoulder. Her eyes met those of an old man sitting on the opposite side of the aisle, three pews behind them.

The man was tall and thin, both to the point that it was almost comical. The starched white collar of his shirt was buttoned tightly over the loose skin of his neck. He wore a dark blue pair of overalls that looked new and no tie. He stared back at her, his thin lips pursed, and shook his head ever so slightly.

They know, Carrol thought to herself, sure that Elvey had told everyone that her only son's family never came to see her. They know we're assholes, and every one of them are condemning us all to hell in their minds right now.

Tearing her eyes from the stranger, she looked at Barry. He sat staring forward, not looking at the preacher or his mother lying in the casket just a few feet away. His face was solemn but not sad. Lost in thought, his eyes looked distant, distracted.

She hadn't witnessed a single tear that he'd shed for his mother. Something told her that she wouldn't. He'd relayed the news to her with the same fatter-of-fact voice he used for business dealings. "Mother is dead. The funeral will be Saturday at one o'clock."

When her son's hand slipped from beneath hers, she dropped her gaze to him. He looked a lot like the younger version of Barry from when they were dating. The angular jawline, the brown wavy hair, and the big dark eyes were all from her husband. She liked to think tender-heartedness and the ability to find joy in simple things came from her.

So far, he'd weathered the funeral better than she had hoped. The gray, foam earplugs helped to lessen the noise, but as the service drug on, he was becoming more restless. She could tell he didn't like being so close to the casket, but neither did she. If she had to, she could take him outside and let him walk around for a while. She knew, however, that if he ever got outside, she'd never get him back in, no matter how cold it was.

She looked to the preacher as he stepped back up to the podium as the song ended, holding his hands up in a call for quiet. The gray suit jacket he wore had seen many Sunday sermons, and the stomach it was stretched across had seen many Sunday suppers. He swiped a hand from left to right across his well-oiled hair as he surveyed the crowd.

"How do you remember a person?" he asked suddenly, his voice filling the small church. "I reckon that depends on how you knew them. I remember Elvey Stivers as a wonderful, caring, giving woman, A God-fearing woman. But of all the battles she fought—and there were many—of all the people she helped—and there were many more—of all the things she did, I can't help but think about all the names that Elizabeth Gail Stivers went by. Each name having its own connotation. 'Elvey,' to her friends, 'Mother,' to her family, 'Mama Stivers' to most of the kids that grew up around her- many of whom are adults here today with children of their own.

"She was a woman who touched a small community in

ways that cannot be measured, that cannot be told by one old preacher. She was a woman well-known and well-loved and one who loved right back in her own unique way. There is evil in this world. I don't have to tell anyone here that." His eyes darted ever so briefly to Barry. "But there is also a lot of good people who stand in the face of that evil. Unfortunately, we've lost one of the good ones."

Carrol closed her hand around Brandon's as the preacher turned to the casket. He took a deep breath, further stressing the buttons on his jacket. "Elizabeth Gail Stivers, we commend your spirit to God Almighty, the risen Lord, and our one and only hope in a lost and dying world. May he keep you and hold you close to his bosom forever and forever. Amen."

A hushed "amen" went up from the crowd. Carrol wrapped Brandon's hand in hers and looked into his eyes. She raised her eyebrows questioningly as she nodded, silently asking if he felt up to standing at the head of the receiving line. They'd talked at length about the process and what to expect. When they'd entered the church, she still wasn't sure he'd do it.

Brandon scratched his head, then tugged at his tie again. He cast a wary eye toward the casket, then looked back to his mother and shook his head.

Carrol offered a smile as she stood. She put a hand on Barry's back, tugging gently at his suit coat as he turned. He looked around without saying a word. His face was as stoic as it had been for days.

"I don't know if Brandon's up for the whole thing up there," she nodded toward the casket as the congregation began to stand. The crowd stood around between the pews, waiting for the family to take their place.

Barry shrugged. "Okay," he said flatly.

Carrol watched him begin to move away but grabbed his arm. "Do you need us there? I feel like we should be there. For you."

Barry shook his head, a thin smile coming to his lips. "Why should today be any different?"

Carrol stood frozen, stung by the comment. The heat of embarrassment and anger rose in her cheeks in equal parts. Her eyes narrowed as she watched him move forward. He walked solemnly to the casket and turned to face the crowd. Sparing her a brief glance, he clasped his hands in front of him and nodded to the preacher.

Carrol put a hand to her forehead as she tried to gather herself. Her mind was reeling. Things weren't great between them, she knew, but saying something like that at a time like this was simply unconscionable. What did he even mean?

Her eyes drifted to the preacher, still behind his pulpit above and beyond the casket. He was staring at her with beady eyes, his brow furrowed slightly. When he looked away, she followed his gaze to the congregation. Everyone was staring at her and Brandon.

"Sweetie," she whispered, struggling to contain her discomfort. "This is something we need to do for your father. Can you stand with me? I'll hold your hand."

Brandon looked at his father, then at the casket. He shrank and closed his eyes, nodding.

"Thank you. You're a brave young man. I'm very proud of you," she whispered.

Brandon offered an uncomfortable smile as she nudged him forward. She took his hand and led him to his father's side, putting him between them.

"And now," the preacher nodded to the pianist, and the first chords of 'Amazing Grace' flooded the church. "The family will receive your condolences."

Carrol squeezed Brandon's hands as the crowd began to slowly make their way down the aisle toward them. She pretended to wipe her eye, giving Brandon a quiet "It's okay."

The truth that she hid from him was that she wasn't sure if it would be "okay" or not. She looked at her husband's cold, expressionless face, and a shudder ran through her.

He's just upset, she told herself. He probably has a lot going through his mind right now, not the least of which is guilt. It's his mother's funeral.

I told him he should check on her.

Brandon glanced over his shoulder at the stranger in the casket. He'd never seen a dead body before, except on television and in video games. This woman didn't look dead. She just looked like she was taking a nap, the way Papa McCluskey did sometimes. Except most of the time, his mouth was open, and he snored.

His brow wrinkled as he studied her to see if she would take a breath. His mother said that she was "at peace," but the expression on her face didn't look anything like peaceful. If anything, she looked a little scared.

His eyes probed the face of the dead woman he didn't know. Someone had applied makeup to her skin, but it looked unnatural and only accentuated the deep lines around her eyes. Her white hair, washed and set, was puffy like a cloud.

She was his father's mother, but he had no memories of her. His father favored her some, but not a lot. She looked small. Small and afraid.

His mother's hand on the back of his head turned his attention back to the group of strangers filing slowly past. Most of them were dressed in what his mother had jokingly referred to as "hillbilly chic." He and his father and the fat preacher man were the only ones in a suit.

From his viewpoint, they all looked tall and skinny. Unnaturally so. There were a few girls in school that were skinny, but not like these people.

He watched their eyes, some filled with tears, some not, as they swept over his family. As each group approached, a pattern developed. They would look at his father, then his mother, then at him. It felt like they looked at him the longest.

When they stepped up, they'd introduce themselves, tell how they knew Elvey, and say how sorry they were for their loss. They'd shake his father's hand, pat him on the shoulder, then take his mother's hand in theirs, giving it a gentle pat. Afterward, they'd simply drop their eyes and file out of the church and into the cold wind outside.

Brandon turned slightly, looking back at the deceased. He gasped quietly. Had her head moved? He bent ever so slightly, examining the position of her head. It might have moved from where it was, but it might not have.

Shaking his head, he turned back to the congregation only to be greeted by an elderly man's face inches from his own. The man had bent at the waist, bringing his big, somber eyes down to Brandon's level. "You okay, Sonny?" he asked in a raspy whisper.

Brandon took a step back, nodding his head. His mother's hand pressed against his back, but it did little to soothe him. The old's man's face smiled, deepening the wrinkles on his pale skin. As the smile grew, two rows of gapped, yellow teeth appeared.

"I'm sorry, sir. Brandon's non-verbal," Carrol said, recognizing the man as the one who had been staring at her during the service.

The smile faded slightly, hiding his teeth as the man looked up at Carrol. "Yes. I remember Elvey mentioning that." He lowered his face back to Brandon, and his smile widened again. Pale gray eyes, deeply set in his boney face, stared at Brandon. A scrawny hand came forward, sneaking from the sleeve of a starched white shirt that had yellowed a bit. Boney fingers unfurled like a party favor.

"Have a candy," he said. His voice was loud, resonant,

and his accent thick.

Brandon stared at the golden cellophane sitting in the man's ghostly white palm. He swallowed, nodding again. A nudge from his mother spurred his own hand into motion. He reached out slowly and took the candy with his fingertips, careful not to touch the man's skin.

"That's a good boy."

A quiet laugh escaped the man's open mouth, bathing Brandon in the smell of coffee and the sweet scent of pipe tobacco. He took a half step back, pressing against his mother's hand.

His gift delivered, the man stood and smiled at Carrol. "Mind you that he don't swallow it. Sometimes the little ones can choke," he said, pronouncing choke as "shoke."

"Uh, how did you know Elvey?" Carrol asked.

"I helped her mind the place sometimes. It wasn't easy with her all alone."

Carrol nodded absently, thrown by the interaction. She forced a smile and thanked the man as her arm snaked around Brandon's shoulders, pulling him to her. She watched the man walk away. He moved with a slow but confident stride despite having a slight limp in his right leg.

A long, deep, nasally "Hnnnn" snatched her attention from the stranger. It was a sound that she knew all too well. It was the sound her son made when he was on the verge of having an episode.

"It's okay," she said, swiping the hair back from his forehead. "It's okay. We're going." She gathered Brandon to her side and apologized as she hurried them through the crowd. By the time they got to the doors, the sounds of his distress were echoing throughout the church.

THREE

May 2020

Brandon Stivers cringed, moaning as the Toyota 4 runner turned from the smooth asphalt onto the dirt road. The sudden change in sound inundated his mind. The roar of the tires on the loose gravel grated on his ears, overwhelming his senses. He closed his eyes and took a deep breath, soothing himself the way the counselors at school had taught him.

"You okay back there, buddy?" Barry Stivers found his son in the rear-view mirror. He hadn't considered how the noise of the gravel road would affect him. "I'm sorry, kiddo. I didn't even think about the road noise."

"Put your headphones on, sweetie. It'll help." Carrol Stivers looked back at her son, smiling. Her smile faded as she turned and looked at her husband. She watched in the mirror as Brandon slid the noise-canceling headphones over his ears.

Brandon eyed his parents carefully from his cocoon of silence. His mother said something, but the headphones prevented him from hearing what she said. The hard lines around her eyes meant she was mad. She was complaining to his father. His father said something back without looking at her. He threw a hand up and let it drop. They were arguing about him. Again.

He followed the tilt of his father's head and saw him looking back in the mirror. His father offered a forced smile. Brandon smiled back. His father moved his head and looked back at the road.

Brandon stared at his own reflection in the mirror and shook his head. He was different from the other kids he knew. Things bothered him more than they bothered everyone else. Sometimes it was hard to think about the same thing for long. Nothing came easy for him, and it wasn't always easy for his dad to hide his disappointment.

In the front seat, his mother said something else to his father. His father shook his head and said something back. She rolled her eyes and then turned to the window. Whatever it was about, the argument was over for now.

Brandon sighed and turned to the window. Outside, trees lined the dirt track, their branches reaching over and mingling with those from the opposite side of the road. The bright sun of early summer yielded instantly to the thick canopy, bathing the car in a diffused light that washed everything with an eerie glow.

Brandon leaned over, looking through the windshield between his Parents. Driving beneath the canopy felt like going through a tunnel. Ribbons of sunlight broke through the leaves overhead, creating a strobe effect of sun and shadows. He closed his eyes and shook his head. Blinking lights always made his brain itch. When he opened his eyes, he turned to the side window, lessening the effect.

Scattered amongst the trees, dark water stood in puddles. A skim of pollen and dust from the road clung to the surface in irregular patches. As they passed one of the larger pools, something stirred beneath the water, sending ripples in every direction. Brandon turned, keeping his eyes on the spot as they passed, but nothing revealed itself.

He looked at his parents to see if they'd noticed it. His

father sat with one hand on the steering wheel, staring out the windshield. His mother was looking out the window on her side of the car. They hadn't noticed.

He looked out the windshield again. They'd made it through the tunnel, and the sky had opened some. Tall, mature trees staked their claim to the space, closing in on either side of the forced incursion. His eyes darted to a rusty mailbox as they approached the first house. The hand-painted address proclaimed it as 134 Darby Camp Road.

His eyes moved to a massive tree in front of them as they slowed, approaching a curve. The lower branches, some of them larger than his thigh, held the roots of Spanish Moss. It hung from the rough bark like an old man's beard, swaying gently in the breeze. If the tree had been in a park, it would have been a good climbing tree. Where it sat, amongst underbrush that had grown tall, and a thick crop of briars, nothing about the tree looked welcoming.

Ahead, on the right side of the road, a small sign caught his attention. The words "watch that child" were painted on a dirty, yellow rectangle of sheet metal. A tangle of vines stood at its feet. Some of them had already started to wind themselves around the bent, rusty pole that supported it. To him, the sign looked like an afterthought. His head turned, staring at the sign as it passed by outside the passenger side of the car.

Watch that child? he thought, his brow creasing deeply. *Not "Children Playing" or "Slow, Children Present." Watch that child. Which child should they watch? Him?* He turned further, but the sign had disappeared into a cloud of dust raised by their car.

Watch that child.

"Well, it is secluded."

"That's the point, isn't it?" Barry replied flatly, not bothering to look at his wife.

Carrol turned back to the window, eyeing a rusted mobile home sitting six feet off the ground on a series of thick, wooden poles. Nature was well on its way to reclaiming the small lot. Weeds stood waist-high in the patches of sun that slipped through the canopy, growing through an assortment of abandoned junk.

Brandon slipped the headphones halfway back on his ears and was greeted instantly by the roar of the gravel beneath the tires. He grimaced but didn't cover his ears again. He wanted to hear what his parents were saying.

"It'll be good," his dad said flatly. His wife had voiced her displeasure about coming here. She'd been loud and adamant, but, in the end, circumstances had defeated her.

Brandon looked back and forth between the two of them. His mother was still looking out the window, and his dad was staring straight ahead through the windshield. He sighed and shook his head.

Tensions between his parents had been on a steady rise since before Christmas when his paternal grandmother died suddenly. The fact that they were getting a whole nother house should have made things better, but it only seemed to make things worse.

They'd had some monster arguments lately, mostly centered on the house they were headed for. The mother of one of his friends had been diagnosed with Covid 19. He had been to their house only the day before, and that was the nail in the coffin of his mother's argument. They'd decided to spend some time "away," and his grandmother's river house was as "away" as they could find under the current circumstances.

"Why is every house up on those poles?" Carrol asked, more thinking aloud than asking a question. Her head turned slowly as they passed another lot, watching an elderly couple sitting on plastic chairs in the shade beneath a dilapidated shack.

"This whole place is in a flood plain." Barry pointed out

the window past his wife. Beyond one of the cluttered yards, a ribbon of water slipped between the mature cypress trees.

She shook her head with a huff. "Perfect."

Barry sighed. "Really, Carrol?"

"What?" she asked. "Who would want to live in a flood plain?"

Barry rubbed his forehead and sighed. "Apparently, a lot of people, Carrol."

"They probably don't have a choice. Just look at these two. They look like a couple of real go-getters." Her eyes washed over an obese couple sitting in the shade beneath another elevated house. The woman, dressed in a faded housedress, offered an unenthusiastic wave which Carrol didn't return. The house had been poorly painted a barn red color. A large script "A" marked the front door in white paint, declaring their allegiance to the University of Alabama.

"Friends of yours?' she asked with a smirk. Barry was a huge fan while she had attended a rival school.

"Could we not do this again? I'm really not in the mood." Barry's eyes glanced up at the rear-view mirror, finding Brandon. He forced a quick smile at his son.

"How's it going back there?" he asked.

Brandon noticed his father's look and nodded, giving him a smile and a thumbs up.

"It'll be a good summer, kiddo. I promise. Man, when I was a kid—" Barry's wife interrupted him with a groan. He looked at her, smiling through his clenched jaw. His eyes found Brandon in the mirror again. "It'll be fun." He spared his wife a glance before turning back to the road.

"Yeah, right."

Barry shook his head but didn't respond.

Carrol let out a chuckle as they approached another house, nodding toward a middle-aged woman in a bikini top and cut-off jean shorts. The woman was watching a shirtless, heavy-set man with a bandana on his head work on a motorcycle. Behind them, a short, green mobile home had been elevated onto poles. "That must bring back memories."

Barry sighed angrily and shook his head. "Dammit, Carrol, why do you always have to do that?"

"What?" she asked, shrugging one shoulder as she turned back to the window.

"Run me down like that." Barry looked at his wife. "Not everyone was born with a silver spoon in their mouth, you know."

"That's not even what I'm talking about."

"Really? Then what was it?"

"I was referring to the motorcy— look out!"

Barry turned from his wife and slammed on the brakes. The car skidded on the loose gravel, coming to a stop inches from an old woman standing in the middle of the road. Bent over a cane, she turned her head slowly to look at them, unalarmed by the fact that she'd just nearly been run over.

"Holy shit." Barry stared through the windshield as a cloud of dust swept past the car and enveloped the woman. "Where did she come from?"

"Hell, it looks like," Carrol quipped as she stared at the old woman, her eyes washing over the faded floral print dress that hung on her thin frame.

Barry got out of the car and hurried to the woman. "I'm so sorry, ma'am. I was talking and not watching the road."

The old woman coughed. "It's all the same. Might have saved me a few months of misery if you'd hit me."

"Well, Ma'am, I'm sorry. I didn't mean to scare you."

The old woman shuffled to him, raising her weathered face to his. Her chin protruded as her toothless gums clasped together. A set of weary eyes set deeply in a basket of wrinkles darted around his face. She nodded her head slowly. "I'll be damned."

"Ma'am?" Barry asked. "Are you okay?" He reached out to take her arm but stopped just short of touching her. He'd always disliked touching old people. Something about their thin skin made his skin crawl.

"I was fine a few minutes ago. Just fetching my mail. I never get the mail this time of day, but today I felt the need to. And now I almost get run down by the likes of you."

"Me?" Barry asked, stepping back. "Do I know you?"

"I imagine you don't." Her eyes narrowed more, deepening the creases around them. "But I know you."

Barry nodded, searching his memory for the woman's name. He looked at the battered shack next to them, then back at the woman. They both had been worn by time since he'd last seen them. A memory of her swam into his mind, but he said nothing. She didn't need to know what he remembered and what he didn't.

"You're that Stivers boy, ain'tcha?"

Barry recoiled slightly, staring at the woman. "I'm Barry Stivers. Yes ma'am. How do you know who I am?"

The old woman shook her head slowly. "I figured you'd come back when Elvey died." She started toward the car, stabbing her cane into the loose gravel with each step. "Was hoping you wouldn't, though I figured you would."

Barry reluctantly followed her slow progress toward the passenger side of the car, a hand hovering just off her back in case she fell. She peered at the glass, waiting for Carrol to roll down the window.

Carrol lowered the window halfway and offered an apologetic smile. "I'm so sorry, Ma'am. We were talking."

The old woman nodded as she studied Carrol's face. She clenched her gums again and craned her neck to look deeper into the car. Her eyes landed on Brandon and narrowed, watching him squirm beneath her gaze. He offered an uncomfortable smile before looking away.

"Look, we've had a bit of a drive. If you don't mind, we'd rather get going."

"Uh-huh. I suspect you would." The old woman straightened as much as she could and looked at Barry. She held his stare for a long time, then shook her head slowly. "Stay out of the muck."

"Excuse me?"

The woman hobbled through a turn and then started away. "You heard what I said," she called without looking back.

Barry looked at Carrol and shrugged. He threw a dismissive wave at the old woman, now gaining the edge of the road. He hurried around the car and jumped in.

"What was she saying?" Carrol asked, watching the woman hobble away.

"Hell, if I know. She's probably just a crazy old bat."

"Do you remember her?"

Barry laughed. "Not hardly. She wasn't exactly in my peer group. When I was a kid, she was probably my age. I don't think we ran in the same circles."

Carrol stared at the woman as they drove away. When she was behind them, her eyes went to the side view mirror. The old woman was hobbling up her driveway, a cane in one hand, her mail clenched in the other.

"That was weird."

Barry shrugged. "I guess if we're lucky enough to get that old, we'll be weird too." His eyes went to the mirror and found Brandon. "You okay, buddy?"

Brandon nodded, but he didn't look too sure.

"It's good. Nothing to worry about. Just a crazy old lady getting her mail." Barry thumbed a bead of sweat from his brow and shook his head.

Though the years hadn't been kind, he remembered the old woman. Ida Mae Sellers had always hated him and his friends and had complained to his mother countless times. Even when he slowed down passing her drive, if she were outside, she'd shake her fist at him, and his mother would get a call. She complained about the noise of his motorcycle, the dust he created as he passed, the time of night he went by, and pretty much anything else he did.

"Home sweet home," Carrol said dryly as they slowed, approaching a mailbox marked Stivers. They turned into the drive that was little more than two gravel ruts separated by grass that hadn't been mown yet this summer.

Barry rolled his eyes as he drove past the house and made a sharp right turn, parking on a bare patch of earth in the shadow of the house. Getting out of the car, he looked up at the rusted screen of the porch and sighed, sparing a glance over his shoulder at his wife and son. He'd made a few trips down to clean things up but suffered under no delusions that Carrol would be happy with the place. Ultimately it didn't matter. They were here, and that was what mattered.

Brandon got out of the car and pushed the headphones off his ears, hanging them around his neck. He stared wide-eyed up at the old house. Resting on pilings taller than he was, it was drastically different from what he was used to and less than what he expected. In his mind, he saw a quaint cottage on the banks of a rushing river. This place was just the opposite.

The green paint on the rough-sawn wood siding had faded to a pale, chalky color. The screen enclosing the front porch was spotted with patches of rust and had several holes in it. One of the holes had been covered with a makeshift patch of screen that was considerably newer than the original, poorly sewn into place with a thin wire. On the far end of the porch, a metal staircase, painted black many years ago, stabbed into the overgrown lot.

"You could have cut the grass," Carrol said, shaking her head as she surveyed the yard.

Barry shrugged. "I was getting the house ready."

"Welcome to Paradise, kiddo," Carrol joked, ignoring her husband as she rounded the car and joined her son. Leaning in, she whispered, "Good thing we got our tetanus shots."

Brandon gave her a quick smile but didn't join her as she headed for the stairs. His eyes washed back to the shade beneath the house. A dozen posts rose from the dry, bare earth to support the structure. Each of the posts wore a thin coating of dark mud that rose three feet high. At the center of the house, next to a large, black drainpipe, cast-off furniture and other assorted junk sat in a heap. Some of the pieces were stained by the mud like the posts, and some only wore a thin veil of dust.

At the corner nearest him, a rusty metal table and four matching chairs sat in the shade of the house. A narrow cord had been fished through one of the legs on each chair. His eyes followed it to a nearby support pole, where it had been tied. On the other side of the house, beneath the staircase, a threadbare hammock hung between two of the pilings.

"C'mon. Let's get unloaded. I've got a lot of work to do."

Brandon looked at his father and offered a sympathetic smile. Barry clapped him on the shoulder and opened the back of the 4 Runner. "It'll be fine."

Brandon turned, surveying the patchy grass that comprised the lawn. Overgrown and dry, it wasn't like the lush carpet of grass they had at home. His eyes swept across the yard and found an old pier jutting into what looked like a swamp. Well beyond that, past the overgrown wetland, he could see a glimpse of a dark body of water.

In the swamp, open pools of dark water stood out like craters in the sea of lush vegetation. The surface of one of them stirred beneath his gaze. His eyes narrowed, waiting for something to break the surface. He expected a fish to jump or a turtle to peek its head out of the water, but nothing happened. He watched until the ripples settled, then sighed. Suddenly curious, he took a few steps toward the pier, but his father stopped him.

"C'mon, son. Your mom packed half the house. Help me lug this crap upstairs. Lord knows she ain't going to help." Barry looked at his son, a suitcase in each hand and one under each arm. "See what I mean?"

Brandon turned from the pier, nodding in agreement. His mother always overpacked, but they usually ended up needing the extra stuff she brought. He grabbed his things from the back seat and headed for the stairs, sparing the pier another long look as he went.

FOUR

"Wow." Carrol put her hands on her lips as she surveyed the room. The living room, kitchen, and dining area comprised the front half of the house, all in one large room. On the far end, a small set of banged-up cabinets almost matched the meadow gold-colored stove and refrigerator that had to be as old as she was. Between her and the kitchen, a small, semi-circular table jutted out from the wall beneath a double set of aluminum windows that looked out over the porch and, ultimately, the river. The table was guarded by four steel-legged chairs that matched the green Formica tabletop.

The rest of the room was taken up by an old sofa, a recliner, and two ottomans that were crowded into the living room area. Neither of the pieces matched in color or style.

A mixed array of faded family photos in various frames littered the walls. They hung on dark wooden paneling with no rhyme or reason.

The sills of all six curtainless windows in the room were filled with a collection of garden gnomes. Coming in every size and shape imaginable, they stared back at her blankly. Carrol rolled her eyes. She'd seen them when she and Barry were dating but had forgotten her mother-in-law's penchant for them. Back then, Barry had explained that Elvey couldn't put them in the yard because they'd be lost in a flood, so she had to keep them in the house.

Finally, her eyes fell to the matted green shag carpet at her feet. Wear patterns marked the paths that Elvey Stivers used the most. From the front door, one led to the kitchen sink. From there, one went to the couch, with an offshoot that went to the door to what had to be a bedroom.

Carrol closed her eyes and took a deep breath, cringing as she considered how many years of dirt was trapped within the carpet. "Mee-maw didn't bother to update the place, I see."

"She was old," Barry said, pushing past her with the suitcases. "She liked things the way they were. Don't be ungrateful for a free house."

"At least it's not one of those trailer houses."

"Even if it was, it's a free house. Mom lived a simple life. It's not like she was a peasant."

"I didn't say she was." Carrol ran her finger along the top of a picture frame hanging next to the door. "But apparently, she wasn't big on dusting either," she mumbled, wiping her fingers on the leg of her jeans.

"The place has been shut up for a while, Carrol. Gimme a break. I offered to have someone come down and clean. Remember?"

Carrol shook her head again but didn't reply. When Brandon entered with his suitcase, pillows, and blanket, she forced a smile. "Welcome to the nineteen seventies, kiddo." She laughed and took another look around the room. "It's just groovy, ain't it?"

Brandon smiled and shrugged, sniffing the air. His nose crinkled as he looked at her.

Carrol nodded. "It's the smell of years of dust and dirt and probably mildew. It's called 'old house smell,' and it's inescapable."

He sat his load down and went to one of the windows on the front of the house. His eyes found the pier, then lifted to the river. From this vantage point, he could clearly see the river. The dark water moved slowly past in a sweeping turn directly in front of the property.

He dropped his gaze back to the pier. The shallow water around it was full of green growth, accentuating dark clumps of tall reeds that looked dead. A smile tugged at the corners of his mouth though he didn't know why.

Lowering his gaze further, he found a row of garden gnomes lining the double windowsill before him, and his smile vanished.

"Your grandmother was a bit eccentric," Carrol whispered, joining her son. "She loved those things. They're everywhere. She might have thought they brought good luck or something. I can't really remember, but there's something about them. She mentioned them often in her—" Carrol caught herself before she revealed the secret letters. Her head jerked around, looking for Barry. When she didn't see him, she offered Brandon a smile. "She said they were lucky."

Brandon leaned over the table and picked up one of the gnomes, leaving a circle in the dust on the sill. The gnome, barely six inches tall, wore a blue hat and held a shovel in his hands. Next to him stood a sign that said "garden." An inscription below the gnome's oversized boots asked, "Can you dig it?"

"See what I mean?" Carrol asked in a whisper as she joined him. "Eccentric is being kind. Actually, she was a little senile if you ask me." She nudged her son and nodded.

Barry emerged from the bedroom and threw his hands into the air. "You two gonna help me unload or what?"

Startled by the sudden appearance of his father, Brandon jumped, and the figurine slipped from his hand. It landed on the carpet with a thud but didn't break.

Carrol bent and picked it up, turning it over in her hand as she stared at it. "You two unload. I'm going to start cleaning this place up. Lord knows it could stand it."

Carrol Stivers folded the comforter and top sheet halfway down on the twin bed. She'd brought Brandon's sheets and pillows as well as his favorite comforter, hoping to fend off a bad reaction to the new environment. She wanted to make the place feel as close to home as possible.

She fluffed his pillow and laid it against the headboard. Stepping back with a sigh, she smiled. Brandon's was the first room she'd managed to completely clean. Between the sheets and a heavy dose of air freshener, it would probably do.

"That's the last of it."

Carrol turned, looking through the open door as her husband dropped the load in his arms onto the floor by the front door. "Where's Brandon?" she asked, emerging from the bedroom.

"He's hanging out on the pier," he answered, going to the window-mounted air conditioner unit and switching it on.

"That old thing?" she asked, rushing to the front windows. "That pier looks like it might collapse any minute."

"It's fine," he said, bending to allow the cold air to blow into his face. "I helped rebuild it before I left home. It was the last project I ever did with my dad."

Carrol looked at him, one eyebrow cocked. "Really? You do realize that was a long time ago, right?"

Barry let out a mocking laugh. "Very funny. The pier's fine. It's plenty sturdy."

"You couldn't know that. It's old, Barry. Did you test it when you were here before?" She watched him carefully, measuring his reaction. He'd made a half dozen trips down here, even spending the night twice, all under the guise of "getting the house ready," but from what she'd seen, he hadn't done much except haul a few pieces of broken furniture out. Suspicions of him having an affair rose in her mind. Again.

He shrugged as he crossed the room to the fridge, plucking a beer from the top shelf. "I know how it was built." He looked at her and smiled. "Besides, I did stomp around on it before. It's fine."

"Still." Carrol turned back to the window. Brandon was sitting on the pier, staring toward the river. "Are there snakes down here? It looks snaky as hell to me."

Barry nodded. "Tons of 'em."

"Seriously?" Carrol asked, a hand going to her chest.

Barry nodded again. "Most of them are harmless water snakes. There are moccasins around, though. If you watch yourself, you'll be fine."

Carrol wiped sweat from her brow and drug a hand through her hair. It was going to be a long summer. "Hopefully, this damned flu thing that's turned the world upside down will pass soon, and we can get back home."

Barry shrugged again as he sat down on the couch. "Who the hell knows." He downed half the beer in three long gulps. "If you watch the news, it sounds like it'll be the end of all of us."

"I doubt that."

"Well, can you at least try to make the best out of a bad situation? I don't want to be here anymore than you do."

"I'm here, Barry. That might be as much as you get from me," she said, gathering items from the pile Barry left by the door. When her arms were full, she headed to the bathroom without looking at her husband.

A garden gnome eighteen inches high and as fat as a gallon milk jug greeted her as she entered the shared bathroom situated between the two bedrooms. It stood on the back of an old toilet with both arms extended in front of him. A spare roll of toilet paper hung on the gnome's left arm.

The gnome's clothes had all been painted red, and a sticker bearing the University of Alabama logo clung to the front of his pointed hat. One edge had peeled and was curled back on itself. Across the front of the base, someone had written, "Neither me nor Bama will take shit off anybody. Use the paper."

Carrol shook her head, remembering the gnome instantly. His name was Big Red, and she hated it. Being an alumnus of a rival school fueled some of her disdain, but mostly she hated it because it was crude and crass. Juggling the load in her arms, she turned the gnome around so Brandon wouldn't see the inscription. He showed no interest in sports, but she didn't want him to see the language.

Much to her dismay, she found two round, pink buttocks staring back at her. Big Red was mooning her. She shook her head and sighed, putting the gnome back where it was. The back was worse than the front.

After putting the supplies away, she turned to leave but stopped. Looking back to the garden gnome, she shook her head. "Who in the hell would even want something like this?" She grabbed it from the back of the toilet and looked at it, turning it in her hands. A thin line ran around the neck of the figure, crossing the long white beard. Big Red took a tumble at some point in his life. His head had broken off, and someone had glued it back on. Carrol grunted, thinking that Elvey missed a good excuse to get rid of it. She shook her head again and shoved it into the small linen closet behind the door.

"Are you going to help me put this stuff away?" Carrol asked, finding her husband still on the couch when she returned to the living room.

"I humped all this crap up the stairs. I'm tired," he said without looking at her. He turned up the beer and finished the bottle.

"Whatever," she huffed. "That reminds me. Did you have the mail forwarded?"

"I did."

Carrol pushed both hands through her hair as she crossed the room, pausing at the front windows to check on Brandon. "We're going to need more bug spray if he's going to hang out around that swamp."

"It's not a swamp."

"It looks like a swamp."

Barry got up and retrieved another beer from the fridge. "A swamp is a backwater, lowland area." He peeped out the window as he headed back to the couch. "That's just a marsh. It's part of the river."

Carrol sighed. Barry loved making asinine comparisons to make himself look smarter than her. "Either way, I'm sure it's full of mosquitoes, among god knows what else."

"I was just messing with you before. I've never seen a snake out there in my whole life. They're around, mind you, but not around the pier."

"That's comforting to know," she said flatly.

"It should be."

Carrol pursed her lips and sighed through her nose as she stared out at her son. The area around the pier looked like the swamps she saw on television, wrought with snakes and alligators.

She closed her eyes, drawing in a deep breath. Her marriage was in trouble. Things hadn't been great for years, but they were manageable. Lately, however, Barry had changed. There was a secrecy about him, a dark brooding that hadn't always been there. On top of that, the world had gone crazy, forcing them to retreat to the one place she'd always hoped to avoid.

Opening her eyes, she looked at her son. With any luck,

she could make it through the next few weeks and get them away from this place without an incident.

Sometimes the waters stir, and when they do, they're stronger than you could imagine. There's evil lurking in that muck. When it calls, people do strange things.

A shudder ran down her spine as Elvey's words ran through her mind. Most, if not all, of the letters she had hidden in the shoebox at home mentioned the "waters." But that was all superstition and backwoods folklore. Right?

As she turned from the window, she saw Barry staring at her with an odd look on his face. The bottle in his hand was frozen halfway to his mouth.

"What?" she asked.

"You okay?"

"No, Barry. I'm not okay, but since when has that ever mattered to you."

He sighed heavily and pushed himself up from the old sofa. "Whatever," he said, heading for the door.

"If you're going outside," she began as she went to the refrigerator, "take Brandon something to drink." She retrieved a can of soda and tossed it to her husband. "And check that damned pier out again. I don't want it collapsing with my son on it."

Barry nodded as he stared at her. "Our son."

Carrol held his gaze until Barry turned and walked out the door without commenting. When the door closed behind him, she pushed both hands through her hair, stopping them on top of her head.

"God, I hate this place already," she sighed. She shook her head and walked into the master bedroom. Her shoulders fell as she took in the small room packed full of old furniture. It was going to take her all afternoon to get the place clean enough to sleep in.

Going to the bed, she grabbed up the flattened pillows, intent to throw them into the living room and replace them with the ones she'd brought from home. She was halfway through the door when she froze, her eyes locked on the long black hair clinging to the threadbare pillowcase in her arms.

Elvey's hair was gray, and it was too long to be Barry's. Dropping the pillows, she sat down on the bed. A hand went to her mouth as she struggled to contain the flood of emotions. Though it wasn't proof of anything, it was suspicious. There might be an explanation, but coupled with his odd behavior lately, it was hard to deny.

"You son of a bitch," she said, rising suddenly. She began stripping the bed, intent to remove anything Barry's whore might have laid on. When the mattress was bare, she grabbed the edge and struggled through the chore of flipping it. She couldn't bear the possibility of sleeping on the stains of a possible affair. The chore done, she stood back, finding an envelope on the floor at her feet.

She bent and picked it up, finding her name printed on it. "What the hell, Elvey?" she asked. She sat on the bed and opened the envelope. It was another letter dated December 13. Two days before she died.

FIVE

Brandon felt his father's presence on the rickety pier before he heard him. He looked up as Barry drew close, offering the beginnings of a smile.

"Be tough to get a boat through that," Barry said, handing his son a can of Sprite. "Mom thought you might be thirsty."

Brandon looked out over the field of weeds and wild grasses growing in the dark mud around the pier. A broken line of dry, dead reeds rose in clumps from the plain of bullrush and ironweed. Their long, thin shoots were dry and brown, standing in stark contrast to the lush greenery. Head high, they reminded him of soldiers standing sentry.

The scene stretched for a hundred yards in either direction along the bank, giving way occasionally to small pockets of murky water. The dark pools offered a glimpse of what lay hidden within the growth of rush and wide-leafed ferns. The useless pier felt more of an intrusion on the wetland than anything else.

Brandon nodded, then extended a finger skyward, moving his hand in circles. It was his request for an explanation of the strange patch.

"Back in the day, they say the river came right up to this pier. I guess over time, sediment just kinda filled in. The river takes a big turn around here. See?" Barry pointed to the river beyond the field of muddy water. To their left, the river was straight and wide. In front of them, it turned sharply and disappeared behind a forested hillside. Their pier was in the center of the turn, and the shallows in front of them clung to the outside bank of the bend. "Silt and dirt got washed up, then things started growing. That collected more dirt and so on and so forth." His eyes washed over the scattering of dry reeds that rose out of the sea of broad, arrowhead-shaped leaves that grew closer to the surface. "All sorts of things settle in the turns, Brandon."

A mosquito buzzed up to him and landed on his arm. He swatted it and thumped the remains away absently. "It's been like this as long as I can remember. We always just called this stuff 'the muck' because you'd need muck boots to get through it."

Brandon watched the color slowly drain from his father's face as he surveyed the wetland before them. His eyes took on a dark, brooding look that left him feeling unsettled. He nudged his father's leg and signed, asking if he were okay.

"What?" Barry asked, pulled from his thoughts. "Oh, yeah. It's fine. There's been lots of construction upriver, I guess. The river's always changing, son. Nothing ever stays the same, even if you want it to."

Brandon nodded, measuring his father's change in attitude. He'd noticed a change in his father since his mother died. There was a darker, unsettled look in his eyes as of late.

"Anyway," Barry said, shaking off his thoughts. "Just give it a little while, son. This place has a way of growing on you. It's not the same as back home, but I think that's the whole point of being here."

Brandon shrugged and nodded, giving his father a smile.

Barry smiled back at his son and mussed his sandy brown hair. As kids went, Brandon caused few real problems. His situation made things more difficult, and it had strained his marriage, but he'd never been hauled in by the cops or been suspended from school. Yet.

He'd long since given up on the dream of a "normal" son and accepted that Brandon wouldn't be like him. Brandon wasn't popular, didn't play sports, and, although he was fifteen, showed no interest in driving. In polar contrast to himself as a youth, Brandon's interest in girls was only fleeting. So far.

"Everything will be okay. I promise," Barry added. Squatting down next to his son, he scanned the weeds. A nostalgic smile slipped across his lips.

Brandon nudged his father and held up a hand, moving two fingers to mimic walking, then jerked his head toward the muck.

Barry's eyes widened, and he shook his head emphatically. He took his son by the shoulders and stared into his eyes. "No, son. Do not try to walk to the river through this. Ever. It's deeper than it looks, and you'll mar up before you know it. There's mud beneath all this growth. It's like quicksand." He stared into his son's confused eyes. "I know I said you'd need muck boots to walk through it, but I didn't mean this stuff. I mean stuff like this. You can't walk through this. I'll show you the places you can use to fish. Okay?"

Brandon nodded, watching his father stand.

"I'm going to start the grill. Supper will be ready in about an hour. It's gonna be Dad's famous burgers. Don't stay down here too long."

Brandon gave him a thumbs-up and smiled. As he watched his father make his way along the pier and up the path to the house, his eyes narrowed. The corners of his mouth pulled into a frown.

Brandon sighed and looked at the can in his hand. He shook his head with a grunt. He didn't like this soda, but his mother had a strict no caffeine rule for him. She didn't care if he liked it or not. His lips curled back in a mocking snarl, and he flipped the unopened can into the swamp in front of him. It fell through the weeds and hit the ground with a wet splat. The can stood for a moment, sparkling in the bright sunlight, then began to sink. The black, soupy mud enveloped the can, consuming it slowly.

A smile slipped across his lips. He'd drawn more pleasure from the scene than he expected. There was something about the way it went down, almost like it was being swallowed. It reminded him of watching a snake devour a meal that was almost too big for it to eat.

When the mud rushed in over the top of the can with a "plop," he chuckled. The sound was funny, almost like a cartoon.

"Hey, come check this out."

Brandon looked around, using his hand to shield his eyes from the sun. His father was standing near the edge of the house in front of an old barbeque grill, motioning for Brandon to join him.

Brandon stood with a reluctant sigh and dusted himself off. His eyes washed over the field of weeds and mud. His father had called it "the muck," and the name fit.

"C'mon," his dad yelled.

Brandon turned from the muck and started down the pier. *Maybe*, he thought, *the summer down here will be more fun than I expected.*

"Check it out," Barry said as his son joined him. He pointed into the open grill. A wad of leaves and puffy pink material sat in the corner of the grill. "It's a rat nest. They make a nest of anything they can find. That pink stuff is insulation. I guess mom had a rat problem." He shook his head, grimacing as he lifted the cooking grate from the grill.

Brandon leaned in, watching intently as his father poked

the nest with the end of a set of tongs. When nothing happened, Barry Stivers gently began peeling back the layers until he made it to the center.

"Damn," he groaned, staring down at the four tiny pink bodies writhing within the nest.

Brandon reached for the nest, but his father blocked his hand with the tongs. He looked up with wide, questioning eyes.

"No, son. Don't touch them. They're nasty. And before you even ask, we can't keep them. They can't be more than a few days old. They'll die without the mother." Barry looked into his son's pleading eyes and shook his head.

Brandon threw his hands up in a gesture asking why he couldn't keep them. He then made a circular motion with his finger, asking for an explanation.

"First of all, they're rats. They're nasty and dirty, and they spread disease, Brandon. Secondly, they're just going to starve to death. We've disturbed the nest. The mother won't come back. They'll make it a day, two tops." Barry shook his head at his son. "And more importantly, it'll be better for everyone if your mother doesn't know there are rats here. I barely got her to agree to stay here in the first place. If it weren't for this damned pandemic crap, she never would have in the first place."

Brandon held his hands up, forming the shape of a box, then pointed beneath the house. He pressed his palms together, begging for permission to keep the babies.

Barry shook his head and sighed. He'd never been able to tell his son no, especially when he really wanted something. His shoulders slumped as he looked into his son's pleading eyes. Brandon was a good kid, though he struggled with understanding why he wasn't allowed to do things that other boys did. He'd thrown his share of tantrums, but they'd learned to work through them over the years.

"Fine." Barry threw a hand toward the house. "Look under

there and see what you can find to put them in." Barry shook his head. "And hurry up before your mother sees you. Jesus."

Brandon clapped his hands excitedly, and a smile slid across his face. He hurried beneath the house and began rummaging through the collection of junk.

"But they stay outside. And let's just keep this between the two of us." Barry shook his head despite the smile pulling at the corners of his mouth. "Sometimes, us guys have to have our little secrets amongst ourselves. Okay?"

Brandon smiled, nodding excitedly as he found an old cigar box. He looked back at his father and gave him a thumbs up.

Barry smiled. He'd find out soon enough if Brandon could keep a secret.

Brandon brought the box to his father, holding it anxiously as Barry grasped what was left of the nest with the tongs and placed it in the corner of the box. The fledgling rats began wobbling around on unsteady legs, exploring their new world.

"Go ahead and close it. If it's dark, they'll settle down."

Brandon nodded, smiling as he slowly closed the box.

"Look, son. Don't get any ideas about raising them. They're not going to make it, and I don't want you getting upset when they die. Do you understand?"

Brandon's shoulders drooped as he looked up from the box. His brow furrowed as he looked up at his father.

"Fine. Go. Find an out-of-the-way place for it, okay?" Barry shook his head. "God knows we don't want your mother looking for something and accidentally stumbling across them."

Brandon nodded eagerly, smiling as he started beneath the house. He stopped when his father called him.

"Not a word," he said, pointing the tongs at his son. "Sometimes women just don't understand, especially your mother. It's not a lie, okay? We'll just 'forget' to bring it up.

Okay?"

    Brandon smiled again and walked beneath the house, clutching the box to his chest.

SIX

Brandon sat up in bed and rubbed his eyes. Rising onto an elbow, he looked out the window and yawned. It was still dark outside, but he couldn't tell if it was late at night or early in the morning. He shook his head and laid back down with a sigh, pulling the covers over his bare shoulders.

Lying in the still darkness, serenaded by the sounds of crickets, his mind replayed the image of the soda can sinking in the muck. A smile crept across his face. There was something oddly satisfying about the way the mud sucked the can down, the way it swallowed it.

A hand went to his head, scratching it. The "itchy" feeling was coming again. Like the one caused by the strobing sunlight. It left him feeling restless and agitated. But this time, he wasn't scared.

As the feeling subsided, his thoughts returned to the wetland. His father's words came back to him from the darkness. "We always just called it 'the muck.'" Brandon sighed as he ran a hand through his short brown hair, sweeping the longer bangs to the left. He didn't know why, but he was sure there was more to the wasteland of muck and weeds than people thought. Maybe it took someone like him to tune into what was happening out there.

He tossed the covers back and sat up. How would other things look sinking into the mud? His mind instantly went to the baby rats they'd found in the grill. How would the muck react to something alive?

Both hands covered his mouth as a wave of guilt washed over him. *No*, he thought. *That would be cruel. They were innocent babies. Helpless.* He shook his head and laid back down, determined to resist the temptation.

Though he felt guilty, his heart raced in his chest at the prospect.

"They're going to starve to death anyway." His father's words rang out in his head again. "Don't let your mother know." Brandon sat back up in bed and cast another look out the window. He began to chew on a thumbnail, weighing the possibilities. *They* are *just rats*, he thought. They're going to die anyway. Just rats. His Father's words came to him again. "It's not a lie. We'll just forget to bring it up."

Sitting alone in the dark, Brandon smiled.

The wood of the pier was cool against his bare feet. The dew had fallen, glistening in the beam of light that he followed to the end. Sitting down, Brandon cradled the cigar box on his lap. He scanned the muck before him, following the beam of light as it passed over the reeds growing in the dark water. The guilty feeling he'd had while collecting the box was gone. Now, there was nothing but curiosity. He needed to see what the mud would do, how it would react.

The light fell on the lid of the box. The faded image of an Indian Chief with a full headdress stared back at him. The words CIGAR CHIEF were embossed above the image, and the words "Best smoke east of the Mississippi" were bent around the bottom of the Chief's portrait. Brandon shook his head, wondering why a Native American would want to smoke a cigar.

The hairless, pink bodies began to wriggle as soon as the light fell on them. Brandon's fingers gently picked one up and held it before him. The tiny pink head moved back and forth, a mouth searching for its mother's tit. In the silence, a tiny squeak filled his ears.

Brandon extended the rat over the edge of the pier and dropped it, following its descent with the light. The tiny body barely affected the surface at all. The rat landed on its side, all four tiny feet groping the air for purchase.

A thin finger of dark mud rose from the muck behind the rat. It arched forward, hesitated a moment, then latched on. The loose skin on the body pulled tight as the finger shrank back into the mud, taking the rat's back half with it. Just before the tiny body disappeared, Brandon heard another gentle, unsuspecting squeak. Then the silence returned.

Brandon stared at the pool of light. His eyes were wide with disbelief. His heart was pounding in his chest. Did that really just happen? A thin smile slipped across his face. He hadn't known what to expect, but it was satisfying on a level he couldn't quite understand. It was both exhilarating and scary at the same time. He picked the second rat and dropped it a few feet from the first.

The mud stirred beneath the pink body, swelled, then enveloped it quickly. Brandon's smile widened as he turned back to the box. He lifted the third out of the nest, holding it in the palm of his hand.

His eyes narrowed as he stared at it, cold to its plight. It was so helpless against him. It was ignorant of its own fate but couldn't do anything if it weren't. He had absolute power whether it lived or died. To the helpless rat, he was a god.

Smiling, he slowly extended his hand over the edge of the pier. Tilting it, he let the hairless baby roll across his palm and over the edge. The mud reacted instantly, grabbing the body and sucking it down eagerly.

He shined his light into the box and found the fourth pink body. It was larger than the other three but still just over an inch long. He stared at it, conflicted. He wanted to watch the mud consume it, but he also knew that it was the last one. Once he tossed this one in, it would be over.

He didn't want it to be over.

His fingertips picked it up by the haunches, holding it up before his face. He could do anything he wanted to it. He could squeeze it, crushing its' hip bones. He could pinch its head off. Hell, he could eat it if he wanted to.

The rat gyrated in the air, mistaking the warmth of his fingertips for its mother's body. Brandon leaned over the edge of the pier and lowered the bait toward the mud, stopping two inches from the surface, and held it there.

When the mud began to swell beneath the body, he raised it another inch. His eyes widened with excitement as a finger of mud began to grow, rising in an unsteady column like a cobra from a basket. He raised the rat another inch, keeping it just out of reach of the wavering sliver of mud.

Yes, he thought. Come and get it. He raised the rat another inch and smiled. The mud began to waiver, becoming unsteady. It swooned back and forth, then fell with a splattering sound. It dissipated into the surface near a cluster of reeds.

Brandon scanned the area with his light, disappointed. He released the rat with a sigh. It didn't fall far before it stopped. He could see the pale body in the dim light of the moon. It hung in the air, hovering above the surface of the muck.

He shifted his light and found a column of mud a foot high rising from the muck. The baby rat lay on the flattened top of the column.

He recoiled slightly but smiled as he did so. He'd hoped for something special, and this was it. The column began to rotate slowly, giving him a 360 degree view of the rat. It reminded him of one of those turnstiles they displayed new car models on during game shows that his mother sometimes watched. His head fell to one side, watching the mud spin. It completed two full circuits before dropping suddenly back into the muck, taking the baby rat with it.

Brandon leaned back on the pier and crossed his legs. Switching off the light, he sat in the darkness. A gentle breeze caressed his face as a rustle arose from the dry reeds scattered about in the muck.

A strange, contented feeling began to envelop him. Everything was alright. His mind was quiet. The ever-present noise that always threatened to overload his sense had gone silent. Everything was quiet now. Peaceful.

Brandon held his hands out before him, examining them carefully in the soft light of the crescent moon that hung in the air above the river.

There was a difference within him somehow. He watched his fingers dance along the skin on his arm, bringing goosebumps to the surface. He swallowed hard, watching the reaction. Things were different now. He didn't know how, but he was and in a good way.

The sound of footsteps on the metal staircase pulled Barry's attention from the lawnmower engine he was working on. He wiped his hands on a cloth as he stood, waiting to see who was coming down. When a pair of sneakers appeared at the end of two skinny legs, an eyebrow arched questioningly. How would Brandon react to the news?

Standing in the shade beneath the house, his eyes went to the cigar box on the ground. He'd found it this morning. The babies were missing.

He closed his eyes and hoped for his son not to have an "episode." Things like this, big emotional events, always brought one on. He could almost hear the righteous indignation in his wife's voice now. If he reacted badly, she'd try to use it as an excuse to leave.

"Hey buddy," he began as Brandon rounded the bottom of the steps and turned to come beneath the house. "Got some bad news."

Brandon stopped, his eyes on his father's. His brow furrowed as he circled his finger in the air next to his head. His eyes went immediately to the place he'd left the cigar box.

"I'm sorry, son. Something must have got to them in the night. I found the box on the ground this morning. I'm sorry. They're gone."

Brandon stared wide-eyed at his father for a moment, then looked again at the cigar box. He sighed and looked back at his father.

"Could have been anything, kiddo. A raccoon, a 'possum, a snake. They were pretty much defenseless little things." Barry went to his son. "I'm sorry. You gonna be okay?"

Brandon shrugged, fighting to hold back a smile. He hadn't considered the fact that anyone else would notice the baby rats' disappearance. Now that his father had created a perfect excuse, all he had to do was play along.

You'll have to be more careful next time.

Brandon's head snapped around, expecting to find someone else beneath the house with them. The words had been so clear that he was sure someone else had spoken them aloud.

"You okay, buddy?" Barry asked. He stared at his son, waiting for a response. If he started crying, all hell would break loose.

Brandon nodded, his brow furrowed curiously, then looked back at the cigar box. The chief on the lid stared back accusingly. The Chief knew the truth, but he'd never tell.

Brandon looked at his dad and shrugged. He went to the

cigar box and picked it up. He gave the Chief one last glance before tossing it into the metal trash can. Dusting his hands, Brandon walked out from under the house and headed for the pier.

A thin smile slipped across Barry's face as he watched his son walk away. Things had gone better than he'd expected.

Barry Stivers sat quietly on the porch of the camp house that had been in his family for nearly a hundred years. He had work to do but couldn't focus on the laptop before him. Through the screen enclosing the porch, he could see Brandon milling about in the yard. He'd been wandering along the bank at the edge of the muck, exploring its length, but stopped suddenly and squatted near the wood line.

Barry closed the laptop and put it aside. Standing, he went to the screen. Brandon was studying something on the ground. Going to the screen door, he pushed it open and started down the steps, keeping his eyes on Brandon.

"What have you found?" he asked quietly, shaking his head. It wasn't out of the ordinary for his son to be enthralled by the simplest of things. Once, he'd spend an hour following the track of an inchworm across their back patio.

Barry reached the bottom of the steps and started across the yard, approaching Brandon from behind. As he neared his son, Brandon looked back at him, smiling.

"Know what that is?" Barry asked with a smile when he saw the chimney of mud protruding from the ground. He squatted next to his son. "That's a crawfish hole."

Brandon's brow furrowed as he looked at his father.

"Some people call them crayfish or craw daddies. We've always called them crawfish. They look like tiny lobsters."

Brandon pointed a finger at the chimney and then showed Barry his palms as an inquisitive look swept across his face.

Barry shrugged. "I've caught them before. You can dig them up too, but that's a lot of work. You can eat them, but you'd have to have a lot to make it worth it."

Brandon's nose crinkled at the prospect of eating something that lived in a mud hole.

"If you want to see one, get the hose. We'll try to get it out."

Barry watched his son spring to his feet and run toward the hose hanging on the pillar behind the steps. He unwound the hose and pulled it back to the hole.

"We gotta be careful, though," Barry warned. "Sometimes snakes use these old holes. Especially if it's hot like this."

Brandon nodded, holding the nozzle over the hole.

"Go ahead. Let 'er rip." Barry watched as Brandon turned the nozzle, flooding the hole. He watched the level rise to the top, then looked up.

"It might take a few minutes. Usually, I'd put a fishing line in it with some bait, but he might come up anyway. Give it a minute."

Brandon rested his chin on his knees, staring at the hole. When the water moved, he looked up excitedly.

Barry's heart stopped as he watched the water in the hole. It pushed upwards, then fell as the dark head of a snake broke the surface.

In one motion, he leaped to his feet and grabbed Brandon, dragging him backward as the snake slithered from the hole.

"My God, son," he said, watching as the long, black body of the snake coiled itself. Its mouth flew open, revealing a white interior and two long fangs. "Stay back! That's a water moccasin. It's venomous. It could kill both of us."

Brandon's brow furrowed as he looked from his father to the snake, now poised to strike. He waved his hand, drawing his father's attention. He moved his hand in a serpentine motion, then pointed a finger downward.

"What? You saw it go in the hole?"

Brandon nodded.

"Shit, Brandon. You could have said that before. Damn."

Brandon's shoulders drooped under the scolding.

"Look," Barry groaned as he ran a hand through his hair. "Everything is not friendly out here, Brandon. Some things can and will hurt you, son." He watched sadness slip over his son's face and rubbed his own with both hands.

He slipped a hand around Brandon's shoulders and pulled him close. "It's okay. You didn't know. I'm just glad you're okay. You've got to be careful." He looked back at the snake. "Jesus, son."

Brandon looked at the snake, then at his father. He nodded sadly.

"You go upstairs, okay? I'm going to find something to kill that damned thing with." Barry watched the alarm rise in his son's eyes and put a hand up to stop his protests. "It's dangerous, son. It has to be done. Now go on."

Brandon plodded across the yard and started up the stairs, watching his father disappear beneath the house. He looked back at the snake and shook his head. *You better run. My dad's going to cut your head off,* he thought. The snake's head dropped to the ground, and it began to slither through the grass quickly, moving toward the river.

He turned, claiming a few of the steps backward as he watched the snake cross the yard. It slipped into a puddle of dark water close to the pier, moving gracefully through the water in an undulating wave.

Barry emerged from beneath the house with a shovel. He saw his son on the stairs and stopped. "Go on inside. You don't have to watch this." He waved his son up the stairs and went to where the snake had been.

Brandon smiled knowingly, then looked back to the water. His eyes found the puddle just in time to see the concentric rings of waves begin to settle on the pool. The snake was nowhere to be seen. His brow furrowed as he stared at the dark water. The only way the snake could have disappeared so quickly was to go straight down.

Had the muck gotten it? Surely something as strong as a snake could escape it. Brandon shook his head. No, he thought. It couldn't.

His eyes narrowed as he stared at the field of wild grasses and mud. Just how strong was it? What could escape it? Could anything? Could a person? Could he?

SEVEN

Brandon swatted a mosquito and thumped the dead body off his arm before returning his attention back to the setting sun. The sky above the cypress trees on the opposite side of the river was streaked with long orange and red clouds. The colors reminded him of the fake coral he often saw in aquariums. Above that, the sky had turned a pale lavender color, like an old bruise.

Sweeping his eyes down, he scanned the other side of the river. The bank rose in a steep incline covered with tall trees. The only break in the woods was to his far left, near the top of the hill. The sun glinted off a window, exposing the large white house.

The river itself made its way slowly through the bend. The surface of the dark water looked still, but he knew it wasn't. It was a river, and rivers always moved.

Sometimes things settle in the bends. His father's words echoed in his mind, and Brandon dropped his eyes to the pier. The vantage point from the top of the stairs gave him a sweeping view of the pier and the field of muck that surrounded it.

A smile slipped across his lips as a sense of welcome swept through him. Although he'd never been here, it felt like a homecoming. His grandfather had lived here. His father had lived here. Now, he was living here. Perhaps it was a homecoming, after all.

He started down the steps, keeping his eyes on the muck. His heartbeat rose with each step, and his smile widened. The lush growth was neat to look at, but it was the black holes that lured him.

Brandon found himself on the bank next to the pier. A warmth spread through him as he stared into the waters. There was a sense of belonging here that he'd never felt before. Here, he didn't have to worry about bullies making fun of him. The stillness in his mind offered by the place was comforting.

A faint buzz came to his ears. He looked around, finding a dragonfly darting around close by. His eyes followed it until it buzzed up to him. A hand shot out and snatched it from the air. The insect buzzed in his hand, but he didn't worry. He knew it couldn't hurt him. Opening his fingers one by one, he surveyed his catch. Two of the translucent wings beat furiously as the iridescent green body struggled against his grasp. The wings came off easily. Brandon smiled.

He tossed the writhing body into the water, watching it closely. The mud swelled, then enveloped the insect. Brandon's smile widened. Something about the movement of the mud satisfied him more than he could understand. It was both smooth and abrupt, liquid and solid. It moved with the grace of a ballerina and the determination of a killer. He drew in a deep breath of the earthy scent and closed his eyes.

When a soft tinkling noise danced to his ears, he opened his eyes and scanned the bank on either side of the pier. There was nothing along the edge of the water. After a moment of silence, he shrugged, turning back to the pier. The noise came again. It was a soft, tinkling sound like two small pieces of metal rattling. Or was it a bell?

Turning from the water, he scanned the yard. He gasped when he saw the dog. It was one of those small lap breeds that yapped a lot. One of his neighbors back home had one like it.

Its white, fuzzy coat gleamed in the shadow beneath his house. *Fucking mutt*, he thought, his eyes narrowing as he stared at the dog.

Get it!

Brandon winced. Looking around, he expected someone else to be behind him. It was the same voice he'd heard while discussing the baby rats with his father. The thought was clear and loud in his head, but like before, no one else was around. He looked out at the field of muck and shook his head, unsure if he liked the new way of thinking.

His eyes went back to the dog, now nosing around their garbage can. A smile slid across his face as the seeds of a notion began to sprout in his mind.

The dog's white fur called to him like a beacon in the twilight. A thin smile parted his lips, and his eyes narrowed as his thoughts grew dark. *Yes, that'll do nicely.*

Get it!

Brandon didn't flinch when the voice came a second time. His eyes were on the dog. His mind was warming to an idea.

He moved quickly. Propelled by the heart thundering in his chest, he hurried along the edge of the yard and rounded the house in a crouch. When he cleared the corner, the dog looked up at him, its tail wagging furiously. When Brandon kneeled and called to it, the dog came running.

Brandon lifted it gently, cradling it in his left arm. The fur was soft beneath his hand and smelled faintly of lilac. The dog was definitely a pampered pooch. It was small and light and trusting.

Stupid mutt, he thought.

Brandon's smile faded as he carried the dog beneath the house. He wanted to go straight to the pier and toss the mutt in, but the notion that he should wait rose in his mind. Someone might see. He'd have to wait until it was dark. He cast his eyes toward the pier. *We'll have to wait. Not long, but a little while,* he thought. *Soon. I promise.*

Carrol Stivers rolled her eyes as she peered into the cabinet drawer. A sandwich bag had been filled with different colored bread ties. "Really?" she asked, lifting the bag out of the drawer.

"What?" Barry asked, not bothering to look up from his phone.

"Bread ties? She saved bread ties?"

Barry shrugged. "So? She thought she might need them, I guess. You know how old people are. Living through the Depression and all."

Carrol tossed the bag into the trash and pushed the drawer closed with her hip. She turned to her husband with a sigh. "The Depression?" she asked with a chuckle. "Do you even know how old your mother was?"

Barry shrugged. "Eighty something."

"Eighty-three, to be exact. She'd have to be a hundred to have lived through the depression, genius."

"You know what I mean. She was thrifty by nature, I guess. Not everybody was born into money, you know."

Carrol leaned against the counter, staring at her husband. "I don't get it. How were you two not closer? You were her only child, and you don't even know how old she was."

Barry sighed and shoved the phone into the pocket of his cargo shorts. "We just weren't. What do you want me to say? We fought a lot when I was younger."

"I'm sure she just wanted what's best for you."

"Maybe so, but our opinions of what was best for me were vastly different."

"Is that why you're not closer to Brandon?"

"What the hell does that supposed to mean?"

Carrol let out a tired sigh. "I don't want to fight, Barry. I was just asking a question."

"A damned loaded question, if you ask me."

"It's true, and you know it."

"What do you want me to do?" Barry stood. "Braid his damned hair or something? We're just fine."

"I don't think you are."

"Well," he said with a shrug. "That's your opinion." He strode to the front door and opened it. "Maybe if you didn't run so much interference, we could use this time down here to get closer. Of course, all you've done since we got here is bitch about my mother's housekeeping, oh, and call her crazy. I'm sure that's really helping."

Carrol opened her mouth to reply, but Barry stormed out the door and slammed it behind him hard enough to rattle the picture on the wall next to it. She crossed one arm over her chest and rested her elbow on it, pushing a hand through her hair. She puffed out her cheeks as she sighed. The ominous feeling in her gut that had been there since Barry suggested coming down here was gnawing at her. Something wasn't right, but she didn't know what.

Of course, there were her suspicions about Barry, but she couldn't stop Elvey's warnings from parading through her mind. But they were too crazy to believe. They didn't make sense.

Turning to the window over the sink, she stared at the garden gnomes and shook her head. She picked the largest one up and weighed it in the palm of her hand. It was eight inches tall, with a belly that hung over its jeans. The caption at the bottom read: I'm in shape. Round IS a shape.

Her lips pursed as she looked around the empty room. She stared down at the gnome and shook her head. Gripping the gnome on each end, she leaned over the sink and smashed it against the divider between the double bowls. The old plaster broke easily, revealing a hollow interior. Carrol turned each piece, inspecting the interior. Both pieces were empty.

When a hand touched her back, she jumped, letting out a yelp. Turning, she found her son standing behind her, a concerned look on his face.

She forced a smile and nodded. Her hands slipped behind her back, hiding the broken figurine. "I'm good."

Using sign language, he asked if something broke.

"Oh," she replied, bringing the gnome from behind her. "Yeah. This guy fell in the sink. I was just cleaning it up."

Brandon's brow creased as he studied her. He nodded, forcing a smile. He offered the sign for "dad," asking where his father was.

"Outside."

Brandon's eyes grew wide at the thought of his father poking around in the shed and accidentally finding the dog. He spun and headed for the front door.

"Brandon?"

He stopped, looking back at his mother impatiently.

"Are you okay? You seem out of sorts this evening."

He signed that he was fine and opened the door.

"Because if you're having—"

Carrol's shoulders slumped as the door closed. She watched through the windows as he hurried across the porch like he suddenly had somewhere to be. She leaned over the table and watched him descend the steps quickly. He disappeared beneath the edge of the porch, then reappeared in the yard below. Barry had taken refuge in one of the lawn chairs next to a sweet gum tree. He looked up from his phone when Brandon joined him, but the smile on his face looked more annoyed than anything else.

Carrol shook her head. "Jackass," she said, staring at her husband. She chewed on her thumbnail while she watched her husband and son interact. Her gut told her that something was off. *Maybe it's a guy thing*, she thought, watching Brandon and his father. *Maybe that's why he didn't come to me.*

She watched Brandon tap his father's shoulder, drawing his attention from his phone so he could sign to him. Barry looked up, watched him, then nodded.

"Hey, you guys," Carrol called from the top of the stairs. Brandon turned and looked at her. Barry finished typing on his phone, then looked up. "Why don't we have a weenie roast tonight? Build a fire, cook some dogs. Sounds fun, right?"

Brandon looked between her and Barry, then shrugged.

"You don't seem very excited. You always loved it at home."

Brandon smiled and nodded, giving her a thumbs up.

"Yeah. Sounds good," Barry finally said. He looked at Brandon. "There's plenty of dead fall around. You up for gathering some wood?"

Rubbing the back of his neck, he allowed his eyes to wander to the small shed just beyond the house. This evening was dragging by. Why couldn't his parents just go to bed early like other old people did?

The baby rats hadn't known what was happening. The mud just sucked them down without a fight. How would it be with the dog, especially a snow-white dog like the one he had tied up in a stinky old sack? Surely it would fight, struggle. Could the mud defeat a struggling animal? It had gotten the snake, but that wasn't a dog.

"Brandon?"

Brandon looked around at his father. He nodded reluctantly. There was no getting around it. He'd have to wait a little longer.

"Okay, you guys do that and get a fire started. I'll get everything ready. Tonight, we feast." Carrol watched the unenthusiastic reaction from her family and shook her head. "I said, tonight we feast!" she repeated, louder as she raised her hands into the air.

When the boys offered an obligatory cheer, she shook her head and retreated to the house.

The sound of the shower coming on told Brandon that it was time to move. He'd suffered through a tense supper with his parents, counting each hour as it passed. He rose from his bed and grabbed a pen light off the dresser. His mother would be in the shower for at least half an hour. Now, all he had to do was get past his dad.

He opened his bedroom door quietly and peeped out. His father was stretched out on the couch watching a baseball game, his hand loosely cradling a bottle of beer next to him.

Brandon smiled. His father had drunk several beers. It would be easy to get past him. Stepping into the living room, he pulled the door closed behind him. He made it to the front door before his father noticed him.

"Where you going, kiddo?"

Brandon flashed him a smile, then signed that he was going for a walk.

"Be careful. You know there's snakes out."

Brandon nodded and produced the light. He absorbed his father's stare for a moment, then nodded again. He ducked out the front door before he had to field another protest.

Oh no, it's dead, Brandon thought when he opened the storage shed. The bag was still and quiet on the floor. He poked it with one bare foot, and it began to wriggle in the sack. He smiled. It was alive for now.

He grabbed the canvas bag and clutched it to his chest. The bag was rough and smelled like mildew, but it had done the job. The tape around the mutt's snout would keep it from barking, but it could still whimper loud enough to get someone's attention. Brandon walked to the edge of the house and checked that the coast was clear. No one was in sight.

A smile came to his lips as he stepped from beneath the house and started across the yard. The grass was damp and cool on his bare feet. Beneath the fabric, the dog began to wriggle again but stayed quiet.

He paused for a moment, listening. The night was a riot of noise as frogs performed their nightly song. Normally, the varying pitches and tones, all coming at once, would make his brain itch, but tonight it didn't. When his eyes fell on the pier, barely visible in the shadows, a realization dawned on him. The noise came from everywhere, with one notable exception. The area surrounding the pier was silent. There were no frogs in the muck.

Brandon scurried across the yard, pausing just short of the pier as a firefly lit up in front of him. The fleeting desire to catch it ran through his mind, but he dismissed it. Back home, he'd be thrilled to run around for hours, collecting them in an old mason jar, but he wasn't back home. He had more important matters to attend to. He swatted the bug away with one hand and went to the pier.

Brandon dropped the bag to the weathered boards and sat down beside it. His hands were shaking as he pulled on the rope holding it closed. The thick twine was rough against his skin, but it felt good somehow, like scratching an itch.

His heart raced with anticipation as he reached inside, finding the dog. He pulled it out by the scruff of its neck and stared down at it. A few soft whimpers escaped its taped muzzle, but they weren't loud enough to cause concern. No one would hear. No one would interrupt him.

His own breaths were coming in excited pants as he held

the dog over the edge of the pier. The sound of his thundering heart drowned out everything else. The dog looked around, its big, dark eyes finding him. Brandon shook his head, offering no sympathy.

It was just a stupid dog. It didn't understand things the way he did. It didn't know the pleasure of watching the muck absorb something. It was a shit-eating mutt. He was giving its meaningless existence some purpose.

Beneath the dog, the mud stirred, shaking the stalks of the reeds noisily as it slithered past them. Their long, dry leaves rattled in the darkness. *So long, shit eater*, Brandon thought as a smile slipped across his lips. He opened his hand and let the dog drop into the churning mud below.

It landed in the muck with a wet plop. Dark mud splashed onto the gleaming white fur. The dog whined, looking up at him for help. Brandon absorbed the fear in its eyes, feeding the sense of power surging through his veins.

Brandon watched as the dog's back legs and hips sank into the darkness. The dog panicked, clawing at the mud furiously. Its struggles only threw mud all over itself, but there was still enough clean white fur to stand out in the dim light. Its cries became more urgent as its front left paw became insnared by the mud.

The dog squinted as Brandon shined the light into its eyes, looking back at him through strands of fluffy white fur. Still unaware of its fate, it whined loudly, begging him for help. Brandon shook his head as he watched it sink. The dog's floppy ears lay atop the mud as its neck sank into the muck. Its nose pushed skyward, struggling until the end.

The last of the white fur slipped beneath the mud. An air bubble escaped, popping on the surface of the muck with a loud squelch.

Brandon's eyes rolled back in his head as his body began

to waiver. He didn't know what being drunk felt like but figured it had to feel like this. He was floating. His body shook as something powerful stirred in his loins. He'd read enough of his mother's "romance" novels to understand what was happening. It was every bit as wonderful as the books claimed.

Brandon opened his eyes to a sky full of stars. His mouth fell open, awestruck. The sky was as dark as soot, and the stars were brighter than he'd ever seen them. They looked bigger, closer. He swallowed hard and sat up.

An unnatural quiet hung on the still air as if the world knew what had happened. There were no frogs croaking, no crickets chirping, no night birds. There was nothing but him and the inky darkness.

He felt around on the pier for the light. The small beam interrupted the darkness like a rude comment. It fell first on the dry reeds. They shuddered as if recoiling from the light. Brandon moved the light from them to the mud, sensing that they didn't like it. He looked where he'd last seen the dog. Of course, it was there, but the beam fell on a flower sitting atop the dark muck.

Five vibrant pink petals surrounded a crown of yellow stamens. The scent of it drifted into his nostrils, and he moaned. He wanted nothing more than to have the flower, to own it, to possess it. One trembling hand extended over the edge of the pier but hesitated. What would happen if he touched the mud? Would he be pulled in? Would it consume him too?

Brandon shook his head, withdrawing slightly. He wanted the flower but couldn't risk falling in. But he couldn't just leave it.

Leaning over the edge as far as he dared, he inhaled deeply through his nose. The flower's scent consumed him, racing through his veins like electricity. His eyes flew open, and he gasped. *Yes*, he thought. He didn't just want the flower. He needed it. He closed his eyes again and took another long sniff of the perfumed air. He needed it like he'd never needed anything.

Brandon opened his eyes and recoiled instantly. The flower hovered before his eyes, glowing faintly in the darkness, inches from his face. His head tilted to one side, and his jaw went slack as he stared at it. It was unlike anything he'd ever seen. Both delicate and strong at the same time, fragile yet powerful.

One hand reached out and found a tall stem growing out of the mud. A tiny charge leapt toward his fingertips as they neared the stem. Brandon recoiled with a gasp but reached out again. The stem broke cleanly a few inches beneath the bloom, and the prize was his. He settled back onto the deck, cradling the flower with both hands.

The soft glow of the flower illuminated the satisfied smile on his lips as he stared down at it. *Yes*, he thought. *Yes*. A low laugh escaped him, drifting into the darkness that pressed in on him and the flower. *Yes*.

Out in the darkness, a clump of reeds began to shake. Then another. One by one, the other clumps joined in until the muck was alive with the noise of them. It sounded like pounding rain or static on the radio, but Brandon barely heard it. All of his attention was devoted to the flower.

EIGHT

Carrol absently turned the page of the book though she hadn't read it. Her attention was on her son, but she didn't want him to notice her watching him. Her eyes peeped over the paperback in her hand and found him lying on the couch, as he'd done most of the morning.

He'd gotten up for snacks twice, finishing neither. He was laying on his back, holding the video game player above him with both hands. The sounds of Pac-Man gobbling the dots drifted across the quiet room. He groaned when the ghost ate his character and dropped the game to his chest with a huff. He sat up, ate a chip from the bag on the coffee table, and shook his head.

Perched in a worn recliner across the room, Carrol turned another unread page. Brandon had been restless all morning, and she was worried. A sudden change in his environment could trigger an episode, but they'd been here three days, and he'd seemed fine until now.

A drastic drop in barometric pressure could also affect him, but she'd checked the weather already. They were in a summer pattern with high pressure, and there were no storms predicted for at least a week.

Her eyes followed him as he went back to the fridge and

grabbed a bottle of water. He opened it and drank most of it over the sink, staring out the window.

She cleared her throat and closed the book. "Are you feeling alright, sweetie?" she asked softly.

Brandon continued to stare out the window, giving no indication that he'd heard her.

"Brandon?" Her brow furrowed when he still didn't answer. "Brandon," she repeated louder.

He turned to her, shaking his head. He threw his hands up, raising his eyebrows questioningly.

"I asked if you were feeling alright?"

He nodded and ran a hand through his hair. He signed that he felt fine and flashed a weak smile that did little to abate her worry.

"Are you sure? You seem a little unsettled."

He nodded again, more adamant, then headed for his bedroom.

Carrol stood. "You know if something's bothering you, you can tell me."

Brandon nodded and signed again that he was fine.

"Is it being here?" she asked. "Because we could go back home. I know change can be hard for you sometimes."

Brandon shook his head and signed that he liked it here.

"It's okay if you don't. You don't have to worry about hurting your dad's feelings. He'll understand."

Brandon shook his head angrily. His hands moved in quick, jerky motions as he signed that he was fine. When he was done, he turned and stormed into his room, closing the door behind him.

Carrol drew in a deep breath and exhaled slowly. Elvey Stiver's words crept into her mind. *They get all antsy in the beginning.* That's what she'd said in her warning to Carrol about the Stivers men when they started to be affected by the dark spirits in the waters. She'd dismissed much of what Elvey said for years, but the possibility that the old woman was right began to take root in her mind.

The phone conversations, always taken while Barry was at work, sounded like the ravings of a lonely old woman bitter because her son never visited. Her warnings about witches and evil spirits that lived in the shallows had been dismissed as old wives' tales and folklore. They were the superstitions of an uneducated old woman who prattled around in an old house, left alone for far too long.

Carrol looked around, noting the shadows in the old house. Her eyes danced on the faces of the gnomes. What was she now but a woman sitting alone in the very same house?

They get all antsy in the beginning.

Carrol rubbed her forehead, staring at the door to Brandon's room. She considered going in and trying to get him to talk but decided against it. A confrontation could make things worse. If it were an episode coming on, which would be easier to deal with, she didn't want to hasten it.

She sighed and closed her eyes, saying a quick prayer for her son. Crossing the room to the fridge, she grabbed a bottle of water and headed for the front door. The idea of talking to Barry about the situation wasn't her favorite idea, but he was all she had.

"Hey." Carrol waved her free hand at Barry as he ran a string trimmer between a series of knotted roots protruding from the ground near the edge of the bog that bordered their property.

He looked at her, slightly perturbed, and shut the machine off.

"Thought you might be thirsty." She extended the bottle.

Barry looked at it suspiciously, then looked up at her. He leaned the trimmer against a cypress tree and took the water.

"Thanks."

"The yard looks good." She watched him drink half the bottle. "What are those?" she asked, pointing at the roots.

Barry followed her point. "Cypress knees. They're the roots from these trees."

"Why do they do that? Come up out of the ground?"

"Other than to make cutting grass even more miserable, I don't know. I've trimmed grass around these same damned things more times than I can count." He rubbed the bottle against his brow and then finished the water. "What's up?"

Carrol shrugged as she accepted the empty bottle. "I don't know."

"It must be something for you to bring me a drink of water." Barry picked up the trimmer again.

"First of all, I was just being nice."

Barry laughed. "That's why I'm suspicious."

"Ass." Carrol shook her head, regretting her decision already. She ran her hand through her hair and scratched the back of her head. "I think something's bothering Brandon."

"What is it?"

Carrol shrugged. "He just seems out of sorts today. It's like he can't be still," she said, intentionally avoiding the word "antsy." That would give credence to Elvey's wild tales.

"Maybe he's just bored."

Carrol pursed her lips and shook her head as she surveyed the yard. "I don't know. It kinda feels like an episode might be coming on."

"You brought his meds, didn't you?"

Carrol nodded. "Of course. I don't think it's come to that yet."

"I don't know. Like I said, maybe he's just bored. He's a kid. They got more energy than us old folks. You want me to get him to help with this?"

She shook her head. "You know lots of noises can over stimulate him."

Barry shrugged. "I don't know what to tell you. Keep an eye on him, I guess."

Carrol watched Barry flip a switch on the string trimmer and yank the pull cord. When the machine roared to life, he went back to his chore.

"Ass," Carrol said again and turned to go back into the house, lamenting her husband's attitude. She'd gotten as much as she expected from him.

Carrol knocked on her son's bedroom door. When he didn't answer, she knocked again and opened it slowly. She found him laying across the bed on his stomach with his back to her. He was wearing his noise-canceling headphones.

Her heart sank. Over the years, he'd learned when he needed the silence the headphones afforded him. The fact that he had them on signaled the coming of an episode.

She bent, looking around his shoulder. Her brow furrowed when she found him coloring. He often colored, but it was the subject matter that bothered her. She recognized the superhero on the page enough to know that he was one of the good guys. This one, however, looked anything but. Brandon had colored his body suit solid black. He'd also added jagged edges to his shield, making it look like a giant saw blade.

She leaned forward and touched his leg.

Brandon turned suddenly, his eyes wide with shock. When his brow creased deeply, she took a step back. There was an anger on his face that she'd never seen before.

"Brandon?" she asked softly, mimicking taking headphones off her own head.

He stared at her for a moment longer, then turned his attention to his clenched fist. It opened slowly, revealing a broken crayon. He tossed the black Crayola into the gutter of the coloring book and sat up, slipping the headphones from his ears.

"I'm sorry." Carrol offered a sympathetic smile as her eyes searched Brandon's face. "I didn't mean to scare you."

He nodded slowly but didn't respond.

Carrol approached him, studying his face. His hair was disheveled and wet with sweat around the temples. "Are you okay?" she asked, sitting on the edge of the bed.

Brandon nodded and signed that he was fine as he turned back to the coloring book. He picked up the tip of the crayon and went back to work.

"You just seem like something's bothering you."

Brandon shrugged.

Carrol leaned over and ran a hand through his hair. "You're sweating." He tried to avoid her hand as it went to his forehead, but she found it with her palm. His skin was cool and clammy. He didn't have a fever.

"You know I just worry about you because I love you."

Brandon nodded as he colored.

Carrol sighed as she watched him work. The darkness on the page concerned her. He'd never used so much black in a picture before. Usually, the coloring pages offered him a respite from the world, and she'd saved every book once he'd finished it.

"Brandon," she began. "You know that if something is going on, you can tell me." She watched him shrug. "I'm always here for you, sweetie. That's what I do. I love you."

Brandon stopped coloring suddenly but didn't turn around.

Carrol stared at his hand, poised inches above the page. His fingers squeezed the broken crayon to the point that his hand was shaking slightly. Seconds passed with agonizing slowness as she watched her son. His whole body was tensed. No, she thought, it's coiled, like a snake.

She withdrew slightly, unsure what he'd do next. Brandon had never been violent towards her before, but the sense that he might began to grow in her chest.

"Brandon?" Her voice was almost a whisper. His body relaxed suddenly, and he went back to coloring. A sigh of relief escaped her, and she pushed a hand through her hair. She watched him a moment longer, then stood.

"I'm here if you need me, Sweetie. Okay?"

Brandon gave her a thumbs-up without looking up.

Carrol walked to the door and opened it but stopped when she heard Brandon move on the bed. When she looked back, he was sitting up, staring at her with tears in his eyes.

"Do you still love me?" he signed.

"Oh, sweetie." She went to her son, hugging him to her chest. "I will always love you." Carrol stroked her hair. "There's nothing in the world that could ever change that."

Brandon pulled free of her grasp and looked up at her, signing, "Nothing?"

Carrol smiled through her own tears. She put her hands on his cheeks, thumbing tears away as she lifted his face to hers. She nodded and planted a kiss on his forehead. "There's nothing between Heaven or Hell that could ever make me stop loving you. Nothing. Nada. Zilch."

Brandon's anguished face stared at her, his bottom lip quivering as he fought to maintain control.

Carrol nodded at him. "Nothing, Brandon," she said again.

"Wouldn't your life be easier if I wasn't the way I am?" When he finished signing, his hands dropped to his lap.

Carrol's heart sank, and her legs grew weak. "Listen to me, Brandon. I love you. You. It doesn't matter who or what you are. You're perfect to me. There isn't one thing I would change about you."

"But wouldn't it be easier?" he persisted.

"You don't make my life hard, sweetheart. I don't even know where you got that idea. You make my life worth living."

Brandon smiled as she bent and kissed his forehead again.

"You're the way God made you, Brandon. Don't ever let anyone make you think that He made a mistake."

Satisfied, Brandon laid back down and resumed his coloring.

Carrol Stivers put a hand over her mouth as she stared at her son. Something was wrong. Something was terribly wrong, but she wasn't sure what. She watched him color for a long time, waiting to see if he'd say anything else. When he didn't, she quietly slipped out of the room, leaving the door open. She interlaced her fingers behind her head as she crossed the living room. The air inside the tiny house was suddenly close, hard to breathe.

Finding herself in front of the double windows in the living room, she stared out over the scene before her. The pier and the swampy area around it, bathed in the midday sun, looked like any other wetland she'd ever seen. Although marked with patches of tall, dead reeds, the abundant growth of grasses and pickerel rush looked as lush as a rainforest.

Her hands went to her temples, massaging them. A headache was building, and it promised to be a good one. She spared the swamp one last look and shook her head before heading to the cabinet to get some ibuprofen.

NINE

The swing his father had hung from the towering white oak was a pleasant distraction, but the novelty had already worn off. Brandon sat on the plank, the crook of his elbows supporting him on the ropes as he swung idly back and forth. He watched the patch of bare earth below him each time he passed. In his enthusiasm, he'd worn the grass down, leaving a patch of bare dirt beneath him.

He couldn't stop thinking about the flower. It withered quickly in the sunlight until it barely resembled a flower at all. He'd clung to the dried-up remains for another day until reluctantly returning it to the muck. The dark mud received it the same way it did everything else, but as the flower sank, he couldn't help crying a little. Even now, a day and a half later, his heart ached for the loss.

"Hey."

Brandon heard the voice but didn't look up.

"Hey, kid. You deaf or something?"

The sharp tone of the young girl's voice shook Brandon from his stupor. He found her standing astride a faded purple bicycle. He put his feet down, stopping himself suddenly.

Her head tilted to one side, shifting the voluminous crop of curly black hair that hung well past her shoulders. One corner of her mouth pulled upwards slightly as she stared at him. "Well?"

Brandon nodded and offered a wave. She was thin but shapely, and his eyes feasted on her. The faded pink tee shirt offered only a hint of the small mounds on her chest. His eyes slid down her body to the cut-off blue jeans that clung to her hips. White threads hung against the tanned skin of her toned thighs.

His mouth suddenly went dry. When he'd first seen the flower, he'd never wanted anything in his life more. The girl before him made that feel like an afterthought. His heart pounded against his chest, and suddenly it was twenty degrees hotter.

"Hey, I got eyes, too," she snapped, catching his stare.

Brandon nodded, dropping his gaze as his cheeks flushed with embarrassment. He'd never experienced such a flash of desire for a girl before and wasn't sure what to do next. His first thought was to run away, but his legs wouldn't move. He took a deep breath to calm himself, then looked at her again.

She did indeed have eyes. Two big, brown soulful eyes that were opened wide, staring back at him from beneath two perfectly arched eyebrows, all framed by a backdrop of wild, dark hair. The thought of running hands through her hair swept through him, and the longing intensified.

"I guess you're not deaf after all." A sly smile slid across her lips. "Or gay."

Brandon shook his head as he stood from the swing, crossing his hands over his crotch. He didn't know if she could see how he felt, but he didn't want to take that chance.

"I'm Amy."

Brandon nodded again and offered another wave.

"I know you're not from around here, but unless you're from Mars, this is usually where you tell me your name."

Brandon dropped his eyes to his feet. For an instant, he'd forgotten that he was the way he was. The sudden remembrance doused his excitement like throwing water on a fire. No girl as beautiful as this one would want anything to do with a boy like him.

Arming sweat from his brow with a sigh, he forced himself to look up at her again. Her head gave him an impatient nod, and he swallowed hard. He put two fingers to his lips and shook his head.

Amy's brow furrowed as she eyed him. "Are you trying to tell me you can't talk?"

Brandon nodded, then dropped his gaze again. Meeting new people was always embarrassing, but it was worse this time. He shrank beneath her stare, wishing she'd just go away yet wanting her to stay at the same time.

"Cool," she finally said, shrugging casually. "A guy who can't talk. That's pretty much like finding a golden goose if you ask me." Her laugh danced on the warm air between them, giving him hope.

Brandon smiled and signed to ask her what he could help her with.

"Oh," Amy sat back on the seat and cocked one leg up on the raised pedal closest to him. "I know some sign language. Not much, mind you. My Aunt Betsy was deaf. I don't know what you asked just now, but I'm looking for a dog. You happen to see one around?"

Brandon shook his head, then looked away as his breath caught in his throat. He thought about asking what it looked like but couldn't bring himself to. If a dog was missing, he knew which one it was. His stomach knotted at the prospect that he might have thrown her dog in the muck.

"Okay. It's cool," her head fell to the side as she stared at Brandon. "Why can't you talk? If you don't mind me asking."

Brandon shrugged and offered her his palms. Explaining that he'd never talked, that there was something wrong with him that the doctors couldn't explain, would take too much effort.

"Born that way?" she asked, nodding. "It's cool. Anyways, I'm looking for a little white dog. A Pekinese or something. I don't know and really don't care."

Brandon shook his head and shrugged. He glanced at the stairs to his house, wanting to run up them and escape.

"It's not my dog or nothing. The old guy that lives up the street from me owns it. He's a weird dude." She put a hand alongside her mouth as she leaned toward him. "Word to the wise, keep your distance from the light blue house down the street. He's a pedo or something." She dropped her hand, grabbing the handlebars. "Anyhow, he put the word out that he'd pay fifty bucks to whoever found the little shit eater. I figured I'd give it a shot. It's fifty bucks, you know."

Brandon nodded.

"It's easier than making fifty bucks the way he'd rather pay for." She grunted and shook her head. "Like I said, he's a weirdo. Really handsy, if you know what I mean. Don't get too close to his fence if he's out there. I'm not sure you being a guy would make much difference to him."

Brandon nodded and took a few tentative steps toward her. He dug a cell phone out of his pocket and held it up, then motioned between them.

"Nope, I don't got no a cell phone. We don't even have a landline at home. Sorry, Charlie."

Brandon nodded, then held out his palm, mimicking writing as he stared hopefully at Amy.

"Okay." Amy shrugged. "I got a minute."

Brandon raced up the steps and returned with a small wire-rimmed pad and a pencil. He wrote his name on the first page and showed it to her.

"Brandon?" she asked, nodding. "Cool." She smiled at him. "How old are you, Brandon?"

He wrote a 15 on the paper and showed her.

"Oh," she said, nodding. "I'm sixteen."

Brandon wrote, "I'll be 16 in a few months."

"That's cool."

He wrote, "I'm here all summer. Maybe longer," on the pad and held it up. After she'd read it, he wrote, "Wanna hang out or something?"

Amy read the note and looked into his eyes. "You get straight to the point, don't you?" She laughed when his cheeks blushed again. "It's cool, though. We can chill sometime, I guess. This place is pretty damned boring." She sat up on the seat and put her hands on her hips. "Not a lotta kids 'round anyway."

Brandon smiled and nodded.

"I guess you live in some big house in some big city far away from here."

Brandon shook his head. He wrote, "Providence. Not far away. This was my grandmother's house. She died."

"Mrs. Strivers was your granny?" One eyebrow rose inquisitively as she studied him.

Brandon nodded as he wrote. "I only met her once, though."

Amy nodded as she read the note. "I live here full time." Her eyes watched his face for a reaction. Some people had their own notions about people who lived on the river. Half of the houses here were vacation homes for rich folks. The other half was home to people who had considerably less.

She smiled when Brandon's face remained neutral. A hint of a smile tugged at the corners of his lips as he stared back at her. "You might be okay after all, for a townie."

Brandon shrugged, unable to hold back his smile any longer. Amy was more than alright by him. His eyes followed her hand as she slapped a mosquito on her thigh, wiping the blood away with her thumb. His eyes lingered on the thin smear of blood she'd missed, and the longing began to well within his chest again. He wanted to touch her smooth skin, to feel it beneath his fingertips.

"Hey," she said, again catching his stare. "You okay? Earth to Brandon."

Brandon wrote, "I'm sorry," on the pad.

Amy laughed and gave him a wink. "It's okay, new guy. You can look, but you can't touch." She turned the handlebars of the bicycle and prepared to leave. "Unless I give you permission, that is." She laughed and pushed off with one long leg. She rode a few feet, then stopped suddenly, looking back over her shoulder at him.

"The reason you cain't talk ain't because you're stupid or nothing, is it?"

Brandon shook his head, stung by the comment.

"Alright, alright," she said, absorbing his incredulous look. "I didn't think so. Just making sure, though." Amy pushed off again and started down the drive. "A girl can't be too careful nowadays, you know."

Brandon watched her until she made the end of the driveway and turned right onto the dirt road. She threw him a wave just before disappearing behind a group of young cypress trees along the edge of the neighbor's house.

He waved back and then ran both hands through his hair as an exasperated sigh escaped him. Bringing his hands to his face, he saw that they were wet with sweat. Amy had ignited a fire inside him that had never been there before. It was odd and exhilarating but also scary, and he had no idea what to do about it.

Brandon rolled over in bed and looked out the window. He knew it would still be dark but checked anyway. Outside, frogs sang their nightly chorus. The soft sound of a distant owl came to him in the darkness. The night sounded different here than it did at home. Everything was different here, but he was starting to like it.

He groaned softly and rolled over. All afternoon his thoughts had flip-flopped between the barrage of new emotions that vied for attention.

An image of Amy formed in his mind. He saw her delicate hand against her smooth, tanned thigh. The thin smear of blood from where she'd swatted the mosquito stood out bright and red. He wanted desperately to touch her, to feel her smooth skin, but the sight of the blood also excited him.

In his mind, he saw them together as if outside himself. He bent and licked the blood from her skin. She looked down at him and smiled, moaning ever so slightly.

When a metallic scent filled his nose, he sat up in bed and looked around. He was alone, but he expected not to be. He wanted Amy to be here. Closing his eyes again, he saw Amy's smiling face, framed by that long, dark, wild hair. He smiled at the thought of her. She was beautiful, but in a different way than he was used to. There was something about her that made him want her in ways that he never wanted anything before.

Brandon's smile faded as the memory of Amy morphed into the flower standing in the pool of dark mud. His hand rose slowly as he reached out for the flower. His fingers caressed the air in front of him, but in his mind, he saw his hand against the flower.

His fingers slid down the stem, preparing to pluck it from the muck. The slight charge he'd experienced when he'd picked the flower from the muck was much stronger now. He grimaced in pain but refused to let go. He groaned as the charge intensified and finally released the stem. It pulled from his hand, dragging the flower further from him.

Brandon got onto his knees, crawling to the end of the bed

as he followed the flower. His hand found the wooden frame at the foot of the bed. When he looked down, he didn't see his bedroom floor but the field of muck at the end of the pier. The rattle of the dry reeds filled his ears. He stretched out, reaching for the stem. The muck stirred beneath.

He tore his eyes from the flower and looked down. Amy's naked body was lying in the mud. A gasp escaped him. The dark mud had wrapped around her chest and hips, depriving him of the view of her private parts.

Brandon looked back at the flower, then down to Amy. When his hand dropped toward Amy to save her, the flower moved further away. He gasped and reached for the flower, but his eyes were on Amy. She was sinking into the darkness but made no attempt to free herself. She smiled up at him and raised one eyebrow seductively.

"You can look, but you can't touch," she whispered, her voice already garbled by the mud. "Unless I give you permission."

The flower began to glow softly in the darkness of his bedroom, drawing his attention from the girl sinking in the muck at the foot of his bed. His desire for the flower grew into a need, surpassing his desire for Amy. He supported himself with one hand on the footboard and stretched the other toward the flower.

"I know you want to do more than look. Don't you?" Amy asked softly. "You can if you want to."

Brandon looked down as she reached up to him. Her dirty hand hung in the soft glow coming from the flower. He nodded slowly. Yes. He did want that. He wanted that very badly.

Amy smiled, parting lips that were now painted a bright red. "Then save me, Brandon. Win me. Be my hero. Can you do that for me?"

Brandon looked back at the flower. He could reach it if he stretched a little further. He could have it. He needed to have it. But what about Amy? He wanted her too. Stretching further over the end of the bed, his fingertips brushed against the stem.

"Brandon," Amy whispered from below him. Her voice was weaker, more distant as she sank deeper into the mud.

He glanced down at her, then back to the flower. It had moved a few inches further away. He looked back down to Amy. She was deeper in the mud now. The ends of her hair, already being pulled into the muck, looked like a tangle of roots.

The intensity of the glow increased, drawing his attention away from Amy. The words *"Let the little whore sink,"* echoed through his mind. *"She's just a white trash bitch, like the dog. Let her sink."*

Amy's plaintive cries pulled Brandon's eyes back to her. He watched as she arched her back from the mud. Her hands swiped across her chest, removing every trace of the mud in one smooth motion. Brandon gasped as he stared down at her bare breasts. In the dim glow of the flower, they were everything he'd imagined they'd be and more.

His hand dropped and grabbed hers. A whimper escaped him as a stabbing pain raced up his arm. The current in the muck was far stronger than that of the flower. His eyes slipped from her smiling face down to her bare breasts, and he pulled.

"It's okay," she whispered, giving him a wink as she rose slowly from the muck. The dark mud slipped from her body, revealing a taunt, flat stomach.

Brandon's eyes followed the retreat of the mud. His heart raced as the slit of her belly button appeared. His breaths were coming in pants as the line of mud neared her hips.

He swallowed hard, disbelieving his own eyes. As he leaned forward, his sweaty palm slipped on the footboard, and he was falling.

He landed hard on his back with a groan. When he opened his eyes, the flower and Amy were both gone. He stared up at the ceiling of his bedroom, his excitement for Amy and the flower evaporating quickly.

Had it all been a dream? Had he imagined it all? He sat up with a disappointed sigh. He looked to his left, where the flower had been. There was nothing but a dark wall. Raising his hands in the pale moonlight, he saw they were as clean as when he'd gotten out of the shower.

Dammit, he thought. *None of it had been real.* Could it all have just been his imagination? The sights, the smells? But he'd felt and seen things. Real things.

He blew out an exasperated breath and got up from the floor. Things were changing. He could feel it. Things were already different.

He crawled back beneath the covers and pulled them up over his head. The tears came in a flood when he began to cry.

TEN

"What 'cha doing?"

Brandon jumped, startled as Amy's voice snatched him from his thoughts. She'd managed to navigate the length of the pier without him noticing. He looked over his shoulder at her but couldn't hold her gaze. He looked away, embarrassed. Last night he'd dreamed of her naked. Now here she was.

He closed his eyes and took a deep breath, trying to compose himself and keep from imagining her naked again, but she wasn't making it easy.

"You okay?" she asked, squeezing in beside him at the end of the pier. "You look kinda wrung out."

Brandon nodded, hoping his cheeks weren't as red as they felt. The touch of her shoulder against his sent his mind reeling. He gave her an "okay" sign and nodded but quickly looked away.

"So, you're just sitting here looking at mud?" she asked, leaning forward to peer into the muck. "I gotta say, it sounds a little boring."

Brandon shrugged as he forced himself to look at her. He signed that it *was* boring, then looked away, but not before allowing his eyes to wash over her. She wore a white tank top that fit snugly and a pair of red running shorts that were short enough to reveal most of her upper thigh.

"So, you want to do something?" she asked.

Brandon shrugged, then nodded, hoping he didn't look as eager as he felt.

"Cool. Let's go."

Brandon stood and offered Amy a hand. When she slid her hand into his, she smiled up at him. "Aren't you a gentleman?"

Brandon smiled and blushed again. Her hand was soft and supple in his. Her skin was warm and inviting.

"What were you thinking about so hard when I came up?" she asked, allowing herself to be helped up. "You didn't even hear me coming, and I wasn't sneaking."

Brandon shook his head. He couldn't tell her that he was thinking about her, about the dream he'd had about her. The image of her bare breasts flashed through his mind, and his heart skipped a beat.

Amy cocked her head to one side and grinned. "You're a little strange. Do you know that?" She let her hand linger in his a moment longer, then pulled it away, making sure that her fingertips danced along his palm.

Brandon's shoulders drooped. He signed the question, "I'm strange?"

Amy laughed as she started down the pier. "I'm not saying it's a bad thing." She looked back over her shoulder at him and smiled. "Maybe I should have said different, not strange."

Brandon nodded, following her across the weathered boards of the pier, taking in her smooth, casual stride. He took a deep breath to calm his racing heart and exhaled quietly.

"Will your folks let you go anywhere?" she asked when he caught up with her.

Brandon nodded and signed, "I'm not a baby, you know."

Amy laughed. "Okay then, let's go for a walk. I'll show you around the 'hood. Try to keep up."

Standing at the edge of the dirt road, Amy looked at the tangle of underbrush before them. "It's a little bit of a rough go. The place is kinda grown up. I haven't been here yet this summer."

Brandon nodded and gave her two thumbs up.

"Just to be safe, you'd better hold my hand. I'll lead you."

Amy held her hand out and smiled. When Brandon hesitated, she arched an eyebrow. "You're not scared to walk in the woods with me, are you?"

When he grabbed her hand, Amy laughed. "Good." She led off the road and into the woods. "Don't let go. You might get lost forever. They say that these woods are haunted."

Brandon stopped suddenly, staring at her questioningly.

"I'm playing," she laughed. "I just don't want you to slip and fall." Amy turned and pushed through the undergrowth, pulling him with her.

Brandon allowed himself to be led. A hint of embarrassment from being helped by a girl hung in his chest, but it was outweighed by the feel of her hand in his. It was soft like he'd imagined it would be.

"Folks call this place 'Big Blue' because, well, it's a big rock, and it's blue." Amy laughed. "It's pretty cool, though."

Brandon nodded, fighting the limbs as Amy released them.

"Back in the day, kids used to come out here at night and go skinny dipping."

Brandon's heart leapt into his throat as the image of Amy's naked body covered with mud popped into his mind. He swallowed hard but made no attempt to reply. Amy was unlike any girl he'd ever known, and he wasn't sure what to make of her yet.

"Here we are." Amy pulled him through the last branches and smiled. She released his hand and swept both arms through the air in front of the massive boulder. "Ta da. I give you Big Blue."

Brandon's eyes bulged as he stared at the rock. Perched on the edge of the river, it was easily as big as his grandmother's house. He stepped forward and ran a hand across the smooth surface. The parts of the stone not covered with moss and lichen were indeed a pale blueish-gray color. He shot Amy a questioning look, then returned to studying the rock.

Amy shrugged. "I don't know what kind of rock it is if that's what you're wondering. Maybe somebody said it was limestone or something. It's not really important, is it?"

Brandon shook his head.

"Gimme a boost." Amy stepped closer to Brandon, bringing her body to within inches of his. "Like this." She interlaced her fingers and held her hands in front of her waist. "I wanna climb on top. Boost me up." She moved closer and put her hands on his shoulders.

Brandon bent and interlaced his own fingers. He gave Amy a nod, and she put her foot in his hands.

"Ready?" she asked with a coy smile.

Brandon nodded.

"Don't drop me," she said, putting her hands on his shoulders. "One. Two. Three." She pushed up into his hand, brushing her stomach against his face.

Brandon took her weight easily, standing frozen as he held her up, her thighs inches from his face.

"C'mon. What're you doing?" She insisted. "Boost me on up."

Brandon strained, lifting her higher. He moaned internally as one leg brushed against his face, wondering if she'd done it intentionally. Part of him hoped she had.

When her weight left his hand, he stepped back and watched her scramble over the top of the boulder and disappear.

He scanned the edge of the rock, expecting her to reappear. When she didn't, he clapped his hands once. He stepped back and scanned the rock again. When he found nothing still, he clapped his hands again, twice this time.

"Settle down, Mister Clapper," Amy laughed as she rejoined him, pushing through the underbrush to Brandon's right. "You're going to wake the dead."

He threw his hands up questioningly.

"There's an easier way up around here. C'mon."

Brandon moved forward and took her arm. When she turned back, he asked her why she made him boost her.

"I don't know." Amy laughed again. "Maybe I wanted to see if you could lift me," she said and disappeared around the boulder. "Come on already," she called through the brush.

The view from atop the boulder was breathtaking. The river stretched out in both directions, slowing in the long, sweeping arc of the bend. High atop a rocky cliff on the far bank of the river, a massive house interrupted an otherwise unbroken forest of pines and mixed hardwoods.

"Pretty cool view, huh?" Amy asked.

Brandon nodded emphatically as his eyes traced the path of the wide, dark river.

"That's your place over there."

Brandon leaned forward, looking past Amy to follow her finger. The yard and the front half of the house were visible. His eyes wandered across the yard and found the pier. From this angle, the field of muck looked like an innocent patch of grass clinging to the banks.

As he watched, a large white bird glided in, flapping its long winds to slow the descent into the wild grasses. His heart leaped into his throat when he realized it was landing in the muck.

He nudged Amy, drawing her attention from his house, and asked her where she lived. He nodded as she pointed past him but stole another glance at the bird. Its wings were beating furiously as it tried to take off again. It was already too late.

Brandon turned, following Amy's gesture. He didn't need to watch the scene to know what would happen to the bird.

"It's just me and mom now. My dad ran off a few years back. The place ain't much to look at, but it's home. I guess."

Brandon turned back to Amy and smiled. He signed, "Home is where the heart is."

She laughed and drew her knees to her chest, wrapping her arms around her legs. "I wouldn't go that far."

Brandon stole a quick glance over her shoulder. The bird's wings, now filthy with dark mud, were still beating, but it was sinking fast. He closed his eyes and sighed, then looked at Amy. Her chin was on her knees, and she was staring across the river. Her eyes were distant, missing the vibrance she'd had only moments ago.

He nudged and asked what was wrong.

"Nothing," she sighed.

Brandon reached out a hand to comfort her but hesitated. He drew it back, reconsidered, then put a hand on her shoulder. She glanced at him and forced a smile, then sat her chin back on her knees.

"Do you ever just get sad for no reason?" she asked.

Brandon nodded, stealing another glance at the muck. Thankfully, the bird was gone.

"I can see that big ole house up there from my bedroom window. Some nights I lay there and stare at it. It's always lit up, you know, like they want folks to see it."

He looked at the house, then back to Amy. He asked who lived in it.

"Who lives there?" she asked, unsure of his question.

When he nodded, she shrugged. "I don't know. I don't even know how you'd even get there. I'm sure there's a long driveway. It's probably paved like a highway. Must be somebody rich."

Brandon nodded. The house was twice the size of their house back home and five times bigger than their little river house. His dad made "good money," but they could never afford a house like that.

He rubbed Amy's shoulder but didn't know what to say. He decided that he didn't like to see her sad. She was still pretty, but the look on her face made his heart ache.

"What do people do to even get so much money?" she asked.

Brandon shook his head as he looked at the house. The owner of the house was probably a lawyer or a doctor, maybe a politician.

Amy sighed heavily and looked at him from the corner of her eye. "Do you think your folks would like me?"

Brandon shrugged. He smiled and told her he wondered if they even liked him sometimes. Her short laugh lifted his spirits. He leaned forward slightly and looked into her eyes.

"What?" she asked, raising her head from her knees.

He told her she was pretty. When she looked away, blushing, his own smile grew.

"You don't have to lie to make me feel better."

"It's true," he signed, nodding. She didn't look like the girls at his school. There was something about her, a genuineness to her looks, that spoke to him. She didn't wear make-up, but she didn't need to. Her hair was windswept, but it looked good on her. There was an exoticness to her that he liked. His eyes found her thin lips, and the urge to kiss her welled within him.

"I'm glad you think so. I don't see it, though."

"You're beautiful."

"Thank you." Amy shook her head and sighed again.

"You wanna hear something funny?" she asked.

Brandon nodded, inching his hand across her back.

"I haven't been by your place in almost a year. I used to stop by now and again when Mama Stivers — that's what everybody called her — was alive. She was a nice enough old lady. A little out there sometimes, but she was nice. She always had snacks and drinks if you asked politely." Amy smiled. "I liked her."

Brandon signed that he'd only met her once, when he was around five.

"Why didn't y'all ever visit?"

Brandon shrugged and looked out over the river. His mother made no secret that she didn't like the old woman, and his father didn't seem to mind it at all. His mother had already boxed up most of the old woman's stuff, especially the garden gnomes. Several of the larger ones had even been broken.

"I get it. Family issues. Believe me, I understand."

Brandon asked if she had ever talked about him.

Amy looked at him and smiled. "She did. Almost every time I stopped by. She'd show me pictures of you." A loud laugh escaped her, and she looked at Brandon. "She had this picture of you when you're a baby, right. You're laying on a blanket naked as a jaybird."

Brandon felt himself flush beneath her cackles of laughter. He withdrew his hand and shook his head.

"Don't go getting upset. She thought it was the cutest thing." She contained another bout of laughter and sighed. "She'd say, 'Look at that little butt. It's like two little yeast rolls.'"

Brandon crossed his legs and rested his elbows on his knees. He covered his face with his hands and groaned.

"It was a cute picture," Amy said, nudging him with her shoulder. He shook his head but didn't look up. "I'm sorry," she laughed. "I didn't mean to embarrass you." Her hand slid across his shoulders, giving him a quick shake.

"It's been nice knowing you, but I might have to just jump in now," he signed and used both hands to mimic diving into the river.

"Don't be embarrassed." Amy put her hand on his arm. "It was a cute butt."

Brandon pretended to prepare to dive, but she pulled him back down beside her, laughing.

"Can we change the subject?" he asked.

"Okay," she relented, subduing her laughter. "What do you want to talk about?"

Brandon pointed to her and nodded.

"My butt?" she asked, her eyes wide with shock.

"No. Just you," he signed, blushing again.

"Oh. There's nothing to talk about, really. I've lived here all my life. To be honest, it's been about as boring a life as you would wish on your worst enemy. We ride the bus to school and home. Otherwise, we hardly ever leave the camp road."

"What do you do for fun?" he asked.

Amy shrugged. "You're looking at it." She leaned back, propping herself on her hands. "Nothing happens down here much. The summers are better. New kids come. New faces to look at, you know." She shook her head as she looked out over the river. "But they always go home, and we all stay here and deal with the rain and the mud that is winter." She nodded. "Oh, and occasionally we get flooded out and have to stay in a red cross shelter, so there's that little slice of heaven too."

Brandon's throat went dry. "Mud?"

Amy nodded. "The road turns to crap. Sometimes the buses don't even run. That's pretty cool 'cause we don't have to go to school and don't get counted absent."

Brandon's pulse slowed, and he relaxed, glad the road was the mud Amy spoke of and not the mud in front of his grandmother's house.

"Sometimes, I do throw crap in the river, though."

Brandon's heart stopped again, and his mouth fell open as he stared at her.

"What?" she asked, staring back at his shocked expression. "You're not some environmental nut, are you? I mean, a few bottles here and there ain't gonna hurt nothing."

"Bottles?" he signed.

"Yeah," she said, puzzled. "Sometimes some of us kids put crazy notes in bottles, put the lid on and throw them in the river. Once, I put my address on a note. Six months or so later, I got a letter in the mail from some kid downriver. I forget where he was from, but they said it was over a hundred miles away."

Brandon relaxed, nodding.

"What did you think we threw in?" she asked with a laugh. "Dead bodies?"

Brandon tensed. He looked downriver, hoping to hide his nervousness.

Amy put a hand on his shoulder. "Are you alright? You seem a little flustered."

Brandon shrugged. So many things were flustering him lately. "Maybe it's the company," he signed. He looked at her and smiled through his guilt. If she knew he'd thrown the dog into the muck, she'd think he was a monster. He was beginning to wonder about it himself.

Amy smiled. "Maybe the feeling's mutual." She leaned forward and gave him a quick kiss on the cheek. "I'm going in. You coming?"

Brandon watched in shock as she stood, ran across the boulder, and leaped into the river fifteen feet below with a loud "Geronimo." He scurried to the edge in time to see her coming back to the surface.

She pushed the gobs of wet hair back from her face and looked up at him. "You coming in or not?" she asked with a wide smile. "The water's great."

Brandon inched closer to the edge. He was a good swimmer, but the furthest he'd ever dove from was the edge of their backyard swimming pool.

"It's okay. I promise." Amy swam back from the boulder, giving him room. She laid back atop the water, the wet tee shirt clinging to her frame. "Don't you trust me?"

Brandon stared down at her. Her brown eyes were locked on his. Her thin smile called to him. When she raised a hand from the water and curled her finger to him, he knew he couldn't refuse. He took one step and jumped in feet first.

The water enveloped him as he crashed through the surface. He opened his eyes but saw only bubbles in a world of green water. He kicked back to the surface and looked around.

His heart leapt to his throat when he couldn't find Amy. He slapped the surface of the water twice, jerking his head in every direction. His first instinct was to get out of the water; that it acted the same way the muck in front of his house did.

He treaded water, spinning in every direction. His eyes scanned the surface, but he still couldn't find Amy. Panic began to rise in his chest, and he slapped the water again with both hands.

His eyes swept the bank, but Amy was nowhere in sight. He found a flat rock jutting out from the base of the border and started toward it. If he could climb onto it, he'd have a better view.

Halfway to the shelf, the water erupted in front of him as Amy surfaced suddenly. She threw her head back with laughter as she pushed her hair back from her face with both hands.

"Did I scare you?"

Brandon stared at her, wide-eyed. He threw his hands up, then signed, "What the hell?"

"I'm just playing." Amy splashed water at him. "Chill out.

You're very tense for a kid, you know."

Brandon watched as she turned and swam toward the rock shelf. Her toned legs churned the water, propelling her quickly. She reached the shelf and pulled herself up.

Water cascaded down the back of the tank top, clinging to her thin frame, revealing the dark bra she wore. Her thin shorts were plastered to her body, accentuating the curve of her buttocks as she rose from the river. There was no outline of panties beneath them.

She turned and sat on the rock, her legs hanging in the water. "You going to join me or what?" she asked with a grin.

Brandon started toward her but felt his excitement growing in his own shorts. "I'm okay here," he signed. Watching her push herself up out of the water was the most sensual thing he'd ever seen, and had pushed his desire for her to grow into a craving.

"Come on. It's a nice place to sit."

Brandon smiled but didn't move. He shook his head.

Amy cocked an eyebrow as she stared at him. A mischievous grin slid across her lips. "Okay then." She gathered her long hair in her hands, sliding them down the length to wring the water out of it. Leaning forward, she combed through it with her fingers before throwing it back with a flick of her head. Pulling a few strands over her shoulder, she twirled the ends playfully. "It's just that this place is called 'The Make Out Seat' for obvious reasons. No one can see you here unless they're in a boat." She swept her eyes along the river. "And I don't see any fishermen about."

Brandon inched closer. His eyes washed over the wet tank top, reviving the images from his dream. His heart thundered in his chest as he watched her, wanting nothing more than to be with her.

"Don't you like me?" she asked coyly.

Brandon nodded emphatically, inching closer.

"Then come and sit with me." She patted the stone next to her hip.

Brandon nodded again, moved closer, then stopped.

As she waited for him, the smile left her face. Her brow furrowed slightly, and her eyes narrowed. "You know, I don't have to beg boys to sit with me." She ran her hands over her hair, arching her back slightly. "Maybe I should just go home."

Brandon swam toward her quickly, stopping just short of the shelf. Her smile returned, and Brandon smiled up at her.

Her feet moved through the water, hooking him beneath each arm. "I got you now," she said with a grin.

Brandon reached out, putting his hands on her legs, just above the knee. Her skin was cool from the water but still smooth and inviting. He swallowed hard and looked up at her. His heart swelled with emotion, and the urge to kiss her overcame him.

His hands slid up her legs and over her hips as he moved closer. He found the rock beneath the shallow water and kicked hard, propelling himself up out of the water. He pushed himself up with his arms until they were face to face. Leaning in, he pressed his lips against hers. An inferno ignited within him, consuming his whole body. It was his first real kiss, but something told him it wasn't hers.

ELEVEN

"That's bullshit, Barry, and you know it."

"What was it hurting?"

Carrol put a hand on her hip, staring at her husband. "The whole reason we came here was for the seclusion. You said we could be away from everyone and wait this whole damned flu shit out. They said it'd be over by the end of summer."

"And?"

"And here is this little girl, who quite frankly looks like a tramp if you ask me, bouncing her ass over here and off goes Brandon. We don't even know her. She could be sick or some other friend of hers. We could just have stayed home if he's going to hang out with everyone who comes along."

"Calm down. Damn. First of all, it was one person. And a 'tramp'? Really Carrol? She's just a little girl."

"I doubt that. She's got a look about her that I don't like."

"What look is that? The look of a girl who might steal your baby away?"

"That's not what this is about, and you know it. Don't be a stupid, macho douche, Barry. She looks like the kind of girl who'd get knocked up and ruin a good boy's life."

"Oh my god," he moaned. "You got her pegged, don't you?" Barry laughed, shaking his head.

"I don't like her."

"Really? I hadn't noticed."

"Look, Barry. The only reason I agreed to come down here was because of the virus. You said it was secluded, that we could keep away from people."

"I didn't say it was deserted."

"I don't like him going off with her." Carrol bit her bottom lip as she shook her head. She lowered her voice and continued. "You know he's not like other boys his age. She could seduce him in a second, and you freaking know it."

"You know, you could have a little faith in him, Carrol."

"Oh, please. He's still a teenage boy, and a girl like that isn't going to make it easy for him to refuse."

"You don't even know her, for Pete's sake."

"Nevertheless, either you talk to Brandon, or I will."

Barry sighed, relenting to his wife's glare. "Fine. I'll talk to him. Happy now?"

Carrol shook her head. "Not even close. More like slightly less pissed off." Carrol stared at her husband until his gaze dropped to his hands. There was no way she was going to let this girl get her hooks into Brandon.

Barry Stivers knocked on Brandon's bedroom door as he opened it. He found his son lying in bed. "Hey, kiddo."

Brandon sat up, casting a nervous glance at his father before dropping his gaze to the hands folded on his lap.

"Look," Barry said, closing the door behind him. He crossed to the bed and sat on the edge. "Your mother, well, we thought I should talk to you."

Brandon nodded and signed, "Okay."

Barry sighed. "First of all, I want you to know I'm not mad. I did get a little worried." He held up his hand to stop his son's protest. "I know that I said you could go with that girl, but you said you were looking for a dog. You get back right at dark, dripping wet. I know you two weren't looking for a dog, and so does your mother."

Brandon shrugged, unable to look at his father.

"Now, I want to tell you something. I'm not saying this girl is like this. By all rights, she seems nice, but sometimes girls can be a little...." he trailed off while he thought of the right word. "Misleading."

Brandon looked up, asking what he meant.

"You know I grew up down here. Sometimes girls who don't have a lot to look forward to will try to secure their future in any way they can. Life is tough here. I got out. You should be glad. A lot of people didn't. This place isn't like our neighborhood back home."

Brandon threw his hands up. "I don't have a clue what you're talking about."

"Brandon, you're fifteen. Things are changing—"

Brandon moaned, shaking his head.

"Stop it. I understand. I went through it. You're becoming a man, and things are different. The problem is that sometimes when you meet a girl, things might not always be what they seem."

Brandon signed that they were just hanging out. His father didn't need to know that they'd had a lengthy kissing session during which Amy allowed his hands to explore her body, albeit above the clothes.

"Okay. Good. We've already had the 'Birds and Bees' talk, so you understand all that. Right?"

Brandon nodded. The talk had been embarrassing as hell but quite informative.

"Now I'm telling you that some girls, especially girls down here, are different from girls you've known from school. Do you know what I mean when I say a girl is 'Fast'?"

Brandon nodded even though he didn't.

Barry stood and made sure the door was secure, then returned to the bed. "Look," he began, his voice softer now. "I know how girls are down here. I've run through my share of them. There were a lot more people who lived here back then. It was a big neighborhood. I'm not telling you not to have a little fun. I'm telling you to be careful."

Brandon stared at his father, unsure how to react. He liked Amy and didn't want to believe she was like that, but at the same time, if she were....

"I can tell by the look on your face that you already like her. That's fine. She's cute, got a nice little shape to her. But remember that we're only here for the summer."

Barry stood and shoved his hands in the pockets of his cargo shorts. He smiled down at his son. "You okay?"

Brandon picked at his thumbnail for a moment, then looked up at his father and signed, "I do like her. She's pretty. She seems nice."

Barry chuckled. "They all seem nice at first." He stepped closer, bending forward slightly. "Once upon a time, I thought your mom was nice too."

A smile escaped Brandon as he nodded. His parents' rocky relationship had been on display for the past few years, but during the last months, neither of them had been nice to the other.

"Brandon, you know I love you. All I'm saying is that things will be complicated from here on out. You're not a kid anymore. If you don't look out for yourself and be careful, you might find yourself in a precarious situation."

Brandon forced an awkward smile and nodded. He gave his father a thumbs up. His eyes bulged when his father produced a small box of condoms and tossed them onto the bed beside him.

"Be careful, son. Do you know what I mean?"

Brandon stared at the box, then up at his father.

"One, you didn't get those from me. Two, if your mother asks, I told you to drop the girl because she's a tramp. Okay?" Barry smiled, then turned and walked out the door, closing it behind him without looking back.

Brandon fell back onto his pillow with a sigh. *Wow*, he thought. *That was almost as bad as the other talk.* His hand found the box and lifted it before his face. A smile escaped him as the thought of using them crept into his mind.

It's not like you haven't been thinking about it, he told himself. He settled into bed as his mind replayed the image of Amy pulling herself out of the water. He knew what he wanted, but what did Amy want in return?

Brandon's eyes darted back and forth beneath his eyelids as he lay sleeping. A bead of sweat gathered and trickled across his temple, collecting other beads as it went. It clung to his cheek momentarily, then ran down his skin and disappeared into the pillow.

In his dream, he was standing on the end of the pier, watching Amy float on the surface of the muck. Her body was covered in a thin veil of mud. It clung to her like a bodysuit, contouring and accentuating every curve. He was breathing heavily, sweating, as his hungry eyes washed over her. She was so beautiful.

Her eyes flew open suddenly, creating two holes in the dark mud. Her eyes were glowing as they stared at him.

"Don't you like me, Brandon?" she asked softly.

"Yes," he answered, speaking aloud.

"Then come and be with me."

Brandon looked at the muck beneath the pier. It roiled and bubbled like a witch's brew. He looked back at Amy and shook his head. "I can't."

"You know," she began, smiling at him. "I don't have to beg boys to be with me. Maybe I should just go home."

"No," Brandon called, reaching out to her. "Don't go."

"Why should I stay?" Her eyes drifted down his body to the bulge in the front of his pajama pants. When her eyes found his again, she was smiling.

Brandon looked down, too, realizing for the first time that he had an erection. He covered it with his hands, then looked back up. The field of muck spread out before him. Amy was gone.

"No," he whined. "Don't go."

"I haven't gone anywhere."

Brandon spun on a heel, finding Amy on the pier behind him.

"I don't ever have to go anywhere. I can stay as long as you want me to stay, as long as you need me to."

Brandon swallowed hard, watching her slow seductive walk toward him. She paused halfway down the pier and pushed the mud off her left shoulder. It fell away like a piece of clothing, revealing the soft, supple skin beneath. She smiled at him as she peeled the mud from her right shoulder.

"You do want me to stay, don't you?"

Brandon nodded, staring at her dumbfounded.

Amy's smile widened, and she wriggled her shoulders slightly. The mud slipped down further, stopping just below the tops of her breasts.

"Do you need me, Brandon?" she asked in a whisper. "Or do you just want to do dirty things to me and leave me behind?"

Brandon swallowed hard again and cleared his throat. A wave of guilt washed over him. He did want to do dirty things to her. Dirty, dirty things. He'd imagined things that made him ashamed of himself, leaving him wondering if he were sick in the head.

"What about you?" he finally squeaked in his own defense.

"What about me?" she asked, griming impishly.

"You know you're driving me crazy doing things like this." He waved a hand up and down her body.

"Oh, I want to do things to you too. You know I do." She arched an eyebrow seductively as she stepped closer. "But I do need you too. I think you need me more than you think."

"I do need you," he admitted.

"Good," she said, smiling. "I can do things you need me to do. Can you do the things I need you to do?"

"I-I think so."

Amy stepped closer, running a finger down his chest. "I think you can too."

Brandon reached for her, but she disappeared. The wet mud that had covered her body fell through his hands and splattered on the deck, splashing onto his bare feet. He looked at his hands in disbelief, then down at his feet. The mud was gathering between his toes and sliding onto the weathered floorboards of the pier.

When the mud on his hands began to move, he looked back up at them. He gasped as it slid up his arms and disappeared beneath his pajama top. A shudder ran through him as it slipped quickly down his body and gathered on the deck behind him.

He turned slowly, finding Amy at the edge of the pier, covered in the mud again. "What?" he asked aloud. "What's happening?"

"That depends on you, Brandon," she whispered.

Brandon watched in horror as she took a step back and dropped into the mud, disappearing instantly.

He rushed to the end of the pier and looked down, finding nothing but the muck. The dark mud was still, but a gust of wind pushed past him, pulling at his hair and rattling the reeds.

Brandon's shoulders fell when he realized she was gone. He shook his head, sighing as he turned from the muck. He froze, gasping, when he saw the outline of a body standing on the porch. The pale glow coming through the open door silhouetted what had to be his father. As he watched, the form turned and stepped back into the house, closing the door behind them.

Brandon sat up in his bed with a gasp, the echoes of the slamming door ringing in his head. He sat in the darkness of his bedroom, listening to the sound of his own heavy breathing. What the hell was that about?

He armed sweat from his brow and laid back down. His breathing began to calm, and his heart rate settled some, but his mind was still racing.

He settled onto the sweaty pillow with a heavy sigh. It was the second night in a row that he'd dreamed about the muck and about Amy. Both were sexualized but also dark and foreboding.

The first part made sense. He'd been scarcely able to think about anything else but Amy since he'd first seen her. There were plenty of pretty girls in school, and he'd had plenty of thoughts, but there was something alluring about Amy that he couldn't quite understand. He hated to admit it, but there was a certain cheapness about her that he found appealing.

The muck was also understandable. Since he'd first dropped the soda can in, it had also dominated his thoughts. The rat babies and the dog had only served to intensify his desire to put more stuff in, to feed it.

The combination of the two had to be his subconscious mind's way of killing two birds with one stone. They were dreams. They weren't supposed to always make sense.

Brandon settled himself down with a long sigh. Yes, he thought. They're just dreams. It's nothing. Just goofy dreams. He closed his eyes and saw Amy, her body covered by a thin coat of mud.

A moan escaped him as he thought of her, and a smile

slipped across his lips. He interlaced his fingers behind his head and drifted back to sleep.

TWELVE

Carrol Stivers stood with her arms folded across her chest. Her breath came in angry pants as she watched her son push Amy on the swing in their yard. She was far enough away from the screen that the shadows would hide her, but they were in the sunshine. She could see them perfectly fine.

She pursed her lips tightly and shook her head. She didn't like it one bit. She'd heard Barry brag about his youthful exploits enough to know that she didn't want her son getting mixed up with a river tramp.

Her eyes washed over the white tee shirt that Amy wore. She didn't have much in the way of breasts, but the shirt was tight enough to show what she had. To an innocent boy like Brandon, they would be alluring enough.

Her gaze shifted to the cut-off jean shorts she wore. They were long enough to keep the pockets from spilling beneath the frayed edges, but barely. Amy had nice legs for a young girl, and the shorts showed every inch of them off.

She watched Brandon push the girl again, then disappear behind the tree. When Amy swung back and didn't feel him push her, she leaned back, looking for him.

"Where'd you go?" she asked in a deep southern drawl that made Carrol's skin crawl. Surely the girl was overdoing it.

She'd lived in Alabama all her life and had never heard someone with that much of an accent.

"Adding to the ruse," Carrol whispered through clenched teeth. "I'm onto you, little girl." She shook her head as Brandon jumped out from behind the tree and grabbed Amy's bare feet. She let out a playful squeal and started to laugh. Carrol turned with a huff and ducked back through the front door.

"And?" Barry asked, eyeing her over his laptop.

"And what?" Carrol snapped.

"You've been spying on them from every available angle."

"So?"

"Did you think they'd screw on the swing in broad daylight?" he asked with a grin.

"From the looks of that girl, she would."

"Wow. That's pretty harsh. Even from you."

"I'm glad you find all this amusing. You, of all people, should be worried."

Barry shrugged. "He's a smart kid. I talked to him. He'll be okay."

"Please," she snapped as she walked past him on the way to the fridge. "You probably told him some ways to get her into bed, knowing you."

"Ouch. That's quite uncalled for, don't you think?"

Carrol grabbed a bottle of water from the fridge and spun, pointing it at him. "I haven't forgotten all the times you've bragged about bagging chicks when you were younger. All the exploits you were so proud of."

Barry shook his head. "That was me. In case you haven't noticed, Brandon isn't me. Anyway, did you ever consider I was bullshitting you? Guys do that sometimes, you know."

Carrol grunted in disgust. "Whatever, Barry. I'm a woman, and I can tell a tramp when I see one." She took a drink of water and pointed to the window. "And that little girl out there is one.

Mark my words, she sees Brandon as a way out of this shit hole place."

"He's fifteen, Carrol. You think he's gonna marry her this summer?"

"I don't know what her plan is, but I'm right, and you damned well know it. What are we going to do if she seduces him and gets knocked up? You ever think of that? Brandon will be on the hook for child support for the next eighteen years. And who do you think will be writing the checks? You will, Barry. You will."

"Brandon's a smart kid. He'll be fine. Jesus, Carrol, just let him be a normal kid for once. They're talking, swinging. They're just hanging out. Stop being a mother hen for once in his life."

"You say that like you know he'll be fine, but you don't."

Barry looked up from his work and shook his head. "What in the hell do you suggest we do?" He closed his laptop and sat it beside him on the couch. "And don't say go back home."

"Why not?"

"Have you forgotten that there's a freaking pandemic? If we were home, he'd be begging to play with his friends. All of his friends. They'd be trying to come over. He'd be stuck at home and driving us crazy. At least down here, there's less people, fewer chances of catching that shit, and he's able to get out and explore. Maybe even glean some joy from this screwed-up summer."

"And how do you know she doesn't have the virus? She might be transmitting it to him right now." Carrol let out a grunt and shook her head. "These folks probably didn't even get vaccinated for polio."

Barry sighed. His wife was the master of thinly veiled digs. Growing up in an upper-middle-class home, she loved to disparage his humble upbringing.

"First of all, the polio vaccination is required to attend public school, which these kids go to. My God, Carrol. We're still in the same county where you grew up too. It's not like we're in Appalachia or something. Damn." He rubbed his face with both hands. "And secondly, Brandon is smart. He's got a good head on his shoulders. You ever think that you're just overprotective and don't want him to grow up?"

"That's outrageous." Carrol took a drink. "Besides, he's got enough of you in him to chase any skirt that will slow down, I'm sure."

"Wow. You're a real bitch sometimes. You know that?"

She flipped him the bird and smiled. "Yeah. I've heard."

"Fine then. You wanted me to talk to him. I talked to him. I don't know what the hell you want me to do now. If you have such a problem, then march your skinny ass out there and tell that girl you don't want your son hanging out with a sleezy river tramp. Run her the hell off. Problem solved."

Barry pushed up from the couch and pointed a finger at her. "But I sure as hell ain't going to do your dirty work for you."

"You'd like that, wouldn't you? He'd hate me for it, and you'd win."

"Win?" Barry shook his head. "I've given up winning with you a long time ago." He threw a hand at her and stormed into the bedroom, slamming the door behind him.

Amy looked up at the house as the sound of a slamming door echoed across the yard. She turned in the swing, looking at Brandon. "Is everything okay?"

He shrugged, sparing a glance up at the house. "They fight a lot," he signed.

Amy reached out and took his hands. "I'm sorry. I know how it is. My folks used to have some real doozies before my dad left. It's rough."

With Amy holding his hands, Brandon was relegated to a nod.

"Is it about me?" she asked, dropping her gaze to their hands.

He looked down, watching her thumb caress the back of his hand. Her nails were painted pink, but he couldn't remember if they were that way the first time he saw her or if it was new. In his mind, he replayed the image of her swatting the mosquito. He saw her thigh, her tanned skin, the blood smear, but he couldn't remember her fingernails.

Brandon pulled a hand free and lifted her chin. He mouthed the word "No," shaking his head emphatically. He signed that they've been fighting for years.

Amy stood with a sigh, tugging at the legs of her shorts. "I'll bet it is. I'm sure they don't like me. Especially your mother. Moms don't tend to like me for some reason." She shook her head and looked at the house. "Look, this whole thing was stupid. I should have known better." She turned and walked away.

Brandon hurried after her, catching her at the edge of the house. He grabbed her arm and turned her to face him.

"It's not you," he signed. "They hate each other. I don't know why, but they do. It's not you at all."

A sad smile slid across her face as she took his hands in hers. "Look, Brandon, you seem like a nice guy. You really do, and I like you. I'm not sure what you just said just now, but it doesn't matter. You're from town. Your folks have money. I'm just a river rat. If he hasn't already, I'm sure your dad will tell you it's okay to have a little fun with me but not to get too involved."

Brandon flushed and dropped his eyes to her hands. He stroked her fingers with his thumb, waiting for his embarrassment to fade. It was exactly what his dad had suggested.

He pulled his hands from her and looked into her eyes. "I like you. It doesn't matter where you're from. You're the most beautiful girl I've ever seen."

Amy rolled her eyes as she pushed a strand of hair behind

her ear. "Please. How can I compare to the girls you go to school with? I'm poor. I don't have money for make-up or fancy hairstyles. I'm sure you're enamored with me because of the way I dress or something, but the novelty will wear off before August comes, I'm sure."

Brandon shook his head. "No, it won't. Don't go. Please."

Amy's expression softened as she looked at him. "Okay," she relented, reaching out and plucking his hands from the air between them. "But I don't wanna hang out here anymore. Your mom has been spying on us since I got here."

Brandon looked up at the house. He hadn't noticed his mother spying.

Amy nodded. "She has. She don't like me one bit. I can promise you that much."

Brandon pursed his lips in frustration. He sighed and finally nodded. When Amy turned and started down the driveway, he followed.

When she stopped suddenly and turned back to him, Brandon almost collided with her. She held her ground and looked into his eyes, their bodies inches apart. "I don't want to cause you no trouble. Why don't you just let me go?"

Brandon shook his head. "I can't stop thinking about you," he told her.

Amy rolled her eyes and smiled. "You're sweet. If you can take it, I can take it. C'mon." They walked in silence, then she looked at him again. "I probably shouldn't tell you this, but I've never liked a boy as much as you."

Brandon put an arm around her shoulders and pulled her to him as they walked. "Are you my girlfriend now?" he asked with his free hand.

Amy stopped and looked at him. "I can be whatever you need me to be," she answered with a wink. "But I'm not gonna make it easy." She slapped him on the chest and spun quickly, and sprinted down the driveway. "You're gonna have to catch me first," she called over her shoulder.

Brandon rubbed the sting in his chest where she'd slapped him as he watched her run. Her long legs flexed and relaxed, putting distance between them quickly. He smiled and took off after her.

Brandon lumbered to a stop on the path and put his hands on his knees, gasping for air. A stitch had started to burn in his side five minutes ago, but he'd tried to push through. Now, the pain was getting serious. He cleared his throat and spat on the ground between his tennis shoes.

Standing, he put his hands on his hips and started walking down the path. He'd assumed Amy would run for a few minutes and let him catch her, but she hadn't. He'd chased her for ten minutes before losing sight of her.

Still panting, he took in his surroundings as he walked. A canopy of tall trees blocked the sun, cooling the air considerably. Had he not already been sweating from his run, it would have been pleasant.

The narrow path beneath his feet was well-worn but uneven as it wound through the woods. Somewhere in the treetops, a bird sang out. Deeper in the woods, another answered. He had no idea where he was in relation to his house or the river. All he knew was that he'd last seen Amy on this path.

Brandon clapped his hands once as he stumbled along, expecting Amy to spring out from behind a tree at any moment to scare him. His legs burned, but the stitch in his side was subsiding. He clapped his hands twice but again got no response, so he continued down the path.

His breathing had returned to normal, and most of the sweat had dried on his forehead when he finally made the small clearing. Amy was sitting on a fallen log amid a patch of florescent green moss. She looked up at him when he entered the clearing.

"You made it."

Brandon nodded, giving her a smile and a thumbs up. "No problem," he signed.

"I'm glad you didn't quit on me."

Brandon watched the moss yield to his shoes as he stepped onto the thick green carpet. He took another tentative step, then deemed it safe enough. He crossed the patch of moss and sat beside her on the log.

"You're a fast runner."

Amy laughed. "Sometimes it pays to be fast."

"What are you running from?" he asked.

Her eyes dropped to the moss as she shrugged. "Nothing. Everything."

Brandon reached out and brushed a swath of hair from her cheek. "What did you mean back at the house?"

She gave him a wry smile. "I'm sure you're not that naïve. You know what I meant." She stood, shoving her fingers in her pockets as she crossed the patch of moss. "That's why you didn't stop, ain't it? That's why you kept running through the woods. You didn't think I had a Parcheesi board out here. Now did you?"

Brandon shrugged when she looked over her shoulder at him. It was hard to tell what girls meant, but he felt pretty sure he understood what she'd said.

"I'm nobody's summer fling, despite what you may think of me. I'm not a whore, so don't think I am."

Brandon stood, shaking his head. "I've never thought that. You seem really nice. I like you." Brandon dropped his hands with a heavy sigh. "You're the one that brought it up."

Amy put a hand on her hip and shrugged with one shoulder. "Like you haven't thought about it. I see the way you look at me."

Brandon shrugged, hoping not to answer, but his head

betrayed him by nodding. He threw his hands in the air and let them drop. "What do you want me to say?" he asked.

"I want you to say that you love me."

Brandon's eyes bulged, but he dropped his gaze quickly, hoping she hadn't seen his reaction. When he looked back up, she was standing with both hands on her hips, staring back at him. Her head was cocked to one side, framed by her wild tangle of hair.

Her eyebrows were raised as if expecting an answer. "And just so you know, I did see the look on your face just now."

"I'm sorry," he signed. "It's just that...." he threw his hands up. "I just met you. I do like you. I'm not going to lie. Yes, I have thought about that, but I never thought you were a whore." He shrugged. "I've never really been in love."

Amy's face softened slightly, and a smile tugged at one corner of her mouth, creating a slight dimple on her cheek. "At least you're honest." She stepped casually toward him. "Most guys would have lied and said that they were madly in love with me just to get me out of my pants."

"You're wearing shorts," Brandon signed with a grin.

Amy smiled as she shook her head. "Anyway." She took another step closer to him, her fingers dancing around the button on her shorts. "I brought you here because it's my special place. I come here a lot. I've never brought anyone here before."

Brandon nodded, remembering the path beaten through the forest. "It's nice," he signed, looking around. The remnants of a campfire, encircled by rocks, sat at the edge of the moss. A pile of empty cans littered the woods behind it. He sighed as sadness engulfed him. This was her sanctuary, but from what?

"You can tell me about it." His eyes washed over her as he offered a weak shrug.

She smiled. "You're a sweet kid, but you don't want to hear about that stuff." She took his hand and led him back to the log. They sat down, and she pushed her shoes off one by one.

"I like the feel of the moss on my bare skin."

Brandon pushed his own shoes off and slipped his toes into the moss. It was cool and refreshing against his sweaty feet. He'd touched moss before, but nothing as deep and lush as this.

"I'm gonna tell you something, but you have to promise not to laugh."

Brandon nodded.

"Say it—ugh—do it with your hands."

Brandon signed his promise.

Amy took a deep breath and puffed out her cheeks as she exhaled. "Sometimes, when it's really hot, I take off my clothes and just lay on the moss naked and look up at the trees."

Brandon swallowed hard but said nothing, unsure where she was headed. A knot tightened in his stomach. He wanted to grab her and kiss her. Her thin lips were soft and pink. Inviting. His hand went to the condom he'd slipped into the pocket of his shorts, making sure that he hadn't lost it on the run.

"It's very freeing to be naked outside like that. I just lay here and look up, and I don't think about anything. It's like I'm connected to nature. Do you know what primal means?"

Brandon nodded. He knew what the word meant but had never really understood it until lately.

"That's how I feel when I'm naked out here. Primal."

Brandon swallowed hard. "Aren't you worried about someone walking up?" he signed.

Amy shrugged. "I don't do it every day, mind you, and nobody ever comes out here. Besides, if they did, I could just run away."

Brandon nodded slowly as he stared at her profile. From this angle, the curves of her features were gentle and smooth, giving her an elegant look. Her full head of dark hair, tangled by the long run, hung about her shoulders in a lush mane that he longed to touch.

One hand moved forward and slipped beneath her chin, turning her to him. He bent in and pressed his lips to hers.

"You're the most beautiful girl in the world." His eyes searched hers, hoping she felt the same way about him.

"Thank you." Amy looked toward the treetops and sighed. "I need to tell you something." When Brandon nodded, she continued. "My mother is sick."

"Sick?" he signed, confused by the sudden change in subject.

"Really sick. Cancer."

"I'm so sorry." His brow furrowed at the thought.

"It's okay. I just needed to tell someone. I don't know what we're gonna do. We can't afford the treatments."

Brandon nodded. His father's warnings tried to surface in the back of his mind, but he fought them back. Amy was just opening up to him. That's all it was. She wasn't asking for anything except a sympathetic ear.

"Look, I have to admit something. It's not good."

His hand smoothed her hair as he offered a sympathetic smile. Despite the sad topic, his heart skipped a beat when he felt her hair in his hand. It was smooth and soft. Her gentle curls rippled beneath his fingers. He felt himself becoming excited but took a deep breath to calm himself.

"I was planning to bring you here to, you know, seduce you."

He stared at her without a response. So far, the plan didn't sound so bad.

"I was thinking that if I did it with you, you'd help me."

Brandon tugged at the neck of his tee-shirt and swallowed hard. His entire body suddenly felt hot. A bead of sweat collected on the back of his neck and ran down his spine. "How could I help? I'll do what I can, but I'm just a kid. There's only so much

I can do." His mind searched for the right words to say as his hands moved quickly between them.

His father's words came back stronger this time, but he pushed them aside.

Amy threw her hands into the air. "I can't even tell what you're saying half the time. Now you're going too fast. I told you I barely could read hands." She rubbed a tear from her eye. "Never mind. It's stupid." She rose quickly and walked away, standing with her back to him. "I'm such an idiot."

Brandon joined her, turning her to face him. He smiled gently, using his thumb to wipe a tear from her cheek. He offered a sympathetic smile. "How can I help?"

THIRTEEN

Hiding from his parents despite the late hour, Brandon laid back on the pier and pressed the heels of his hands into his eyes. He wished his mind to stop and go back to the way it used to be. Even the incessant noise was better than this. He always wondered what it would be like to be "normal," but now he didn't envy his classmates.

He wanted the whirling menagerie of thoughts about Amy to stop. His life used to be so simple. He could lose himself for hours in a book or studying a map. Everything else in the world would disappear. But this. This was torture. The onslaught of thoughts, of desires, overlapping and vying for his attention was maddening. This, this was unreal.

Tears pressed out around his hands and ran down his cheeks. How could this be real? It couldn't be happening. It had to be another one of the crazy dreams he'd been having about Amy and the muck. It had to be a dream.

It is not a dream, Brandon.

He pulled his hands from his eyes and craned his neck to see who was behind him. All he saw was an upside-down pier. No one was standing behind him. When the reeds rustled in the muck, he spread his feet and looked between them. He saw darkened shapes moving in the shadows but little else.

Sitting up, he wiped his eyes. *Did you say that?* he thought, his eyes fixed on the reeds. After several minutes of staring, he sighed and shook his head.

Damn. Now I'm talking to freaking weeds, he thought. He armed the sweat from his forehead and pushed the hand through his hair. Crossed his legs in front of him, he hung his head, paralyzed by indecision. Every thought of Amy brought a fresh ache to his body. He needed to touch her, to feel her body against him.

His mind, however, begged for the muck, wanting nothing more than to watch something else disappear into its dark mud. Every line of thought came back to the muck, to the sensation it gave him when he fed it.

"I thought I'd find you down here."

Brandon scanned the dark field of wild grass and mud before him. His eyes narrowed, straining in the darkness.

"Brandon."

He jumped, startled by his father's voice. He looked around and shook his head, thankful for the company and not at the same time.

"It'll be okay, son." Barry Stivers ambled down the pier and sat beside his son. "It will."

Brandon threw his hands up. "How do you know?" he signed.

"Because things are never as bad as they seem. The whole 'darkest before the dawn' thing." Barry nodded at his son and smiled.

Brandon held his hands up to begin signing but hesitated. His face twisted with indecision. He started again, then dropped his hands to his lap and shook his head.

"Let me guess. You're all tied up in knots, and it has something to do with the girl. Amy, is it?"

Brandon shrugged and nodded at the same time.

"I'm gonna go ahead and guess that you two either hooked up or came really close to it."

Brandon dropped his eyes to his hands. They hadn't exactly had sex, but they had lain naked together, and she'd let him touch her body. His fingertips could still feel her skin as they roved over her body. It was the most thrilling time of his life until she'd started talking.

"It's okay, son. It's a normal, natural thing. The feelings you're having, they're normal. Every guy has gone through this."

Brandon let out an embarrassed sigh but said nothing.

Barry chuckled quietly and put a hand around his son's shoulders. "Would I be wrong to assume that she asked you for something, you know, afterwards?"

Brandon's head jerked up. How did he know?

Barry nodded and let out a long, contemplative sigh. "I'm not surprised. Honestly, it's sort of a trick that females pull on us guys."

"She didn't ask for money or anything like that." After he finished signing, Brandon wiped the sweat from his face.

"I figured that by the way you've been acting all evening." He patted his son's back and then withdrew his arm. He clasped his hands before him and sighed again. "Did she ask you to help her do something?"

"It doesn't make any sense," Brandon signed, his hands shaking.

Barry nodded knowingly. "No, it don't." He stared out over the darkened field of mud and weeds. "It doesn't make sense because you don't know the whole story."

Brandon twirled two fingers in front of his face, begging for elaboration.

"It's the muck, son. It's not just mud and grass, but I suspect you already know that."

Brandon gave a slight nod, conceding the fact without

revealing what he'd done.

"You see, there's more to it. A lot more." Barry cleared his throat and shook his head. "It's not a normal place. The muck will give you things, but it always wants something in return."

"How?" Brandon asked.

Barry rolled his neck around his shoulders, his spine cracking noisily as he groaned. "I took a pain pill for my knee. All this extra work and going up and down the stairs isn't good for an old body."

He rubbed his eyes and pinched the bridge of his nose, stifling a yawn. "I'll be turning in soon, but I wanted to talk to you about what's been going on. It's a long story, son. Some of it's legend, some of it may be bullshit. I don't really know. People around here have been telling it for a long time. I suspect no one really knows the whole truth."

"Amy said there was a witch."

Barry shrugged. "There's more to it than that." He cast his eyes toward the dark water beyond the muck. "This is strictly between us. Your mother cannot know a single word of it. Understand?"

Brandon nodded.

"I'm deadly serious. Not a word. If she gets even a whiff of this, she'll snatch you up and head home quicker than a cat can lick its ass. You'll never see your little girlfriend again."

Brandon nodded again, more emphatically.

"My mother told me that a long time ago, something happened. In the early days before this place was really settled much, I don't even think we were a state yet. Anyway, upriver, there was a big stone house. There's not much left of it now but a few foundation stones out in the woods. I've seen 'em. They're plenty big too. There's still a spooky feeling about being there.

"Anyhow, A bunch of women built the place, if you can believe that. The few people who lived around the ferry crossing there thought they were nuns. Maybe they told them they were, I don't know. Anyway, they lived there and kept to themselves for a long time. Years. Nobody knows how long. They never went into the tiny town. They raised their own food and stuff. Wore black all the time. Never had visitors. You get the picture."

Brandon nodded. The women sounded like the goth kids at school, except for the farming.

"So, anyway, as more and more settlers moved into the area through the years, people began to ask questions about this weird group of women. Eventually, people started to talk about them being witches."

"So, they were witches?" Brandon asked, eager to believe Amy's story.

"I don't know what they were. Grandmother and Mama thought they were, but that's just what they were told by their people. Back then, folks weren't very smart, educated, I mean. If you showed your ankles, you'd probably be labeled a witch."

Barry fanned a mosquito from in front of his face and scratched his head. "Eventually, things got tense, I guess. One night a few men from town decided that they were witches, and that just didn't sit right with their Puritanical Christian ideals. They probably finally drank enough to find their courage if you ask me. That's more often the case. I always imagined them with torches and pitchforks, like in the movies, but I don't know. Anyway, they marched up to the old house to confront the women, but no one was there. They'd already left. They searched the woods and found them behind the house, gathered around a campfire. The men chased them into the river, and they drowned."

"Why did they chase them? Did they want to kill them?"

Barry shrugged. "I suppose if they thought they were witches, they wanted to do something about it. Hell, maybe burn them at the stake or something. I don't know."

"How do you know they drowned?" Brandon asked eagerly.

"Because their bodies washed up right out there." He pointed a finger into the darkness in front of him. "You see, we're in the middle of the bend. The current creates a natural eddy. It's why the bodies ended up here, just like it's why all this mud washed in here. Things gather in the bends, son. Good and bad. It's the natural flow of things."

"What did the town do?"

"That's the thing. The men never came back to town. I reckon people were scared, so they waited a while. They never found hide nor hair of the men. They searched the woods but found nothing. They did happen upon a half dozen or so of the biggest turtles they'd ever seen. Legend has it that they were tall as a wagon wheel."

"That sounds like a fairy tale."

Barry chuckled. "That it does, son. That it does." He looked out over the muck and shook his head. When the wind picked up, his eyes went to the patches of dried reeds. He counted them. There were still nine, just as there'd always been.

"If they were witches, how did they drown? Couldn't they just fly away?"

Barry offered his hands. "I don't even know if they were witches. Maybe they really were nuns. Hell, if I know." He cleared his throat and spat into the muck. "They said that nobody wanted to touch the bodies for fear of being cursed. They were all tangled up in tree roots and branches and stuff, so they stayed put for weeks. Eventually, I guess they just sank into the mud at the bottom of the river."

"I threw the rat babies into the mud. I couldn't help it."

Barry looked at his son. "What?"

Brandon signed his confession again, slower this time.

Barry stared at him, surprised by the sudden admission.

His son's cheeks glimmered with wetness in the faint light of the waning moon. His breaths were coming in panicked rasps.

"I kinda figured you would."

"What?" Brandon asked. "You knew?"

Barry nodded. "I've known about this stuff all my life, son. I've grown up with it. You see, it calls to some people but not others. If you answer the call, it gives you what you want, but there's always a catch. I figured if I brought you here, you'd eventually feel the pull and feed it. I'm sorry, son, but I thought you'd get your voice, that you'd be able to talk."

"Obviously not," Brandon signed.

"Yes. I see that."

"What did I get?" Brandon asked.

Barry shrugged. "With it just being baby rats, probably not a lot."

Brandon rubbed his forehead. "There was a bunch of random junk before that." He looked at his father and took a deep breath before signing that there was a dog too.

Barry's eyebrows shot up. "That's bigger, but it's not like a wishing well, son. The muck has a way of giving you what you want, not what you need. Once you're connected, you always will be."

"Connected?"

"Didn't you see a flower?"

Brandon nodded.

"I thought it looked familiar, but it was withered by the time I noticed it." Barry closed his eyes and moaned. "Anyway, you gave it something, and it gave you something."

"Amy?" Brandon asked.

"I don't know, son. Maybe. But remember, there's always a catch, a give and take." He investigated the darkness and then shook his head. "All these years since I've been gone, I've come to realize that it can be a bad place. It seems like it's not, but that's how it lures you in."

Barry turned to his son, staring into his eyes. "It's all about the muck, son. It's always looking out for itself. He wiped a tear from the corner of his eye with one crooked finger. "It makes you do things that you might not otherwise want to do. But you can't help it. It's like a circle. Everything comes back to this place. Always."

"Like you?" Brandon signed.

Barry nodded reluctantly. He tore his eyes from his son's, staring into the night. One by one, the clutches of reeds began to rattle. When one fell silent, another one in a different area started. He didn't have to look up at the trees to check the wind. There was none. It wasn't the wind rattling the dry reeds. It was the dark magic that was the muck, and it knew he was back home.

"I really don't want to know what Amy asked you to do for her, but you're my son, and I have to know. If you don't want to tell me, I won't try to make you." Barry watched his son pick his thumbnail. He wasn't going to tell. A dry smile slid across his unshaven cheeks.

"All I'm going to ask is that you make damned sure it's worth it. Maybe Amy was what you got. I've seen her. There're worse things a teenage boy could want for. But maybe it brought her to you to benefit itself. That's the pisser." Barry slapped his son on the shoulder as he stood. "Make sure you think things through, son." He turned and started down the pier but stopped when Brandon clapped his hands. He turned and walked back close enough to see in the darkness.

"Did you ever put anything in the muck?"

Barry sighed. He'd put plenty of things into the muck, but his son didn't need to know that. "I did." He shoved his hands into the pockets of his shorts. "A stray cat had kittens in an old chifforobe under the house there."

"What did you get?"

A cynical chuckle escaped Barry as he looked at his son. "I shocked the world by beating out Billy Mathison for starting quarterback my senior year in high school. It was wonderful. I got everything that came with it, prestige, girls, everything." He shook his head. "Wanna know what else I got?"

Brandon nodded eagerly.

"Remember that huge scar on my right knee? I got that from the surgery to reconstruct it after being sacked in the second game. There was also this cute little candy striper that volunteered at the hospital. Later on, she became your mother." Barry gave his son a dry smile. "Remember what I said. There's always a catch." Barry turned and walked away, leaving Brandon alone in the darkness. "Always."

Brandon looked into the muck. The dark shapes of the reeds looked like so many soldiers standing guard. Had the dark magic of this place really sent him Amy?

He wiped the sweat from his brow as the craving for her began to grow within him again. He could still feel the softness of her skin against his hand. He closed his eyes and inhaled deeply. There was a light, musky scent in the air. The smell of her body. He clenched his fists, fighting the urge to go to her house and have his way with her as his body began to tremble. There was a deep desire but also an anger at being denied what had been gifted to him.

She'd been given to him. He should be able to have her, and more than being allowed to touch her naked body. He wanted it all, to possess her, to have her in the ways he wanted. He dug his fists into his eyes as his frustration turned into tears. Nothing was going the way he wanted it to.

He took in a deep breath and exhaled slowly. When he opened his eyes, he saw movement in the darkness before him.

A dark shape stood in the shadows. He thought it was one of the clumps of dead reeds, but when it moved again, he realized that the shape was vaguely human. The figure moved silently through the muck, staying far enough away that he couldn't quite make it out.

His head followed the shadowy figure as it moved from right to left. When it came to a stop, he squinted his eyes, staring at it. *No,* he thought. *It's just my mind playing tricks on me. Or another dream. This isn't real.*

He covered his face with both hands, sighing through them as he tried to collect himself. When he dropped his hands, the dark figure was standing directly in front of him, just past the end of the pier. He gasped, crawling backwards on the weathered boards.

He caught the sight of movement out of the corner of his eye and turned to his right. Another figure, just like the first one, was standing beside the pier. He froze, staring at it. Dark mud slid up and down the gentle curves of the shape, giving it the ability to rise from the muck.

The shape of them reminded him of those dolls that were stacked inside each other or maybe a giant bowling pin.

He swallowed hard and turned to his left and found another one. Drawing his knees to his chest to make himself smaller, he sat frozen as more approached, gliding silently in the darkness. They took up places between the others. When they'd all come, there were nine of them. Though they had no eyes or even faces, he could feel the weight of their stares on him.

Brandon closed his eyes and took a deep breath. He let it out slowly and opened his eyes again. The shapes were still there. His shoulders drooped, and he sank onto the weathered boards of the pier. Somehow, he knew that running away would be pointless. There would be no escaping them.

The figure at the end of the pier moved closer until it was touching the edge of the wood. It leaned forward, looking at him. Brandon slowly gathered his legs beneath him and rose to his knees. His eyes were glued to the shape before him, unable to look away.

He leaned forward, extending an uneasy hand toward it. Everything in his mind had gone silent. There was no worry or fear. Even his maddening desire for Amy was gone. There was nothing but him and the shape before him and a dark silence.

His hand moved slowly, drawing closer to the shape.

"Brandon."

His head jerked around, finding his mother standing on the porch. She was silhouetted by the light coming through the windows behind her.

"Come on in, sweetie. It's getting late."

Brandon turned back to the muck, but the shapes were gone. A disappointed sigh escaped him, and his shoulders drooped. He stood, still searching the muck.

"Brandon, it's too dark to be out. Come in. Please."

He shook his head and clapped his hands once to let his mother know he'd heard her before taking another look around. The muck was as it had been before, dark and silent. He took a deep breath, inhaling the scent. It was thick and musky. Smiling, he turned and hurried down the pier.

FOURTEEN

A long shower while his parents enjoyed their morning coffee on the porch went a long way to relieving some of his tension. Brandon decided he couldn't help Amy, at least not like she wanted him to. He wanted to help her, but what she asked was too much. It was crazy. He'd spent most of the walk to her house figuring out what he was going to say. He'd let her down easy, and hopefully, they could still be friends. They still might even have sex.

"Hey."

Brandon looked up. His eyes found Amy walking toward him. His eyes washed over the coral bikini top clinging to Amy's tanned skin, and his resolve disintegrated. She offered up a wave and smiled at him, and he knew he'd burn down the world if she asked him to.

"Good morning," she said as he approached. She pressed her body to his and stretched onto her toes, kissing his lips eagerly. "I couldn't stop thinking about you last night."

"Me too," he replied, dropping his eyes to the red dirt road at their feet. She was the only female other than his mother to ever see him naked, and she was the first live person he'd ever seen naked.

"Do you still like me?" she asked shyly as they began to

walk.

Brandon nodded. "Of course."

Amy smiled and squeezed his hand. "Good, because I think I fell in love with you last night."

Brandon nodded in agreement. "Me too." He probably fell for her the day they went swimming, but he didn't see the need to reveal that.

"Do you think I'm crazy?" she asked, swinging their hands between them.

Brandon shook his head.

"It's real, you know."

Brandon nodded and signed, "I know," with his free hand.

"Your grandmother knew too."

Brandon nodded again. He listened to the sound of the gravel beneath their feet as they walked in silence, replaying the conversation he'd had with his father in his mind.

"I guess the only question is whether or not you'll help me."

Brandon ran his free hand through his hair, then sighed, "I'll help."

"I know it sounds like a terrible thing, but it really isn't. I've racked my brain, Brandon. It might be the only way to save my mom. She's dying."

Brandon raised his hand to sign something but dropped it back to his side.

"You'll see. Just you wait. You'll see." Amy looked at him and shook her head. "What do I have to do to convince you?" she asked.

Brandon swallowed hard but gave no response.

"Do you believe me?"

He nodded.

"Do you believe I'll do what I said?"

He nodded again but was less sure.

She put a hand under his chin and turned his face to hers. "I'll do anything you want me to." One of her eyebrows arched slightly, and a seductive grin slid across her lips. "Anything."

A smile slipped across his lips as his body erupted with desire, aching for her. His eyes narrowed as a thought occurred to him. If he helped her, he could do anything he wanted, whether she wanted to or not.

Amy gasped as he grabbed her roughly, pulling her to him. When he pressed his lips to hers in a hungry kiss, she knew he'd do anything she asked him to.

―――――

"Are you sure about this?"

Amy reached up and took Brandon's hands, lowering them to his side. "You just stay put right here. Watch and listen. You'll see what I mean." The concern on his face brought forth a smile. She leaned forward, delivering a long, passionate kiss. "I'll be okay. Really."

She ran her hands through her hair as she stepped from behind the overgrown Azalea bush and began strolling down the gravel road. She slowed her pace as she approached a rusted chain link fence, surveying the littered yard it contained. She usually avoided the man who lived here like the plague, but today she needed him to be. He would prove her point for her.

As she neared the beginning of the fence, a smile tugged at the corners of her mouth. Mr. Simmons was already headed her way. A scrawny chihuahua followed close behind, yapping incessantly.

"Dam ain't you a purdy thang?" he asked, his eyes feasting on Amy.

She rolled her eyes, ignoring him as she strolled along.

"Tits are coming in nice."

"Leave me alone, Mister Simmons."

"I ain't doing nothing. Yet. I could be if ye were willing,

though."

Amy shook her head but didn't reply.

"Look, my check will be in soon. How about I give ye fifty bucks for letting me stick a finger in you."

"You're sick."

"Not knowing what ye little cooch smells like is making me sicker." He threw his head back and laughed, revealing a row of gapped yellow. "I bet it smells good too."

"Leave me alone," she insisted. "I got a right to walk down the road without being leered at by an old pervert."

"I ain't no pervert. I just say what everybody else is thinking, and you know it." He kicked at the barking dog next to him. "Shut up, Barney."

"How about you go to hell?"

"How about you go down on me?" he asked, groping the crotch of his baggy work pants. "I'd give you a hunnerd bucks." He leaned on the fence and leered at her. "I know yer people are sick. You could use the money, and I know it."

Amy stopped and looked at him, her face a mask of revulsion. "You're a sick, sick bastard. Don't you ever speak my family's name again."

"Damn, yer a feisty one. I like it with they put up a little tussle." He reached for her, but she stepped back. "Let me just rub on you a minute."

"You lay a hand on me, and that little pecker of yours will be harder to find than it is now."

"I don't need to find it," he laughed. "I said shut up, you damned mutt." He kicked the dog, and it retreated, yelping. "Anyways, all I need is for you to find it."

Amy shook her head and started walking again. He followed her along the inside of the fence.

"That shitter you got there is awful nice looking too." He reached the end of his fence and threw up his hands. "Wait," he called, pleadingly.

"What?" Amy asked, half turning back to him.

"Look." Simmons rubbed his chin and looked around. "I'll give you two hundred bucks if you come in the house. Half an hour. That's more than a grown hooker makes."

"There ain't enough money in the world for me to let you see me naked, you sick old bastard, much less put your grimy, filthy paws on me." Amy spun and walked away.

"Oh yeah," he called after her. "We'll see. You'll need money, and you'll see. I'll have yer cooch yet, you little bitch."

Brandon seethed in anger as he watched the old man. Every word struck him like a fist until he shook with fury. He stepped out from behind the shrub and started down the road after Amy, moving quickly.

Simmons stopped at the edge of his house and looked at him. His eyes narrowed slightly, then a dirty grin slid across his lips. "Hey, you. C'mere."

Brandon watched him approach the fence but kept walking.

"Hey boy, you wanna earn a quick fifty bucks?"

Brandon looked at him and shook his head.

"I'll give you fifty bucks cash if you give me a hand job."

Brandon flipped him off as he walked past.

"To hell with you then," Simmons snapped, throwing a hand at him. "You probably don't know what the hell yer doing anyway."

"See what I mean?" Amy asked as Brandon joined her around the bend from the old man's house.

"Why doesn't anybody do anything?" Brandon asked.

Amy shrugged. "They just ignore him. Every girl down here is told at an early age to walk on the other side of the road.

He still talks, but at least he can't grab you."

"He's a real asshole," Brandon signed, looking back over his shoulder toward the house.

"He's been doing that shit as long as I can remember. I was like five when he started. Five years old. I didn't even know what he was talking about. I asked Mama, and she told me to stay away from him."

"He should go to jail."

Amy shrugged. Her eyes locked on Brandon's, and an eyebrow slid upwards slightly. "Or worse."

Brandon pursed his lips as he looked at her. Trading the old man for Amy's mother's life suddenly felt like a deal. If it helped him have Amy, so much the better. He closed his eyes and nodded.

Brandon sat on a swing in the shade beneath Amy's house. He'd politely declined her offer to meet her mother because the look in her eye told him she didn't really want him to. Also, he tried to avoid sick people if he could. Meeting new people was awkward enough. Their being sick would make it ten times worse.

He picked at a flake of paint on the metal armrest with his fingernail. It popped free, revealing a tiny patch of rust. He took the flake between his fingers and ground it to powder, watching it fall to the bare earth between his feet.

He sighed and looked out over the river. Amy's house was closer to the bank, with a nice view of the open water. A towboat chugged upriver, pushing a half dozen rusty barges filled with coal. Shielding his eyes from the sun, he squinted to read the name of the boat, painted on the cabin just beneath the twin smokestacks. The boat was named the Madison Nichole. That's a pretty name, he thought and began to wonder who the girl might be to deserve to have a whole boat named after her.

"Here we go."

Brandon startled, snatched from his thoughts by Amy's voice. He looked around to find her standing next to him with a glass of lemonade in each hand and a notepad squeezed beneath one arm. She'd suggested the drinks, and he'd asked for the pad. If he was going to go along with her plan, he needed to make sure they were on the same page. There were things he needed to say that he couldn't leave up to her limited ability to read sign language.

He took the glass, sipped it, and set it aside. She joined him on the swing, sitting very close, and handed him the pad and a blue pen. He looked at the letters WAHA, then rolled the pen between his fingers. Western Alabama Hospice Associates was printed beneath the letters.

He looked at Amy, finding a deep sadness in her eyes as she stared out at the river. He took a deep breath and started writing on the pad. When he'd filled half the first page, he handed it to her.

She read the first question and looked at him, nodding. "Yes, I'm one hundred percent sure I want to do this." She read the second line and sighed. "Yes, I know what it is," she said, making sure not to use the word "murder" like Brandon had written. "But I don't have any other choice."

Brandon watched her read the next question.

"No, I haven't planned it exactly. I needed help, and I wanted to see if you'd help. And yes, I know it's going to be hard to do." She slapped the pad on her thigh and looked at him. "This feels too much like an interrogation."

Brandon shrugged, signing, "I'm sorry."

Amy rolled her eyes and grunted before going back to the pad. Her head jerked up suddenly, staring at him with wide eyes. "You talked to your dad about this?"

Brandon pointed to the pad, showing her he didn't give any details. "Okay, but he knows something is up. If people start asking questions, he'll figure things out."

Brandon shook his head. "He won't tell. He's done it too?"

"What?" she asked.

"Not a person. Some kittens." He signed, then pointed to the line on the pad where he explained that there's always a catch.

"What do you mean?" Amy asked, eyeing him suspiciously.

"That's what he said," Brandon signed. "You get what it gives, but it takes from you too."

"What did your dad get? And lose?"

Brandon told her about him winning the quarterback position, only to blow his knee out.

"Have you done it?" she asked, watching him intently.

He nodded.

"Get out!" she exclaimed, clutching his shoulder. "What did you ask for?"

"It's not a wishing well. My dad said it gives you what you want inside. Not what you need."

Her brow furrowed. "What did you get?" she asked.

Brandon looked up at her and smiled. "You."

Amy's eyes filled with tears as she stared at him in disbelief. "Me?" she asked. "Why not the ability to talk?"

Brandon shrugged. "I'm okay not talking." *I'd rather get laid*, he added to himself.

Amy threw her arms around him, squeezing him to her. "That's the sweetest thing anyone has ever said to me."

Brandon embraced her tightly for a moment, then pushed her back. He stared into her eyes as he signed, "Now I'm just waiting on the catch."

Amy's shoulders drooped as she looked at him. She laid a hand along his cheek and stroked his skin with her thumb. "Do you think I planned all this? That I'm using you?"

"I don't think so. I hope not."

Amy shook her head. "I'm not." She ran both hands

through her hair as she settled into the swing. "I don't think I did or am. I mean...." She sighed heavily. "Mama had cancer, like, four years ago, but she kicked it. It was in remission. She only told me it was back a few weeks ago, but she's known a lot longer. She already made plans and stuff."

"Maybe my dad was wrong then."

Amy wiped her eyes with her fingertips. "I don't think he is."

"What is it?"

She took a deep breath as her eyes washed out over the river. "When my daddy left four years ago, we went to see Granny Stivers. There were rumors, you know. People talk. Mama thought maybe if they were true, we'd use it to come into some money. She was scared, wondering how she was going to support us." Amy shook her head. "Anyway, we rustled up my dad's old coon dogs. They were really just lazy flea bags, if you ask me. We hogtied their feet and put duct tape around their mouths so they couldn't howl. When it was good and dark, we hauled them to your granny's house, and she helped us throw them in the muck. I couldn't watch, but Mama did."

"What happened?"

"Mama went over to Mississippi and bought a couple of lottery tickets, but we never did win anything. Eventually, she gave up and got a second job working nights at the Dollar World."

"Nothing happened?" He asked. "Nothing at all?"

Amy puffed out her cheeks as she exhaled slowly. "I've been wondering about it, but now it makes sense." She turned to him, pulling one leg onto the swing between them. She watched Brandon's hand instantly go to it, caressing her thigh, and smiled.

"I don't know if boys do this, but girls measure stuff."

Brandon's cheeks flushed, and he dropped his gaze to his hands. Like most boys he knew, he'd done plenty of measuring of certain things himself.

"So, 'round about that time, I was measuring stuff. My chest, my waist, my butt. I'd write it all down in this little notebook. For a long time, I did it every week. When nothing changed, I started doing it every month. Then every couple of months. Nothing ever grew."

Brandon looked up at her, his brow furrowed with curiosity.

"I haven't measured anything in over a year, but I bet if I did, it would pretty much be the same. I might have gained a pound or two, but that's it."

"What does that mean?"

"Things usually change in that time frame. Sometimes a lot." She sighed. "I started measuring stuff when I was fourteen."

Brandon's brow creased deeper as he did the math in his head.

Amy nodded. "My hair is the same length, I'm the same height, my boobs are the same size, my butt. Nothing's changed."

"So you're really eighteen?"

"I don't think I am. This is exactly how I looked when I was fourteen."

"But that was four years ago, so you're eighteen."

"I suppose," she said with a shrug.

"But you said you were sixteen."

"I look sixteen, don't I? I feel sixteen. What was I supposed to tell you?"

Brandon closed his eyes and ran a hand through his hair a few times. "So," he signed, looking at her. "This is what you got?"

Amy shrugged. "I'd rather we won the lottery. I guess deep down, this is what Mama wanted for some reason."

"But if nothing changes, you'll always be beautiful. Forever young."

Amy pursed her lips. "But you won't."

Brandon sank into the swing, deflated. That was the catch. He'd gotten Amy, but he'd grow old, and she wouldn't. He'd lose her in the end, after all.

"I'm sorry," she said, lacing an arm around his waist. She leaned into him and rested her cheek on his chest. "I didn't really believe it until just now."

Brandon stroked her thick crop of hair as he gathered his thoughts. Once he aged to eighteen, twenty-five at the latest, they'd make an odd couple. His heart began to ache, and tears welled in his eyes as he considered losing her.

"I'm so sorry," she whispered.

FIFTEEN

Amy picked up a rock the size of her thumb from the road and looked up at the window on the end of Simmons' house. The light was on, and she'd seen him pass twice already.

She rubbed the dirt from the rock as she held it between her thumb and pointer finger. The dirt turned to powder, falling gently to the ground at her feet. She weighed the rock in her hand, then flung it at the window. It hit the window dead center, sending a spiderweb of thin fractures in every direction. Her eyes bulged as panic swamped her. She considered running but forced herself to stay put by the fence. A shadow appeared in the window, then the curtains parted. She heard Simmons cursing as he examined the break in the window.

She picked up a smaller rock and flung it at the window. It hit the glass next to the broken one and bounced off.

"What the hell?" Simmons complained as he cupped his hands and peered out the dirty window. She stood in the last vestiges of the evening sun and waved her arms to get his attention.

Simmons pressed his face to the window, staring at her. His bushy eyebrows rose instantly as his eyes bulged with disbelief. A dirty grin slid across his face as he recognized her.

Amy smiled as she watched him rush from the window.

The front door opened seconds later, and he hobbled down the metal staircase in a hurry.

"Well, well, well. Lookie what we have here."

"Look, Simmons, shut up and listen. We need money. As much as it sickens me to say so, I think me and you can work out a deal of some sort."

A lascivious grin slid across his unshaven face. "I knew ye'd come around. You got plenty of what I need, and I got the money you need. It's a match made in heaven."

Amy grunted in disgust. "Hell is more like it."

"Either way's fine by me." A pink tongue slipped across his lips as he stared at her hungrily.

"Shut up and listen, you old pervert. If I have to say this twice, I might come to my senses. You know where the old Stivers place is?"

"I do."

"I'll be over there tonight."

"Naw, that place's spooky and shit. I done heard all kinda crazy stuff about that place."

"It gets dark around nine. Come at nine-thirty."

"I ain't doing it. You come upstairs."

"Yeah, right, and have you tie me up and keep me in a cardboard box. Hell no. I ain't that dumb."

"I ain't going to come over there. Not for some skinny shit like you. Besides, some folks have moved in over there."

"They're not home tonight. It's about as private a place as I could find. I don't want anybody to know what lows I've had to stoop to."

Simmons shook his head as his eyes studied Amy's body. "I don't like this. Sounds a lot like some kind of trick."

Amy arched her back, tugging at the bottom of her tee-shirt. The fabric stretched across her chest, revealing that she wasn't wearing a bra.

Simmons gasped quietly. One hand went to his crotch as he leaned against the fence.

"Look, you old asshole, I'll be there on a blanket out on the pier from nine-thirty until ten. I'll be naked and waiting. Bring three hundred dollars cash."

Simmons licked his lips again as his eyes fed on her. "Three hundred? That's a lot of money for a little thing like you." A smile parted his lips despite his complaints.

"That's what I said. Take it or leave it." Amy turned to walk away but stopped suddenly. She looked back at Simmons. "You got time to take a shower, so I'd get to it." She turned and walked away. "Clock's ticking, you old bastard."

Brandon sat on the edge of his chair, kneading an orange squishy ball as he stared down at the pier from his front porch. The sun was already disappearing behind the Cypress trees on the far side of the river when he saw Amy make her way to the pier. In the gathering darkness, he watched her spread the blanket across the weathered boards. His whole body ached to be with her, to be laying on the blanket beneath the stars, but he knew he couldn't. Not yet. There was still some work to do.

It had taken two days of begging and pleading to get his father to agree to take his mother to the drive-in. When he finally agreed, it took the fact that "The Notebook" was playing to convince his mother to go with him. They wouldn't be back for at least another two hours, maybe longer if they didn't end up in another fight.

He squeezed his fist around the ball, straining his eyes to see in the gloom. Amy was moving about on the pier, but he couldn't tell what she was doing. He wondered if she was taking her clothes off like she'd told Simmons. He asked her about it, but when they'd last spoken, she hadn't made up her mind.

Brandon armed sweat from his brow and tried to swallow,

but his mouth was dry. He raised the bottle of water at his feet and was about to drink when a muttering from his driveway floated to him on the still evening air. It was probably just about nine-thirty. Simmons wasn't going to risk being late, but he was complaining about the walk.

Brandon's eyes shifted to the pier. He could barely make out the dark rectangular shape jutting into the muck. There was no hope of distinguishing Amy.

His eyes followed the sound of Simmons' shuffling across his yard. The long walk had winded the old man, his breaths coming in labored gasps. He stopped once, put his hands on his knees and coughed. When he recovered, he continued toward the pier.

Brandon sat deathly still, listening to the sound of the heartbeat pounding in his head mingled with the incessant croak of countless frogs. In the stillness of the night, he found no solace. He was a little sad for the old man, even though he was a pervert, and scared, mostly for Amy. If something went wrong, both she and Simmons could end up in the muck. What a disaster that would be.

Brandon shook his head, relinquishing a quiet sigh to the night. He considered saying a prayer but reconsidered. God wasn't going to help them with what they were about to do.

A tiny spot of light appeared near the edge of the yard. Simmons was close to the pier. Amy's voice. She sounded angry, but he couldn't tell what she said. The light went out, and Simmons complained about not being able to see.

Brandon stood from his chair and crossed the dark porch. He slipped down the steps and headed for the wood line. The plan was for him to sneak around the edge of the yard and hit Simmons in the back of the head while he was distracted.

Amy wanted him to use a hammer, but he thought that might kill the old man, lessening the effect. In the end, they'd decided on the hickory ax handle he'd found beneath Amy's house. It was stiff and hard enough to disorient Simmons, but it probably wouldn't kill him.

They'd also added two low posts to the right side of the pier and tied a rope between them. If things went awry, Amy was to move to that side of the pier.

Moving quietly along the grass, Brandon strained to listen for voices but heard only frogs and crickets. He cursed their infernal racket, wishing they'd take a five-minute break.

He found the tall water oak silhouetted against the night sky and hurried to it. His hands found the trunk and slid down the rough bark to the base. Panic gripped his heart when he couldn't find the ax handle. His fingers groped the dark grass, sweeping from side to side.

He looked up when he heard the boards of the pier groan as Simmons mounted them. His hands swept wildly around the base of the tree. He was about to give up when he found the handle. He closed his eyes and sighed thankfully.

The sound of steps on the pier was his cue to move up. Things were moving fast, but that was good. It would leave less time to think about what they were about to do. Brandon grabbed the handle and hurried closer to the pier, crouching behind a young cypress tree.

"You better not be messing with me, you little bitch."

"Shut up. Keep walking. I'm out here. I wanted to see the stars, that way, I'd have something to look at other than your ugly face."

Simmons laughed quietly. "I'll shut you up in just a minute." He pulled his shirt off and dropped it on the pier. "You better be naked, or I'll tear your clothes off you. I'm going to make you a woman tonight." Simmons' lustful chuckle swept across the muck. Beyond the pier, the reeds began to rattle gently in anticipation.

"You bring the money?" Amy asked. Her voice was level and calm.

"I got it, but you ain't getting it 'till afterwards."

"Show it to me."

Simmons slipped out of his pants and dropped them on the pier. "I'm going to show you something, little missy."

The pier groaned as Simmons moved forward, one hand outstretched, groping the darkness for Amy.

Brandon moved closer to the edge of the pier. The sound of the reeds shaking sent a rush through his chest. Maybe tonight, he thought, everyone will get what they want except for old man Simmons, of course.

"Where the hell are you?"

Amy stepped back, putting as much distance between her and Simmons as possible. Her heels found the end of the pier. She'd gone as far as she could. She squatted in the darkness, hugging the short pole they'd added, and waited. "You're closer than you think."

That was the cue. Brandon crept from behind the tree and hurried onto the pier just as the sound of the reeds intensified.

"What the hell?" Simmons asked.

Amy stood and struck a match, revealing the fact that she was indeed naked.

Simmons moaned, forgetting the noise coming from the muck. "Come to Daddy." He lurched forward with his arms open, but Amy dropped the match into the muck, sinking the pier back into darkness.

"Dammit, girl. Stop playing games. We had a deal."

Brandon's bare feet barely made a sound as he closed the distance on Simmons, but he could have been wearing boots, and no one would have heard. The reeds were practically screaming now.

"Here I am." Amy struck another match, illuminating the

target. Her eyes shifted from Simmons to Brandon as he raised the stick into the air behind the old man. She smiled. As Brandon brought the club down, she blew out the match.

Brandon decided not to take any chances and put his full weight behind the swing. The force of the impact traveled down the three-foot handle and into his hands. A sickening thud filled the night. Simmons collapsed onto the pier with a weak grunt.

Brandon, in the darkness, listening for movement. None came from Simmons, but bare feet were shuffling toward him from the end of the pier.

A hand touched him in the darkness, then a naked body was against his. He pulled her to him, relishing the heat of her excitement on her skin. His hands wrapped around her and found her butt. His fingers dug into the toned muscle and yanked her closer.

"I'm okay," she whispered, her hands running through his hair. Amy laughed quietly. "He never laid a finger on me."

Brandon's hand found the back of her head, sinking into the crop of wild hair. He brought her to him, and their lips met in a hungry kiss.

Amy allowed the moment to linger before pulling away. A thumb ran across his lips, wiping the wetness from them. "We'd better hurry before he wakes up."

Brandon reluctantly let her slip from his arms and then dropped to the pier, feeling for Simmons' body. His hand touched a hairy back, and he recoiled with a grunt of disgust. In the darkness, he couldn't tell if the wetness was blood or sweat. Either way, it was gross.

"He's still breathing." Amy reached out to Brandon and led his hands back to Simmons' body.

"Get on that side," she urged quietly. Brandon did as instructed, and they drug Simmons the few feet to the edge of the pier. He was heavier than expected, but they got him into position without much trouble.

Sitting in the darkness, his hands clutching an old man's upper arm, Brandon noticed that the reeds had gone silent. Had they intentionally helped them, or were they just reacting to what he and Amy were about to do?

"Okay. On three. One. Two. Three."

Brandon pushed his half of the body, grimacing as it landed in the muck with a wet squelch. It was done. Over.

He'd murdered a man. No matter what he did for the rest of his life, he'd always be a murderer.

The clump reeds closest to them began to shake, then the rustling spread quickly across the muck. The sound grew until it was louder than the chorus of frogs from either side of them. To Brandon, it almost sounded like rain or a thunderous applause.

"Now, the clothes," Amy whispered. She crawled along the pier. "I've got his pants." She stood, rifling through the pockets. "The sonofabitch was going to stiff me. He didn't even bring the money."

Brandon's hand found Simmons' shirt and handed it to Amy.

"I mean, it doesn't really matter, but I could use three hundred bucks all the same, know what I mean?" She moved to the end of the pier and tossed the clothes in. "Well, it's done," she said, dusting her hands.

Brandon moved toward her voice and gripped her wrist. He pulled her to him and wrapped his arms around her. His lips found her in a frantic kiss, and his hands slid down her naked body, exploring her eagerly.

He stopped suddenly as the thought occurred to him that he and Simmons both wanted the same thing. Both of their lusts for Amy's body had led them here to the edge of the muck. Now, one of them was being consumed by the dark mud beyond the pier, and one was enjoying the prize they both wanted so badly.

"It's okay," Amy whispered in the darkness. She took his hand from her hip and placed it over her breast. "I promise. Everything's going to be okay. And I always keep my promises."

Brandon smiled as the apprehension fled his body, replaced by a full-blown desire to feel Amy's naked body against his. As he peeled his shirt off, he felt her hands on his skin, then her lips were kissing his chest.

"Trust me," she whispered as she pulled him down to the blanket with her. "It'll all be okay," she added just before her lips found his again.

Just beyond the end of the pier, feet from the entangled bodies of the young lovers, dark mud closed in on the remnants of Grover Simmons without making a sound.

SIXTEEN

Brandon lay on his bed and stared out the window. Thin, wispy clouds slid gently past the waxing crescent moon. Barely twenty-four hours had passed since they'd pushed Simmons into the muck, and he had made love to Amy. He'd never forget the sound of the ax handle striking the old man's head, but it was a memory easily replaced by what he and Amy had done afterwards.

He felt guilty, but not as much as he thought he would. The thing that was keeping him awake was the two-day separation from Amy. She'd insisted on it to avoid drawing suspicion to themselves. If people started asking questions, the first thought would be that Simmons went too far and one of the girls did something. The next logical step would be to add her boyfriend to the blame. They hadn't been seen by many people who would talk, so laying low would prevent any loose lips from putting them together.

It all made sense when she explained it, but then again, she was lying naked beside him on the pier after making love. He would have agreed to anything.

Brandon turned from the window with a moan. Not seeing Amy was harder than he thought, and he cursed how easily he'd agreed with the forced separation. No one was going to ask questions. No one would ever know what happened to the dirty old bastard. As far as anyone could tell, he'd just vanished. There was nothing to connect them to him.

Even if someone suspected them, no law enforcement officer would believe the story of the muck and witches and dark spirits. He'd seen it in action and barely believed it.

Brandon let out a frustrated moan. *Even if they did notice that he was gone*, he thought, *nobody would raise a fuss. He was a despicable human being.* They'd actually done everybody a favor. They'd spared countless girls from his vile tongue and possibly more.

He closed his eyes, imagining Amy. She was lying in bed in a tee shirt and a pair of panties the same coral color as her bikini top had been. The color practically glowed against her smooth, tanned skin. He moaned again as frustration swamped him.

A smile slipped across his face as he relived their time together on the pier. It was the single greatest feeling he'd ever experienced, greater even than smelling the flower from the muck. The flower had given him a surreal, floating feeling that felt good in a spiritual sense. Being with Amy was real, tangible. It was primal and connective. She'd awakened every nerve in his body and left him feeling complete. Now, she was all he could think about. She was all he wanted, and not merely in a physical way. Being with her was like finding a piece of himself that he never knew was lost.

Brandon sat up in the bed and slammed his fist into the mattress. He shoved his other hand through his hair twice, then grabbed a handful. Holding his hair in his fist, he took a deep breath to calm himself. He had to keep it together one more day, then he could be with Amy.

He stood suddenly, dropping his hands. Another day? He'd never make it. Today had been torture. He'd slept well past noon only to be awakened by his mother, who was sure he was "coming down with something." She'd taken his temperature three times, sat with her hand on his chest to measure his breathing, and even used the penlight to look at his pupils. Physically he was fine, but mentally he was barely holding it together. She'd also asked how he felt a hundred times.

Amy turned the knob slowly, wincing as the metallic click of the plunger echoed in the darkness. She waited for a voice to speak, but nothing came.

She pushed the door open and peeped inside. The room was dark except for a small pool of light cast by the 40-watt bulb in the lamp on the nightstand. A half dozen bottles of prescription pills stood around the base of the lamp, reminding Amy just how sick the woman in the bed was.

Her eyes went to the soft hum coming from the darkness on the far side of the bed. She found the small, clear oxygen line coming from the concentrator, following it across the bed and up to the cannula in the woman's nose. So far, she only needed the oxygen at night, when she was sleeping. The doctors said it would help her rest.

It'll be okay, she thought. *Soon.* A smile tugged at the corners of her mouth. *I fixed it. It's going to be better soon.* Amy crossed the room and sat gently in the wooden chair that matched the other three still out at the kitchen table.

She watched the gentle, rhythmic rise and fall of the woman's chest for a while, then looked up at her face. She'd lost a few pounds, but it looked good on her. Her hair, once as dark as Amy's, had a smattering of gray, especially at the roots. She'd had a rough go at it lately, but things were going to be better soon.

She sat back in the chair with a quiet sigh. Her thoughts drifted to Brandon, and a thin smile escaped her. He was a simple soul, kind and gentle, and he loved her. Shaking her head, she closed her eyes as a pang of guilt swept through her.

She could tell by the way he looked at her and the way he'd been with her on the pier that he honestly cared for her. He'd helped her with Simmons and, in doing so, had saved the only other person in the world who cared about her.

Opening her eyes, she looked at the pitiful soul lying in the bed. Brandon had helped her when no one else would. He deserved better than to be put in a situation like that, but what choice did she have?

She moaned internally as she dropped her head back, staring at the circle of light on the ceiling above the lamp. Part of her wanted to be with Brandon, but it was better this way. She couldn't risk drawing suspicion to them. It had been part of the plan all along, but she hadn't anticipated how hard it would be. He was the nicest boy she'd ever been with. Too nice to be mixed up in all this.

Amy pushed her hands through her hair and interlaced her fingers atop her head. Her emotions were raw, and her nerves felt like the naked ends of electric wires. So much had happened in such a short time. Her mind couldn't process all of it, and her whole body ached from the stress.

They'd pushed Simmons into the muck, then made love on the same blanket she'd used to lure the old man to the pier, but she felt no remorse. She'd traded the life of a filthy, nasty pervert for the wonderful, caring one next to her. It was a deal she'd make a thousand times over if she had to.

She lowered her hands but brought a thumb to her mouth, chewing on the nail as she watched the woman's steady breathing. She was resting comfortably. She'd be fine alone for a bit. Besides, the cancer was probably already gone anyway. The muck would break the spell and kill the cancer. Things were already getting better.

Brandon moved slowly along the road, telling himself that the sound of the gravel crunching beneath his feet wasn't that loud. The air was thick and humid, bringing sweat to his brow almost as soon as he'd stepped out of the house. To his left, deep in the woods, an owl called to his mate but got no answer.

The smell of the red clay dust hung in the air, entering through his nose and tickling his throat. Brandon cleared it as quietly as he could and spat as he walked along the road toward Amy's house.

She'd probably be asleep, but that was okay. He'd be closer to her. If her light were on, he'd go to her. They could make love again. If the house were dark, he wasn't sure what he'd do. The one thing he was sure of was that he couldn't keep away.

The toe of his tennis shoe kicked a rock, sending it skittering down the road. He stopped, listening further down the way. Well past Amy's house, a dog barked, then fell silent. He strained his eyes, scanning the unlit road before him. The dark woods to his left marked the edge of the road, yielding a soft glow to the lighter colored dust at his feet. In the pale moonlight, the road took on an eerie, netherworld look.

Brandon licked his dry lips and started walking again. He swallowed hard and stifled a cough, wishing he'd brought a bottle of water.

When Simmons' rusted fence loomed out of the darkness, Brandon paused again. He hadn't considered that he'd have to pass the man's house to get to Amy's. His eyes went to the dark windows, and he nodded slowly. The old man was gone, but no one would ever know where.

Good riddance, he thought as he hurried past the fence. Simmons had been dealt with, but his place still had a dirty feel to it.

Amy stepped into the shadows alongside the road, carefully watching the figure making its way toward her. Who would be out at this hour, she wondered? And at Simmons' place, no less.

She often took late-night walks down the road and had never seen another soul until tonight. She paused in the shadows, cursing the inconvenience.

She squatted next to a tree, resting her shoulder against the rough bark. A thumbnail went to her mouth as she watched the figure. It had stopped in front of the old man's house but then hurried past. Whoever it was, they were coming toward her now, and there was less than fifty feet between them.

She tried to sink further into the shadows, but a knot formed in her left thigh. She grimaced as she stretched her leg out before her, rubbing the cramp.

The figure moved ever closer with each furtive step. They were going somewhere but weren't in a hurry. Amy chewed at her nail anxiously as she took in the shape and size of the figure. They were short and, judging by their shoulders, a man. Her head tilted to one, and her eyes narrowed as she watched them grow closer.

Her heart leapt into her throat, and she gasped when she recognized the person sneaking toward her. It was Brandon. What was he doing? Why was he at Simmons' place?

"Hey," she said in a loud whisper as he drew even with the tree she was hiding behind.

He sprung away from her, putting his fists in the air in front of his face.

"It's me," she whispered with a chuckle. "I didn't mean to scare you."

Brandon dropped his fists, peering into the shadows. A smile came to his face as Amy stepped forward. The faint glimmer of moonlight caught in her eyes, producing a sparkle for an instant as she moved toward him.

"Whatcha' doing out so late?" she asked.

Brandon moved to her, signing close so she could see. "I

wanted to see you."

She eyed him suspiciously for a moment, then smiled. "I can't stop thinking about you either."

Her body fell into his, and her arms wrapped around his waist. He put his arms around her and gripped her tightly. The faint smell of coconut on her hair enthralled him. He inhaled the scent deeply and moaned.

"I know it was my idea to stay apart, but I'm glad you came." She dropped her gaze and laid her head on his chest. "Especially after...." she trailed off.

Brandon nodded, wondering if she meant after the thing with Simmons or what they'd done together afterward. He buried his face in the crook of his arm and coughed quietly. *Damn this dust*, he thought.

He wrapped one arm around her shoulders and one around her waist as he squeezed her body to his. The loss of one day with her gave him a greater appreciation for the way she felt. Her body was strong and muscular but soft and comforting at the same time.

He cleared the tickle growing in his throat as he clung to her. Turning his head, he coughed. "I love you so much," he said.

Amy's body tensed at the sound of his voice. She pulled back, staring at him with wide eyes. "Did you just say something?"

Brandon rubbed his throat and cleared it again. "D-did I?" he asked tentatively.

Amy's eyes widened more, sure now that the voice was coming from Brandon. Her mouth fell open as she stared at him in amazement. "You can talk?"

Brandon raised his chin into the air, probing at the side of his neck with his fingertips. He beamed at Amy, overjoyed with his newfound voice. "I think maybe I did."

Amy stepped back from his, staring in amazement.

"It's a miracle," he said, but his joy faded quickly when he saw the anger rising in Amy's eyes.

"It's not a miracle, you bastard. Were you playing me?"

"What?" Brandon cleared his throat again. "No?"

Amy's eyes searched his in the dim light. "Are you for real?"

Brandon nodded. "I've never spoken a word before."

"Then how can you talk now?" she asked, eyeing him suspiciously. "What did you do?"

"I didn't do nothing," he answered, confused.

Amy gasped as a thought occurred to her. "You son of a bitch," she snapped, shaking her head.

Brandon opened his mouth to speak but never got the chance. Amy's hand sailed through the air and landed on his cheek with a loud crack. He never saw the hand coming, but he felt the sting instantly. By the time he recovered from the shock of being slapped, Amy was running down the road toward her house.

He cleared his throat again and spat. "Shit," he said, shaking his head as he went after her.

Brandon followed Amy down the narrow driveway to a small cabin sitting slightly askew atop its pillars. He saw movement in the darkness beneath the house and followed it.

A thin shadow stepped from behind one of the pylons, hand raised to strike. Brandon reacted quickly, stepping back to avoid the slap. As the hand sailed past his face, he grabbed the body of his attacker and clutched it to him.

"Let me go, you asshole."

Brandon held Amy in his arms, giving her a violent shake. "Stop." She went limp in his arms. "I didn't do anything. I don't even know what you're talking about."

"Yeah, right. All the planning, all that time, and you come along and steal it."

"Steal what?"

"And we thought you were some innocent kid. What the hell was I thinking? You freaking played me good, you dirty bastard."

"Look, Amy, I don't know what you're talking about."

She spun in his arms and pointed a finger in his face. "Right. We push—" she looked around, lowering her voice to a whisper. "We push Simmons in the muck, and suddenly you can talk."

Brandon's jaw dropped. "Do you think that's what did it?"

"What the hell else would do it, genius? Unless you been talking to Jesus...."

Brandon's arms went limp, freeing Amy. "That's not what was supposed to happen." A hand went to his throat, absently rubbing it.

"No shit, Sherlock." She shoved him back with both hands, causing him to stumble and fall. "Go on and go. I still got a dying mother upstairs, but at least you can talk."

Brandon clambered to his feet and grabbed Amy's arm as she spun to leave. She tried to snatch free, but he held her. "Stop it."

"Go to hell, asshole."

Brandon stared at Amy though she refused to look at him. He'd dreamed of a sappy reunion and even hoped for the chance to make love again, but all of that was gone now.

"I didn't have a clue this would happen."

"Yeah, right." Amy tried to snatch her arm free, but Brandon held it. "You're hurting me, asshole."

"Do you promise not to run away?"

"Whatever. Freaking jerk."

Brandon loosened the grip on her arm. When she didn't move, he released her. He shook his head. "I didn't mean for this to happen."

Amy ran both hands over her hair and shook her head. "I

should have known better."

"Better than what?"

"To trust you fucking Stivers."

Brandon clenched his jaw and shook his head. "You know, I get it. You've had a rough life—"

"Oh, spare me the bleeding heart bullshit," she interrupted. "I don't need your sympathy."

"I guess you don't. You know I didn't do this for myself. I was trying to help you and your mother."

Amy held her hands up between them. "You know what, just forget it."

"Forget it?" Brandon stepped closer to Amy and lowered his voice to a whisper. "I helped you chunk an old man into the freaking swamp to save your mother."

"Did you? Did you really? Or were you just looking to get laid?"

Brandon recoiled slightly, stung by the harshness of her tone and the fact that what she said was at least partially true. Without the possibility of having sex, he probably wouldn't have helped her at all.

"Okay, fine then." Brandon backpedaled a few steps. "I know I didn't do anything. You're upset. I understand. But don't blame me for your whole freaking life."

"Go to hell."

"I may because of you. But right now...." He stepped forward and grabbed her.

"Let me go, you bastard."

Brandon put his hand over her mouth as he half carried her, half drug her deeper beneath the house. He pushed her against one of the pillars and pressed his body against hers.

"What are you going to do, rape me?"

"No," he said in a throaty whisper. He wanted to take her, to make her do what he wanted. The muck had given her to him.

She was his, and he had every right. She was his. Her body was his.

Amy laughed as she watched his anguished face. "I didn't think so." She slid a hand up and patted his chest. "Run to your mommy like a good little boy. Tell her your good news. Celebrate while my family slowly dies because of you."

Brandon raised a clenched fist but didn't swing. He looked at Amy and shook his head. When he released her and walked away, he heard her laughing. The sound of it followed him all the way home.

SEVENTEEN

Carrol Stivers looked up from the letter before her with a worried sigh. The first light of dawn was coming softly through the rusted screen on Elvey Stivers' porch. A light fog had rolled in from the river, hiding the pier and the muck that surrounded it from her view.

She sat in silence, listening to the dampness drip from the trees. Somewhere out over the river, a crane let out a squawk.

For a moment, she could almost see why her mother-in-law loved this place or at least stayed here when she could have left. There was a calmness to it that felt good.

Shaking her head, she pushed the peacefulness of the moment away. It was all a cruel charade. She knew that now. The danger was in what lay hidden by the fog and the muck. Whatever magic it held had gotten a hold on Brandon. She could see the change in him. He'd gone from a gentle, sweet boy to an agitated, restless teen in the time they'd spent here. She was sure it had something to do with Amy but also couldn't rule out her husband's involvement.

The one thing she knew for sure was that the truth was in Elveys' secret letters. The last note she'd left in the bed as much as said so. She hadn't come out and told her, probably in case Barry found it, but in her own way, she'd let Carrol know. But the letters were back in Providence.

The only way she could figure this out was to go through the letters. She didn't want to leave Brandon but didn't think he was in any immediate danger. If Barry was involved somehow, he'd be okay. The man was a bastard, but even he wouldn't endanger his own son.

Carrol signed the letter and sealed it into an envelope. She wrote Brandon's name on the outside and stood. Creeping back into the house, she was greeted by Barry's loud snoring. She tiptoed across the room and slipped into Brandon's room.

A smile parted her lips when she saw him. He was sleeping peacefully, lying on his side and curled into a fetal position. Her heart swelled with love, and she considered waking him and taking him with her. He'd resist, she knew. He was in love with the girl down the road and wouldn't go quietly. That would probably wake Barry, and everything would become much harder.

She sighed quietly as she approached the bed. Bending, she slipped the letter beneath his pillow. Brandon stirred but didn't awaken. She risked a kiss on his forehead, then left, telling herself that she was doing the right thing. She had to find out the truth to save her son from whatever evil had its grip on him, and she couldn't do that here.

"Good morning, kiddo."

Brandon nodded through a yawn as he staggered toward the fridge. His body was heavy, like he was wearing a lead suit. His fight with Amy hurt on so many levels that he'd barely slept at all.

Late in the night, as his exhausted body began to drift, anger began to rise in his chest. He'd killed a man for her and helped dispose of the body. He wanted more of what they'd done on the pier. He deserved more. She'd promised.

This morning, however, all he felt was a heavy sadness. He genuinely liked her and hated to see her so upset. Of course, he hadn't planned for things to happen the way they did. She knew it was little more than a crapshoot. He'd explained it. This wasn't his fault.

Barry Stivers watched his son pull a bottle of orange juice from the fridge and pour himself a glass. Brandon looked haggard. The events of the last few days were wearing on him. He hadn't said so, but talking them into going to see the drive-in movie signaled that he and the girl had settled on a plan. Since then, Brandon had been preoccupied and withdrawn. There was no doubt that he was having regrets about what they did. He just hoped what he was about to tell him didn't push him over the edge.

"Look, son," Barry began. "I got some bad news."

Brandon choked on his juice, suddenly remembering he had some news too. He sat the glass down and coughed into his fist.

"You okay?" Barry Stivers looked at his son. When Brandon nodded, smiling, he continued. "Your mom left. She was gone when I got up this morning. I guess she called someone to come get her because the four runner is still here. She went back home, I guess. It's no secret that she doesn't like it down here."

Brandon stared at his father, taking in the battered look in his eyes. His hands flew up out of habit. "She left us?" he asked. Coupled with their near-constant bickering, this was bad news.

He sighed and ran a hand over his tangle of hair, confused and relieved at the same time. He'd always imagined she'd take him with her if she ever left his father. Now, however, he was glad she didn't.

Brandon thumbed the side of his glass, the joy of his own surprise fading. He couldn't reveal his secret now. The timing was terrible. He forced a smile and asked his father if he was okay.

Barry smiled. "It's all good. Really. It's just that I don't know how things will play out from here." He shrugged and rubbed his palms together. "Anyway, I just thought you should know because I don't know how much longer we'll be here."

Brandon's heart sank. All thoughts of his parent's divorce evaporated, replaced by the possibility that they'd leave soon. The notion that he'd never see Amy again hit him like a gut punch. Yes, she was mad at him, but he was clinging to the hope that he could make it better somehow.

He went to his father and gave him a one-armed hug, then asked if he was okay again. When he smiled and said he'd be just fine, Brandon asked if he could go see Amy.

Barry gave his son a sympathetic smile and nodded. "Yeah. It's fine, son. You go. Have fun. Don't let this crap worry you none. It'll be okay. It will."

Brandon thanked his father and hurried back to his bedroom to change. Now he had to talk to Amy. After grabbing a pair of shorts from the floor and slipping them on, he turned for the door but stopped. After a moment's thought, he went back to the bed and lifted the edge of the mattress, grabbing a condom from the box hidden beneath. There was still hope that he could salvage things with Amy.

As he dropped the mattress, the corner of an envelope slipped from beneath his pillow. He swallowed hard and pulled it free. His name was written on the front in a familiar script. It was a letter from his mother.

Brandon rubbed his forehead as he stared at the letter. He flicked the envelope back and forth, tapping it on his fingertips while he considered his options. He should read it now but didn't want to deal with the emotional upheaval it would surely bring. Right now, he needed to make things right with Amy. The letter would have to wait.

He shoved the envelope back under his pillow and hurried out the door. He'd read it tonight after he'd sorted things out with Amy.

Carrol Stivers burst into the spare bedroom and hurried to the closet. She pulled the shoebox containing Elvey's letters from its hiding spot and carried it to the bed. Flipping the lid off, she stared down at the stack of envelopes. They were now the writings of a dead woman. The last will and testament of Elvey Stivers.

"What the hell are you talking about, Elvey?" She shook her head, wondering why she was here. If something was going on at the river house, she should be there to watch over Brandon. Barry couldn't be trusted to look after him, but there was something in the old letters that she needed to know. Now all she had to do was find it.

She'd almost forgotten the note that Elvey left under the mattress until things started to get weird. She didn't like the girl who'd been hanging around Brandon or the fact that Barry was almost being tolerable. That whole trip to the drive-in wreaked of a setup. He was up to something. She was sure of it.

Lifting the first letter, Carrol shook her head. Was the final letter just the continued raving of a lonely, sick old woman? Was all this a waste of time? She slid the letter from the envelope and began reading it again, this time watching for hints that she might have dismissed before.

Brandon's heart stopped when he saw the Hillburn County Sherriff patrol car pulled to the edge of the road. The dust it had raised settled on the back windshield as it sat parked directly in front of the Simmons house.

He took a sip from the water bottle in his hand and crossed to the other side of the road. The policeman was nowhere in sight, lending him the hope of slipping past unnoticed.

As he drew even with the patrol car, the front door to Simmons' house opened, and a policeman stepped onto the porch. He was a meaty man with a ruddy complexion and dark hair. His right hand held a plastic pet carrier. The chihuahua inside barked relentlessly, shaking the carrier. He gave the policeman a nod but kept walking.

"Hey, kid."

Brandon's throat went dry, and his heart stopped again. He looked at the policeman, his palms raised questioningly.

"Come here a second, if you don't mind."

Brandon complied as casually as he could. He took another drink of water as the deputy struggled down the rickety steps and came through the gate.

"You know the guy who lives here?"

Brandon shook his head.

"No?" The deputy shook the carrier. "Don't you ever shut up?" He opened the back door to his cruiser and sat the dog inside. Closing it, he rounded the back of the car and approached Brandon.

"You don't know this guy?" he asked again, jerking a thumb toward the house.

Brandon shook his head again and signed, "I'm not from here."

The deputy drew in a deep breath. "Great." He leaned in. "Are you deaf?" he asked louder.

Brandon stepped back. He pointed to his ear and nodded, then put two fingers over his mouth and shook his head.

"Oh, sorry." The deputy rubbed the back of his meaty neck and looked back at the house. "I don't know sign language, but maybe we can muddle through this."

Brandon forced an innocent smile and shrugged.

"You must be one of the summer people."

Brandon nodded.

"You see an old guy walking around?"

Brandon shook his head. He looked at the house and asked, "What happened?" with sign language.

"You asking what happened?" the officer asked. When Brandon nodded, he continued. "Hell, if I know. Probably nothing. Got a call about a dog barking all night. No one came to the door. I figured the occupant died in their sleep or something, you know. Stuff like that happens a lot with these older folks. Anyway, the door was unlocked, so I went in."

"You find them?" Brandon asked.

The deputy shook his head. "Not a sign. Thanks anyway, kid." He produced a card from his breast pocket and handed it to Brandon. "If you see anything, give us a call."

Brandon took the card, looking at it as he backed away. He threw the deputy a wave and walked away.

Brandon Stivers climbed the metal staircase to Amy's house feeling like a man going to the gallows. In a few scant hours, Amy had slapped him and refused to see him, his parents were probably headed for a bitter divorce, and now the cops were at Simmons' house. His whole life was falling apart, and there wasn't anything he could do to stop it.

He pushed through the screen door and approached the bright orange wooden door. Taking a deep breath to calm himself, he knocked twice.

The woman who opened the door looked vaguely like Amy but much older. Her hair was more gray than black, and her eyes carried the weight of worry. When she smiled, however, he knew she had to be Amy's mother. She was the one dying.

"Is Amy home?" Brandon asked. The sound of his own voice was still strange to him, but he liked it. It had a slight raspy tone like his father's but wasn't as deep.

"You must be Brandon." Her smile widened.

"Yes, ma'am."

Her head tilted to one side slightly as she took him in, still smiling. The look in her eyes said that she was thinking of better times when she was young and boys came calling for her.

"You really do look like your old man when he was your age. Damn."

"Excuse me?" Brandon asked, confused. The woman was probably close to his father's age, but had they known each other?

"Never mind. It's nothing. Just an old woman rambling on. I'll see if Amy's awake."

"Yes, ma'am. I'll wait downstairs on the swing if she'll see me."

The woman nodded and moved the door slowly, watching him until it closed between them. Brandon stared at the door for a moment as hushed but insistent voices filtered out to him.

Turning, he sighed and walked across the porch. It was out of his hands now. If she'd see him, he might be able to fix whatever was wrong. If she didn't, there was nothing he could do.

Amy's bare feet dismounted the metal staircase slowly. She stopped halfway down and closed her eyes, preparing herself to face Brandon again. Last night had ended on a bad note. The plan with Simmons didn't work, and she'd lost her temper, risking everything.

Amy bent, looking beneath the house. Brandon was on the swing. His elbows were propped on his knees, his fists tucked beneath his chin. His eyes were closed, his breathing slow and rhythmic.

She hurried down the remaining steps and went to him, kneeling in the dry dust in front of him. "Brandon," she whispered.

His head jerked up instantly. His eyes fluttered, blinking

away sleep. A wide smile parted his lips when he saw her. He opened his mouth to speak, but she put a finger to his lips.

She leaned in and kissed him, her hands digging frantically through his hair. "I'm sorry," she said, breaking the kiss. She slid her arms around him and clutched him to her.

"It's okay," he whispered, burying his face in her hair. Her body was trembling beneath his grasp. "It doesn't matter."

She pulled back, cradling his face in both her hands. "Can you forgive me?" she asked, her bleary eyes searching his. "I'm so sorry."

"There's nothing to forgive. I was never mad at you. I love you."

Amy closed her eyes, pushing a lone tear down her cheek as she shook her head. "I love you too. I'm sorry."

Brandon took her hands in his and pulled her onto the bench with him. "Everything's fine if you're okay. Are you okay?"

"Everything's not okay. I mean, I love you, and we're okay, I think, but that's about all that is."

Brandon nodded. She didn't know half the story. "What happened? What did I do?"

Amy wiped her eyes with her fingertips, then slid them down her face and covered her mouth. She stared out at the river, shaking her head slowly.

"When you started talking, I thought you stole my wish, that somehow you'd gotten what you wanted, and I wouldn't."

"I don't...." His voice trailed off, unsure what to say. "My dad said that it doesn't work like that anyway."

"I know, but it was my mother's last chance."

"How is she? She seemed well. Maybe a little tired, but okay."

Amy shook her head. "She says she's okay, but I know she isn't. Neither of us slept much last night. I think she's gotten worse."

"It didn't work at all?"

Amy shook her head. "Not even a little."

"How could it not work?" he asked. "It just makes sense that would be what you got."

She threw her hands up and let them drop to her lap. "I don't know how it works. You know more about it than me."

Brandon rubbed his temples. A headache was forming in the center of his brain. "My dad told me that it's not a wishing well; it gives you what it wants to give you." He looked at Amy and nodded. "And that there's always a catch."

"I've been thinking about that. Since we both pushed Simmons in, maybe we both got part of something. Maybe that's why Mama wasn't cured."

"Maybe. I mean, I can talk now."

"I know." She offered him a smile. "I am sorry for slapping you."

"It's fine. It didn't hurt or anything," he said with a grin.

Amy caressed the cheek she'd slapped. "This morning, I was getting out of the shower, and I happened to catch a glimpse of myself in the mirror. I went and dug out that old tape measure. I was an inch bigger around the chest than I was when I last measured. Just a few minutes ago, I was a little bigger."

Brandon's eyes dropped to the front of her baggy tee shirt, then diverted back to her eyes. He couldn't stop the smile from tugging at the corners of his mouth.

"You know what that means?" she asked, ignoring his glance.

Brandon shrugged but didn't venture a guess.

"The thing is done that happened when me and Mama tossed those mutts in the muck. I guess I'll age normally now?"

"Who the hell knows anymore." The news wasn't bad for him, but Amy's mother was doomed. "My dad said it's an evil place, and I'm starting to see why."

"Do you wish you'd never come down here?" she asked, her eyes frantically searching his face.

"Not even a little bit."

Amy hid her face in her hands and began to sob. "But Mama's still sick. She's dying, Brandon."

Brandon felt his body deflate, unable to stop an exhausted moan from escaping. Every time one situation resolved itself, another problem arose. His father's words echoed through his head.

"There's always a catch, always."

He slid an arm around Amy and pulled her to him, stroking her hair as she lay against his chest, crying. His mind was turning summersaults, leaping from one problem to another, trying to solve them all at once.

When the idea that he could simply leave and go home with his mother flashed into his mind, he considered it. In the end, he decided that running away wouldn't solve anything. If the police started questioning Amy about Simmons' disappearance, she might take him down with her, especially if he abandoned her.

No, he thought. *I don't want to leave.*

What he wanted was for the police to go away, Amy's mother's cancer to disappear, and to lay with Amy again and forget about the whole world. Was that too much to ask for?

Brandon took a deep breath and lifted Amy from his chest. "Look, I know you're upset, but I have to tell you something."

"What?" she asked, wiping tears from her cheeks.

"On the way over here, the cops were at Mister Simmons' place."

"What?" she asked, grabbing his arm.

Brandon nodded. "They said a neighbor called about that damned dog of his barking."

Amy shook her head as she sat up. A thumb went to her

mouth, and she started chewing on the nail. "Shit. We should have thrown that shit eater in with him," she said around her thumb. "Did they ask you any questions?"

"Just if I knew him. I pretended like I couldn't talk."

"That was smart," she said, smiling.

"They asked if I knew him. I said I was just down for the summer." Brandon shrugged. "Then the guy gave me his card, and I left. He didn't seem very interested."

Amy pushed her hands over her hair and interlaced her fingers behind her neck. "There's no way they can connect anything to us. Is there?"

Brandon shook his head. "He's gone, and so are his clothes. I don't guess anybody saw anything. It just seems like he disappeared."

"It won't take much questioning for them to find out what a gem of humanity he was. Nobody liked his dirty ass anyway."

"That's pretty much what I thought. I think if we're smart, we'll be fine."

"Jesus, when it rains, it pours."

"Tell me about it," Brandon said. "My mom went back home this morning. Dad looked pretty ragged. I think they're going to get divorced soon."

Amy put a hand on his cheek. "Yeah. I'm sorry. How you doing?"

Brandon's brow furrowed. "What do you mean, 'Yeah?'"

"You said they fought a lot. I could see it coming."

Brandon shrugged, satisfied with the answer. "It'll be okay. My dad said I should tell you because he doesn't know what she'll do about custody. I guess he'll stay here 'till things are sorted out."

"You're not leaving, are you?" she asked, panic in her eyes.

"I don't want to. I don't think my mom will make me if I say I want to stay, but you never know." He considered the letter she'd left him, wishing he'd read it.

"My God. It seems like everything is working against us, doesn't it?"

"Maybe that's the 'catch' my dad talked about."

"Why do things have to be so complicated?" Amy asked.

Brandon shook his head. "I don't know." He stared out at the river over Amy's shoulder. The dark water slipped past silently, ever moving. His eyes found a piece of debris and followed it for a while.

The roots of the headache were slipping across the front of his head. For so long, his life had been so simple, almost perfect. Now, he had a girlfriend, and he could talk, and things were more confusing than ever.

"It'll be okay," he said quietly, knowing that things wouldn't be. So much had changed. He had changed, and he wasn't sure it was for the better.

EIGHTEEN

Amy peeped over her sandwich at Brandon, watching as he devoured his lunch like he hadn't eaten in days. "You must have worked up an appetite," she said with a devilish grin. His father had scarcely cleared the driveway before their clothes were off. They'd spent hours together, only driven out of bed by hunger.

Brandon nodded, smiling himself. "I guesso, but it's a really good sandwich."

"I have many talents."

"And so far, I like all of them."

Amy laughed and took a bite of her food. "I need to go check in on Mama. A nurse comes by in the morning a couple days a week, but she's off today."

"Want me to come along?"

Amy's smile faded as she shook her head. "It's okay. You can stay and have a nap."

"I don't mind."

"I know you don't wanna come. You're just being nice. Besides, sometimes she's not well, and I wouldn't want anyone to see me like that."

Brandon dropped his food to his plate and wiped his mouth on a napkin. "Isn't there anything anyone can do?"

Amy shook her head. "I mean, we've made some calls and

stuff. There are some places, but she doesn't want to go. She said if she's going to die, then she wants to die at home."

"How long does she have?" Brandon asked, almost in a whisper.

"I don't know. I mean, she's already weaker than she used to be. She needs oxygen when she sleeps now. She looks sick even though she says she's fine."

"What would it cost for the medicines and stuff?"

"Geesh." Amy rolled her eyes. "Thousands, probably. My dad was a piece of crap, but he always worked places that had insurance. Since he left, we haven't had any."

"There's got to be places. I've seen stuff on T.V. a lot of times."

"That stuff's mostly for kids. Anyway, she doesn't want to go away. She's worried about me."

"If you had a safe place to stay, would she go?"

"We don't have any relatives around here. There are some friends, but I don't know…."

"What if you stayed here?" Brandon's mind reeled with the possibilities, and a smile escaped him.

Amy shook her head, smiling herself. "As much as I'd like that, she'd never go for it. She doesn't know y'all. Plus, now that it's just you and your dad, she'd never allow it. She don't trust men."

"That's understandable," Brandon sighed.

"It'll be okay," Amy said, standing.

Brandon stood and went to her, pulling him to his chest. "You don't believe that, do you?"

"No," she whimpered. "Not even a little bit."

Brandon fluffed the pillow on the hammock tied between two of the poles supporting his grandmother's house and settled in with a tired sigh. The emotional turmoil, lack of sleep, and this morning's fun with Amy had drained every ounce of energy from his body. He felt guilty for taking a nap but was also thankful for the opportunity.

The shade offered enough respite from the blazing sun to make it tolerable, and his eyelids became heavy as soon as he lay down. A dragonfly buzzed up to him, but he didn't notice. He was asleep before it grew bored and flew away.

Brandon's eyes opened suddenly, staring at the joists beneath the house. Two cracked, dried-out cane fishing poles hung on rusty nails, their lines hopelessly tangled. Faded red and white bobbers swung in the breeze of the coming storm.

He sat up and looked around. The air was cool and heavy with the scent of rain. He shook his head to clear the sleep, but it didn't help.

"What woke me up?" he asked, stifling a yawn.

"Brandon!"

His eyes flew wide at the sound of his mother's voice. She sounded angry. Was she back? Surely, she hadn't come back already.

He rose from the hammock, scanning the yard. There were no cars in the drive. He stepped out from beneath the house, still looking around. Everything was bathed in a strange yellow hue. His eyes went to the sky, expecting to see a storm front. Sometimes the color meant hail was close, but not this time. A different storm was brewing.

"Brandon!"

The scream echoed about the place. His mother wasn't just mad. She was furious. A door slammed on the porch, and he looked up at the house.

"Mama?"

"There you are, you little shit." She stared down at him, her face contorted by rage.

Brandon watched in horror as her fingers pushed through the screen wire, ripping it from top to bottom. His mother's head appeared in the opening. Her hair was disheveled, but it was the redness of her eyes that scared him.

"What have you done?' she asked.

"Nothing, Mama."

"Nothing?" she asked through clenched teeth. She shoved her hands through the hole in the screen, leaning down towards him. Her arms were extended before her, her fingers splayed. An unrolled condom hung from each fingertip, flapping in the steady breeze.

"Does this look like nothing to you?" she screamed.

"Mama, I can explain."

"Explain? Explain how you've been sneaking around screwing your stupid little brains out with that whore?"

"She's not a whore!" His voice was angry and mean.

"She's a little whore. You know she's just using you. She's just letting you dabble in her to steal everything."

"No. You're wrong."

"She's got you under her spell, doesn't she?" She threw her hands at him, loosening the condoms.

Brandon watched them flutter to the ground, shocked into silence.

"She's a whore and a witch. She's tricked you, but she hasn't tricked me."

"What are you going to do?"

"You know what happens to witches, don't you? Surely you're not that d-d-dumb." She threw her head back, releasing a cackle. When she'd finished laughing, she stabbed one finger toward the pier.

Brandon swallowed hard as he turned slowly, following her point. The wind picked up suddenly, tearing at his hair. Pain exploded in his chest, and his breath turned to fire in his throat when he saw the thick, wooden cross standing just shy of the pier. Amy was hanging on it.

Her body was slumped forward, held in place by large rusty nails that had been driven through her wrists. Blood ran down her naked body, seeping from the clutch of thorns that had been stretched across her breasts.

"What did you do?" Brandon screamed as he started running toward the cross. "Amy."

"There's nothing you can do now, boy," Carrol screamed. "What's done is done."

Brandon's hands fell on Amy's bloody feet as he made it to the base of the cross. His fingers slid gingerly across the thick, rusty nail that had been driven through both of them.

"No!" he cried. "No. Amy." He gripped her legs, trying to lift her, but only managed to smear them with blood. "Please, no." He fell against her legs, sobbing. "No. No."

"At least you got what you wanted," his mother screamed from the house. "You dirty little bastard."

"It's okay."

Brandon's head snatched up at the sound of Amy's voice.

"I'm so sorry," he sobbed, stretching to reach her. His hand landed on the thorns wrapped around her waist, and he recoiled.

"At least you got what you wanted," she said, smiling.

"What?" Brandon looked at her, then back at his mother. He turned back to Amy wiping tears from his eyes.

"I'm sorry." He looked at the blood on his hands and began to shake.

Brandon's body erupted from the hammock as a hand touched him. His arms flew out as he sprang up, gasping.

"Easy now," his father said with a chuckle.

"What?" Brandon asked, confused. He looked at his hands. They were clean. He looked up at his father, then looked

at the pier.
Barry Stiver's jaw hung open as he stared at his son. "Brandon?" he asked timidly.
Brandon rubbed his face with both hands and swallowed hard. He took a deep breath and blew it out slowly, trying to control his panting. He armed sweat from his brow and looked at his father, and nodded.
"Did you just say something, or am I losing my mind?"
Brandon stared at him, considering his options. He wiped tears from his eyes and nodded.
"You did say something?"
Brandon nodded again.
"I'm not having a stroke?" He leaned into Brandon. "Pupils not fixed and dilated?"
Brandon shook his head.
Barry Stivers rubbed his mouth with the palm of his hand. "Can you do it again?"
Brandon smiled. "I can."
Barry moved quickly, wrapping his son in a powerful embrace. "Oh, my God." He hugged his son until his back ached from bending over, then released him. When he pulled back, tears were on his cheeks.
"Please don't have a heart attack, Dad."
Barry laughed and put a hand to his chest. "I thought I was for a second there, or a stroke or something." He shook his head, a broad smile painted on his face. "When? How?"
"Yesterday, and I think you know how."
Barry pumped his fists in the air. "I knew it would work."
Brandon nodded. "It worked." He looked down at his sweaty palms. "Dad," he said as he began to cry, "I think I need some help."
Barry opened his arms, "C'mon, kid. Get in here."
Brandon fell into his father's arms, allowing himself to be

engulfed by his embrace. Barry shook his head as his eyes drifted to the pier.

There's always a catch.

Barry Stivers turned up the bottle of beer in his hand and finished it. It was his second since they'd come inside, and Brandon began to unfold his dilemma.

He let out a heavy sigh and nodded slowly. "Well, you've got yourself into the thick of it, ain't you?"

Brandon nodded as he drug both hands down his face. He looked at his father and said, "Yes."

Barry leaned forward on the couch and rested his elbows on his knees. His head drooped, staring at the floor. "Okay. Give me a bit to sort through all this."

"Shouldn't I get Amy? She should be in on the decision. After all, she's got a big stake in all this too."

Barry looked up. "I suppose, but not just now. I want to think things over."

Brandon looked out the window. The sun was getting low. The day was getting away from him. "I think she should be here."

Barry leveled his gaze at his son, examining him intently. "Look, Brandon, I know you want to see her. That's understandable. It's fine, really, but we need to make sure this thing works out for us. For you."

"What do you mean?"

"I mean what I said. I'd love to help Amy and her mother, I really would. My first priority, though, is you." Barry Stivers pointed his finger at his son. "I mean it."

"I know, Dad, but I'm not going to abandon Amy."

Barry held up a hand to quieten his son. "No one is asking you to. That's not what I'm saying. All I'm saying is that we have to be smart. Something like this could turn sour very fast."

Brandon's brow furrowed as he stared at his father in disbelief. "You think Amy would hang me out to dry, don't you?"

"I don't even know her." Barry looked down at his hands as he rubbed his palm together.

"But I do," Brandon insisted.

"Son, this is a very complicated situation. There is a lot happening right now." Barry sighed and rubbed his face with both hands. "I've got to tell you something that might upset you." He stood and went to the fridge, grabbing another beer. He twisted the top off the bottle and leaned against the counter.

"I talked to our lawyer this morning. Your mother is in the process of filing for divorce."

Brandon's shoulders drooped. "I figured as much."

Barry took a long drink and shrugged one shoulder. "I guess anyone could see it coming."

"Amy said she saw it coming."

"Did she now?" Barry arched an eyebrow, staring at his son.

Brandon shrank beneath his father's gaze. "Like you said, anybody could see it coming. She heard y'all fighting the other day."

Barry gave a dismissive shrug. "Anyway, your mother isn't coming back."

"Is she okay?"

"Your mom? Yeah. She's fine. I mean, I haven't talked to her, but I'm sure she is."

Brandon stood. "Should I call her?"

Barry threw his hand up. "It'd be one hell of a shock, don't you think? She'd probably think I was up to something to trick her."

Brandon sat back down. That was true. It wasn't like she'd recognize his voice.

"I'm not telling you not to contact her. All I'm saying is that a call might be a bit of a shock." Barry closed his eyes, shaking his head gently. "I mean, she's the one who left us. You can text her if you want, though. It's up to you." He raised the bottle to his lips but didn't drink. "In situations like this, things can turn ugly. Things get done and said that people don't really mean. Divorce isn't usually pleasant for anyone involved."

"I wouldn't think so."

"I wouldn't mention any of this other stuff to her."

"God, no."

"Good." Barry scratched the stubble on his chin. "I've got about fifteen beers in the fridge, and I think I want to get after them. I'm gonna figure something out. I promise."

Brandon forced a smile. "Thanks, Dad."

"Go. Text your mom. I'll be on the porch." He grabbed another beer from the fridge and wandered out the door.

Brandon looked around the empty house. Things already felt different. Long shadows stretched across the floor, giving the room an ominous look. He shook his head and looked at the phone in his hand, wondering if talking to his mom would make things better or worse.

She'd certainly want him to come home, but there was no way he could do that. Things had to be handled here, and there was no way around it.

Brandon wandered into his room and sat down hard on the bed. So much needed his attention, but all he wanted to do was lay down and sleep until it was all over.

He crawled onto the bed and laid back on his pillows. How the hell did things go so wrong so fast? This place was supposed to shield them from the craziness going on in the world, but it felt a hundred times worse than whatever flu was going around.

He curled his arm around his pillow and found the unopened envelope from his mother. He pulled it from beneath the pillow and rolled onto his back. His eyes followed the neat script. His mother had written his name and drawn a heart beneath it.

Holding the envelope above him with both hands, he stared at it. Chewing on his bottom lip, he thought about his mother and all she'd done for him, how she'd sat in so many doctor's offices next to him. Finally, he shook his head and sighed. Ripping off the end, he slid the neatly folded letter out and opened it. There were two pages of his mother's handwriting. Apparently, she had a lot to say to him.

NINETEEN

Brandon yawned and stretched as he rolled over in his bed. The valium his father suggested he take had brought the first peaceful night's sleep in a week. He snuggled into his pillow with a contented sigh, drifting slowly toward consciousness.

"Good morning, handsome."

Brandon's eyes flew open, finding Amy perched in a chair next to his bed. "Uh, good morning," he said, a surprised smile slipping across his lips. He sat up, rubbing sleep from his eyes as he stared at her. The morning sun filtered through the window, highlighting the smooth, graceful features of her face. Her dark hair, tamed and pulled into a ponytail, shimmered in the sun.

"Is this a dream?" he asked, his voice a hushed tone.

"I don't think so," she whispered, smiling.

"How'd you get in?" he asked.

"The door was unlocked. I knocked a few times, but nobody answered. So here I am."

"How long have you been here?"

Amy shrugged. "A while, I guess." She stood and approached the bed, pulling the covers back. "Mind if I join you?"

Brandon cast a cautious glance at the door. It was closed. He smiled and raised the covers, sliding over to make room for her.

"It's not a big bed."

"That's fine by me."

Amy toed her shoes off and slid beneath the covers. She laid down with her back to Brandon and pulled his arm over her. "Can we just lay here and hold each other for a while?"

"We can do anything you need," Brandon replied, though he felt himself already becoming excited.

Amy smiled, snuggling into him. "I thought you might come back over last night."

"I wanted to, but my dad told me that he and mom are getting divorced. He was drinking, and I didn't think he should be alone."

"I understand."

"How's your mom?"

Amy shrugged beneath his embrace. "About the same. A nurse came today, so I decided to check on you."

"I told my dad."

"About what?" she asked, looking back at him.

"Everything."

Amy rolled quickly to face him. "What?"

Brandon shushed her. "Look, he knows all about the muck, or the mud or whatever you call it. He's dealt with it before. He can help us."

"Don't you mean he can help you?" Amy rolled over and threw the covers back. She tried to stand, but Brandon grabbed her arm and pulled her back.

"I mean, he can help us. I told him as much."

Amy laid back down reluctantly, turning her back to him. "I can't believe you told him. About Simmons and everything?"

"Yes, everything." Brandon blew a tired sigh into her hair. "This stuff is driving me crazy, Amy. I'm having nutso dreams when I do sleep. I feel like a thousand-pound weight is pressing down on me. My dad had to give me a valium so I could fall asleep last night."

"Like I don't have problems? How do you think I sleep?" she snapped.

"I know you do." He slid closer, hugging her to his chest. "Before we came down here, I had a few friends, but it's not like I was popular. Some girls talked to me, but I was damaged goods, you know. I've never really had a girlfriend."

Amy stroked his hand as it held her and shook her head.

"My life was a lot simpler, like a little kid. My parents shielded me from a lot of stuff, I guess. I don't know. Maybe I was the weird kid people thought I was."

"Don't say that."

"It's true. You know how on those videos, a football team lets a messed up kid dress out, and they pretend he's part of the team? That's how my life was. I was just a messed up kid that everyone was pretending to like."

Amy squeezed his hand but said nothing.

"You're so beautiful, Amy. Your hair, your eyes." He swallowed hard. "Your body. All of you. All I want is to be with you, to hang out and talk to you. I love you, and I feel like everything is working to keep us apart."

Amy closed her eyes, shaking her head. "That's what I want too, and for my mom to not die from this damned cancer."

Brandon held Amy, his mind racing as he searched for ideas. "What can we do? I mean, we tried."

"I don't know, but I can't just let her die."

"Well, if she'd let you stay with someone, she could go and get treatment, but you said she won't."

"She's hard-headed." Amy shook her head and sighed heavily. "No, she's just scared. To be honest, so am I."

"If we could come up with a boatload of money to pay for the treatments here. Isn't there a hospital close by?"

"There is," Amy sighed. "But short of winning the lottery,

where are we going to come up with that much money? To be honest, we're having trouble keeping the lights on as it is."

Brandon shook his head. He didn't think things were that bad. "We've already tried the muck."

"It didn't work because we pushed him in."

Brandon rose onto an elbow, staring down at her. "The cops are already looking into Simmons' disappearance. We can't do anything like that again. It would definitely cause suspicion."

"I know."

"I mean, two people from this little place going missing." Brandon shook his head.

"I said I know."

"Besides, your mom would have to do it."

"I know that too."

Brandon laid back down, pulling Amy back to him. He closed his eyes, losing himself in the moment despite their troubles. Her hair smelled good. Light and flowery. Her body was warm against his.

She snuggled back, pushing her body against his with a tired sigh. "This is nice."

"It is." Brandon smiled, but it was short-lived. His mind replayed the sound of the ax handle hitting the back of Simmons' head. He closed his eyes, wondering if he could do it again. The first time, he didn't know what to expect. Now he knew how it felt. How it sounded.

He looked at the girl in his bed. Amy was still, and her breaths were now coming in a low, steady rhythm. She'd fallen asleep.

Brandon closed his eyes, absorbing the presence of her body against his. She fit perfectly against him, like a piece in a puzzle. As sleep began to tug at the corners of his mind, the words of his mother's letter tried to surface, but he pushed them away. Some of what she'd said made sense, but some of it didn't.

His father had warned him that during a divorce, people said and did things in the throes of anger, jealousy, and even spite. A lot of his mother's letter sounded like that.

He sighed, releasing the tension building within him. It didn't matter. What mattered was that Amy was here in his arms, in his bed.

Brandon sat on the couch, holding Amy's hand. It had taken a full day, but she'd warmed to the idea of letting an adult handle the situation. In the end, she'd been as exhausted and sick of dealing with the whole situation as he was.

The result of the freedom from their worries was two days of bliss. They were like a young couple on their honeymoon if they honeymooned in a rural, swampy part of Alabama that didn't have much to offer. They'd ridden bikes, taken walks, and laid in the hammock.

Brandon nudged her with his shoulder playfully, offering her a knowing smile. They'd also managed to go through the entire box of condoms his father had given him.

"Okay," Barry said, stopping his pacing suddenly. "We have three factors that must be dealt with. We must deal with all three or none at all. There's your mother's cancer, my divorce, and you two being together." Barry looked at them. Adding such a frivolous thing as teenage love to the others felt ridiculous, but his son had insisted on it. "That's the deal?" He looked back and forth between the kids. "Okay?"

Amy nodded, and Brandon shrugged.

"First and foremost, the cancer—" he pointed at Amy, "How can we fix that?"

"Are you an oncologist?"

"No. I'm a banker."

"Then it'll take a miracle."

"Have you come up with any ideas between you two?"

Barry looked at the kids, a pang of jealousy in his eyes. "And cool it with the lovie dovie stuff already. This is serious."

"What's the matter?" Amy asked with a grin. "Jealous?"

Brandon watched the tense stare between them for a moment before interrupting. "What is this?" he waved his finger between the two of them.

Amy laughed, patting him on the chest. "I'm just being silly."

Brandon looked at Amy. She held his gaze. When he looked at his father, Barry looked away.

Brandon's brow furrowed, then relaxed. "Anyway, I guess we have to have her put something in the muck."

Barry pursed his lips. "That's problematic at best, as you've already seen."

"It's the only way unless we've got thousands of dollars you want to get rid of."

"Not hardly, although that would really piss your mother off." A sinister chuckle escaped him. "Look, you're old enough to stay by yourself, Amy. I could swing a loan that would pay for the bills and stuff for a couple months while your mother went to an indigent facility."

Amy's eyes dropped to her lap. "Mama's sick, and she didn't make that much, to begin with. She couldn't pay for a loan too. I suppose I could get a job somewhere...." She flicked the end of one nail against the other. "But that doesn't do anything about the other problems."

"What if you brokered a deal with Mom that let you keep this place? Surely, she doesn't want it. That takes care of the divorce and us." He looked at Amy and smiled. "Then we just get Amy's mom to toss something in the muck."

"Someone," Barry corrected. "Anyway, it's complicated, son," Barry said. He put his palms together, placing his fingertips against his lips. "Do you remember when I said things sometimes get ugly?"

"Yeah."

"Well, they're starting out that way." Barry sighed. "My lawyer called this morning. She's officially filed, and going after everything she can get. Even the stuff she hates, like this place."

"Damn," Amy said with a chuckle. "What did you do to piss her off?"

Barry dropped his hands, staring at her unamused. "Things are complicated when you're a grown-up. I'd rather not go into it."

"But why is she all angry all of a sudden?" Brandon asked.

"All of a sudden?" Barry asked, standing from his chair. "She's been angry for years, Brandon. Maybe you haven't noticed."

Brandon shrugged his concession, dropping his gaze. Of course, he'd seen their arguments, but she'd always been nice to him.

Amy patted the back of his hand. "Your dad's right. It doesn't matter. Mom's sick, you guys might lose this place in a divorce. It doesn't matter what happened. Does it?"

"It doesn't. Now let's get back to the matter at hand. Your mom needs a miracle. Now outside of someone with an inside track to Jesus Christ, the muck is the closest thing we have. It's not the best option, but it may be our only one." Barry sat on the edge of the chair and looked at Amy. "Brandon said you guys put some dogs in the muck a while back?"

She nodded. "My Dad's lazy hunting dogs."

"So, she realizes what we're dealing with. I mean, she knows what the muck does?"

Amy shrugged. "I don't even know how much she believes. Maybe she was just trying to get back at him or reduce the number of mouths to feed."

"Okay, your mom's situation might be the easiest to deal

with. If I'm able to keep this place, I have no objection to staying here. I will be working remotely for the foreseeable future anyway. Long-term, I don't know, but for a while, I'm here. That means Brandon's here for now."

Amy smiled at Brandon. "Okay. That sounds fair enough."

Brandon smiled back at Amy, but when he looked at his father, he found himself under an angry stare. "What?" he asked.

Barry shook his head. "Oh, I was just thinking. My divorce is a whole nother story. I'm going to have to do something. I've advised my lawyer to be as generous as we can, within reason. I don't know if it'll be enough."

"Should I talk to her?" Brandon asked.

"Didn't you text her the other day?"

Brandon's eyes roved around the room, looking everywhere but at his father. "I. Uh. No."

"Why not?"

"I knew if I did, she'd want me to come home. I didn't want to have to tell her I wanted to stay here." He rubbed the back of his neck with his free hand. "I didn't want to hurt her feelings."

Barry sighed and leaned back in the chair. "You need to talk to her. I'm going outside to get some air. Come find me when you're done." Barry stood and walked out the door without looking back.

"Me too. I need to go check on Mom."

"No. Stay."

Amy shook her head. "You need to talk to your mom, and you don't need me hanging over your shoulder. I can come back later if you want."

Brandon nodded. "Okay," he sighed. He clung to her hand as she stood. "All this just sucks, you know."

Amy nodded as she pulled away. "Yeah, it does. But maybe it'll all be over soon."

TWENTY

"You know, playing in a fire will make you wet the bed."

Squatted next to the fire, Brandon flinched as Amy appeared out of the darkness behind him. When he saw her, a thin smile came to his lips, and he tossed the stick in his hand stick aside.

Dressed in a pair of white cut-off jeans and a bikini top, she came to him. Cradling his head in her hands, she pulled him to her, his tear-stained cheek resting against her bare stomach. A warm hand found the back of her thigh and slipped up to her butt.

"Look, I'm just going to say this once, and I'm going to go." She shook her head and took a deep breath as she stared into the fire. "Things would be easier for you if we just don't see each other." Brandon's body tensed beneath her hands. He started to protest, but she held up a hand to stop him. "I know your mom is going to make you come home. I don't blame her. My mom would do the same thing. She loves you."

"If she loved me, she'd let me stay here with you. That's what I want. I told her, and she wouldn't hear of it." His mother had said many things in her letter, but some of them were hard to believe.

"Look, Brandon, your folks are getting divorced, and

it seems like a nasty one's a-brewing. Me and you trying to be together is just complicating things for everybody."

"I don't care."

She offered a thin smile. "Yes, you do, and that's fine."

"What about your mom?"

Amy shrugged. "We'll figure it out. We've made it this far alone. The nurse left some pamphlets. We were looking through them this afternoon."

"How is she?"

Amy shrugged one shoulder as her hand stroked Brandon's hair. "Sicker. She didn't get out of bed at all today."

"I hate this."

"So do I."

"Amy," Brandon took her hands in his as he stood. "I want to be with you."

"I want that too, but it's just not going to work out. It's eating my guts out. I cried in the shower. I couldn't let my mom see me. I have to be strong for her. I have to concentrate on her. I don't know what else to do." She pulled away, turning to the fire.

"You know," Brandon said, joining her. Reaching around from behind her, he clasped his fingers together just above her shorts and pulled her close. "I've never had a girlfriend before. All my life, I've been different. Every time I met someone new and told them I couldn't talk, they'd always get this look on their face. Pity, like they felt sorry for me. I mean, I'm different. I look at the world different than most people. In a lot of ways, though, I was as normal a guy as anybody else. Nobody ever saw that. I've always been the weird kid who couldn't talk." Brandon leaned forward and kissed her cheek. "But when I met you, and I told you I couldn't talk, I didn't see that look in your eye. You didn't feel sorry for me." He moaned, shaking his head. "It's like you get me, you know. Me being the way I was never bothered you."

Amy shrugged. "You seemed like a normal guy. To

be honest, most of what guys say is pretty much just bullshit anyway."

Brandon chuckled, wiping a tear from his cheek with the back of his hand. "I think that's pretty much what you said."

"Look, I understand what you're saying. I'm a river rat. Most of the time, we just stay down here, and you never notice that you're poor because everybody else is in the same boat. Sometimes, though, we go places, and people seem to just know. It doesn't matter how I dress or act. I'll always be a girl from downriver." She reached back and caressed his cheek. "What did you think when you first saw me?"

Brandon smiled. "I thought you were the most beautiful girl I'd ever seen."

"Oh, please. I probably looked like hell. I'd been riding my bike all morning looking for that stupid dog."

"Really. My first thought was how much it was going to suck to have to tell this beautiful girl that I couldn't talk and have to endure that same look from you too."

"You didn't."

Brandon squeezed her tighter. "No. I didn't." He sighed over her shoulder and stared into the fire. "I was all screwed up by the muck. I'd put some stuff in. Random junk, some baby rats, then the dog you were looking for. It was all in my head."

"I imagine so." Her hand slipped from his cheek, and began playing with a lock of his hair. "The day after me and my mom put the dogs back in, I came to make sure they were still gone. I didn't exactly know what to expect. But there was this flower."

"Yes, the flower. My dad said that's how it connected with you, or whatever it did."

"I was just staring at it. Next thing I knew, your granny come out and picked it. She said to take it home and give it to my Mama. She said she'd like it, so that's what I did."

"Was my grandmother a nice lady? I only met her once, and I barely remember it."

Amy smiled. "She was nice, but not like baking cookies and patting you on the head kinda nice. She'd always tell you the truth, you know. Even as a kid. Even if it hurt your feelings. Some folks didn't like her. Lots of folks thought she was crazy."

Brandon nodded. "My mom said she was senile."

"Oh, she wasn't senile. Not by a long shot." Amy turned in his arms and looked into his eyes. "Later on, near the end, I'd come by and bring her flowers. Just honeysuckle or some wild daisies or something growing along the road. She liked wildflowers the best."

"Thank you. I guess she was lonely down here by herself."

"One time, she told me about you."

"That I couldn't talk?"

She nodded. "And that you were handsome and smart and that you were a good kid."

"She knew me more than I knew her," Brandon said, staring into the darkness beyond Amy. His brow furrowed as he wondered how his grandmother knew so much about him? Had his father told her? Given their relationship, it didn't seem likely.

"The last time I saw her, it was cold," Amy continued, pulling Brandon from his thoughts. "Really cold. I came by, and she was sitting on the porch. I asked if she wanted to go in. She said she didn't, so I fetched her a blanket. I sat with her for a while. She didn't say much. She was just staring out at the river.

After a while, I was about to go, and she turned to me and said, 'Amy, life is like that damned river out there. It's wild and unpredictable. You never know what's going to come floating past. Most of the time, it's just plain old shit.' I laughed because it's always funny to me when old people cuss. Anyway, she said that then she said, 'But sometimes, if you're lucky, something really nice will come downriver.' I never believed that." She put a hand along his cheek and stared into his eyes. "But I believe it now."

Brandon pulled her to him again, their lips meeting in a passionate kiss. "I don't want you to go."

"I should. It would be better for you, but I don't think I can." She reached up with both hands and pushed her fingers through his hair.

"Okay, okay, you two. Knock it off before I get the hose. Damn." Barry Stivers lumbered down the steps with a sandwich in one hand and a beer in the other. "How's your mom?"

Amy shrugged as she and Brandon pulled apart. "The same, I guess." She sat in the chair that Brandon offered, and he pulled one up beside her. Barry sat on an upturned five-gallon bucket on the opposite side of the fire.

"Good. So, where are we at with a plan?"

"We decided that our being together matters. I don't want to leave Amy, Dad. I can't."

"I didn't know that was an option." Barry looked back and forth between the two of them, then his eyes settled on Amy.

"It never really was," she said with a shrug, dropping her gaze to the fire. "I just suggested it to make things easier for Brandon."

"How magnanimous of you."

"Don't be an ass."

A chuckle escaped Barry as he shook his head. "To tell you the truth," he began around a mouthful of ham and cheese on wheat bread. "That's the easiest to fix. The problem is *your* mom and *my* divorce." He looked at Brandon. "Your talk with Mom go okay?"

Brandon leaned forward in his chair, putting his elbows on his knees. "About like I expected. Texting your own mom is weird." When he looked up, his father and Amy were locked in a stare as if an unspoken conversation was taking place.

Barry took a bite of his sandwich as he turned his attention back to his son. "She want you to come home?"

Brandon nodded. Amy's hand began rubbing his back. "But I don't want to."

Barry took another bite of the sandwich and chewed it as he stared into the fire. "Well," he began after washing it down with a long swallow of beer. "It's out of my hands. I've told my lawyer what I wanted; this place, custody of you, and at least half my stuff. He said he couldn't promise anything, least of all custody of you." He leaned forward and tossed the remaining sandwich into the fire, watching the flames char it to black.

"But look, you'll be sixteen soon. You can drive down on weekends if I'm able to keep this place. It won't be too bad. You two can still see each other. You can talk on the phone or text." He shrugged, "Or whatever kids do nowadays."

Brandon felt Amy's hand stop moving on his back. "Amy doesn't have a phone."

Barry shrugged. "That's easily remedied."

"What about Amy's mom?"

"She'll have to 'feed the beast,' so to speak." Barry threw a palm into the air. "There's no way around it."

Amy stared into the fire. "What?"

"I said she'll have to—"

"I know what you said," Amy interrupted. "But what does she have to put in to cure cancer?"

Barry pointed his bottle at her before lifting it to his lips and finishing it off. "That's the million-dollar question, now, ain't it?"

"The cops are already snooping around because of Simmons." Brandon looked at Amy, but she was lost in thought, watching the flames dance in the fire. He turned to his father. "We have to be careful."

Barry nodded. "Yup." He stood with a groan. "But in

both situations, we don't have a lot of time. Something's got to happen soon, or we'll all be screwed." He looked at Amy, his eyes narrowed slightly. "And not just in the fun way."

"It has to be a person," Amy said, a smile tugging at the corners of her lips. She turned and looked at Brandon. "A life for a life."

"That's crazy. We can't do that again. Dad?" he pleaded but only got a noncommittal shrug.

"There are only so many dogs and cats around."

"No. There has to be another way." Brandon shook his head. "There has to."

Barry leveled his gaze at his son. "It was okay with the old pervert because you wanted to get laid, but not now?"

"Dad!" Brandon protested, embarrassed.

"Look. I get it. You're human. Things happen. They make sense at the time. Trust me. I know. We've stopped being rational a long time ago, and everybody here knows it. We're long past normal."

"That's not it at all. He was a bad guy anyway. And old."

"So, find someone else who's old and greedy and mean. Shouldn't be hard to find. The world's full of folks like that." Barry stood and started toward the house. "But whatever is decided," he called over his shoulder. "Needs to be decided soon."

Brandon turned to Amy and made her look at him. "I want to help, I really do, but this is dangerous. We could go to prison."

"And my mom is dying."

"I know, but there has to be another way."

Amy burst into tears and fell against his chest. "I wish there were. Do you think I like this? I'm not cold-hearted. Some crazy girl out for kicks. I'm not a monster, Brandon, but if it saves my Mama, then I'll do what I have to. With or without your help."

Brandon pushed her off his chest and brushed the hair from her face. Her cheeks were wet with tears, and her big, soulful eyes were looking to him for answers. His resolve began to wane immediately.

"I'll do it by myself, okay?" Amy began. "You don't have to be involved. If things go bad, it'll just be me and my mom who takes the fall." She shrugged. "Maybe if she goes to prison, they'll have to give her the treatments that will save her."

"What about you?"

Amy shrugged. "What about me? I'm just a poor girl from downriver, remember?" She pulled away and turned toward the dark river with a huff. "I'm no fool, Brandon. I know how this goes. I'm just a summer fling. You're not the first boy to notice me."

"It's not like that at all."

Amy shook her head. "You'll go back home with your mother, and maybe you'll miss me. Hell, maybe you'll come down a few weekends, and we'll screw all night. But you'll move on and meet someone else and probably marry a girl from a nice family and have a passel of good-looking kids and have a wonderful fucking life without me."

Brandon recoiled slightly, stung by the sharpness of her tone. "Where did that come from?"

"Never mind." Amy tore from his grasp and stood, walking toward the pier.

"Not, never mind." Brandon got up and followed her into the darkness. "Why are you mad at me?"

"I'm not mad at you, Brandon," she spat. "See, you have something to lose. I don't. If Mama dies, it's just me. I'll be alone with nothing."

"You'll have me." Brandon tried to embrace her, but she resisted.

"No, I won't. Your mother will make you go back home. You'll protest, but you will because you know how screwed up this whole damned place is. It's a shithole, and we're all just river trash washed up on the banks. Deep down, you know you're better than this place, just like your mom. That's why she didn't want you involved with trash like me."

"Don't say that."

"Can you look me in the eye and say none of it's true?" Amy leaned closer to him, staring into his eyes. "Say it."

Brandon opened his mouth to speak but closed it. "I don't think...." he trailed off, dropping his gaze. He'd never thought of Amy as trash, but a lot of the people around her fit the bill.

Amy shook her head, a sad smile slipping across her lips. "See. I told you. I'm good enough to fuck, but not good enough for your friends to see you with." She shook her head, clenching her teeth as she stared back at him.

"You want to know what the worst part is?" Tears began to roll down her cheeks as she pointed her finger in his face. "I knew better. I stinking knew better. It's like we're from different countries or something. You've never known want and probably never will." She pushed past Brandon, walking toward the driveway. "I thought you were different, but I see now that I was wrong. Just leave me alone. You've got some packing to do. Go home to your mommy."

Brandon called after Amy as she disappeared into the darkness, but he didn't go after her. He stared into the night, knowing she wasn't coming back but wishing she would. He rubbed his face with both hands as he turned away from the house toward the muck. He sighed, shaking his head. The pull it had on him was growing stronger again. He could feel it welling within his chest. Despite all his moral high speech, deep down, he wanted desperately to feed the darkness again. He wanted the high again.

He closed his eyes, and his mind took him back to what he and Amy had done on the pier after dropping Simmons in. It was intense and exhilarating in ways he hadn't imagined. The sight of her body, the smell of it, the soft sounds that escaped her.

There was more, he thought. The act of doing what they did out in the open, flaunting their lust before anyone who cared to look, thrilled him. The fact that they did it on the pier, surrounded by the muck, was exhilarating. He could feel it pulling in around them as if watching, enjoying their lasciviousness. The muck was feeding off their lust, and he was feeding off its darkness.

As he stared into the darkness, the dry reeds began to rattle. As the sound of them intensified, the desire to find Amy and take her began to well within his chest.

Closing his eyes, he allowed the muck into his mind. When it began to speak to him, he listened. She is yours, the voice said in a whisper. You deserve to have what you want. She promised.

Sweat beaded on his forehead as his body began to tremble. She did promise him anything he wanted. She was his, gifted to him by the muck. He did deserve to have what he wanted.

His eyes flew open suddenly, and his smile disappeared. He knew what he wanted, and it was Amy. Turning, he sprinted into the darkness, skirting the corner of the house. He ran down the darkened drive and onto the gravel road, catching up with Amy quickly.

"What do you want?" she asked, walking with her arms crossed over her chest.

"You." Be grabbed her arms and pulled her to him. His hungry mouth found hers, extinguishing her protests. Her arms found his chest and pushed against him to no avail.

Holding her in his arms, he moved her to the side of the road. When her back came to rest against a tree, he pressed his body to hers. His hands moved up her body and clenched her face.

"You're hurting me," she complained. "What the hell's wrong with you?" she asked, her breaths coming in scared pants. Her wide eyes stared back at him.

"You," he said again and kissed her. "You're what's wrong with me."

"Go home, you damned brat."

"No." His mouth fell on hers forcefully. "I want you, and I'm not going to lose you."

"Leave me alone." She wriggled a hand free and raised it to slap him, but he caught it without taking his eyes off hers.

"I have a plan, but first things first."

Amy's resistance faded as he pressed her against the tree, grinding his body against hers.

"Are you sure?" she asked.

"Yes," he said, his hands yanking at the waistband of her shorts.

Amy gasped as he yanked the snap open and shoved them over her hips. She wrapped her arms around his neck, clinging to him as a devilish smile parted her lips. "Tell me what you've got in that dirty little mind of yours," she whispered.

TWENTY-ONE

Barry Stivers looked at his lawyer, watching as he perused the papers on the large mahogany table between them and the opposing counsel. His lawyer was short, overweight by at least seventy-five pounds, and had oily hair and acne scars. Even the suit he wore looked cheap.

He sighed and looked at the tall, well-built man in the expensive, tailored suit that sat opposite them. Conrad Shaw had been their personal lawyer for years but resigned from the position to handle Carrol's divorce proceedings. They'd both known him since college. He was deathly efficient.

Barry looked back at his council, catching his stare. He nodded. When he got a questioning look, he nodded again. The lawyer shrugged and pushed the stack of papers to Conrad.

"I'm sure you'll find these last revisions more than accommodating. You'll see that my client has been more than generous. Exceedingly so, if you ask me."

Conrad Shaw glanced through the papers, stopping occasionally to check against his own papers. After making it through the stack of papers, he looked at Barry but couldn't hold his gaze.

"I've worked very hard for a long time to get where I am. I'm also not too proud to admit that Carrol stood by my side every day, and there were a lot of good days."

Carrol Stivers stared at her husband, finally seeing the darkness within him that he'd kept hidden for so long. For so long, there had been a part of him that he kept from her, a shadow he never revealed. Even in the early days of their marriage, when they were young and in love, a part of him was always inaccessible to her. She'd always thought it was because of his upbringing, a self-defense mechanism, but now saw it for what it was.

He'd been touched by that place in ways she couldn't fathom. Elvey knew it. She also knew that leaving there was no remedy for its pull.

"What?' he asked quietly.

Carrol shook her head, knowing he'd never give that place up, no matter what it cost him.

Barry watched her reaction and sighed. "And while things, admittedly, weren't great at the end," he looked at Conrad as he spoke, "It doesn't erase those days that were good. I don't want to fight over every dime and drape. If it must be over, then let's all be civil about it."

"Very well said," his lawyer added.

Barry looked at him, not trying to hide his contempt. He was only here as a pawn. He'd known all along how things would play out. Turning, he smiled at Conrad.

"Does everything seem acceptable to you?"

Conrad cleared his throat. "I think, at a preliminary glance, it seems generous enough. Of course, I'd have to consult with my client in private about the matter."

All eyes went to Carrol. When the phone on the table in front of her started to vibrate, everyone's eyes diverted to it. Barry watched her face as she reached for it. Her brow furrowed as she raised it. When she saw the number, her eyes grew wide. Her eyes darted from the phone to Barry, then back to the phone.

Barry smiled, interlacing his fingers on the table before him.

"I have to take this," Carrol answered the phone, turning away from the table as she put it to her ear. "Hello."

Barry sat back in his chair with a shrug. He idly picked at his fingernail but was paying close attention to the hushed conversation.

"This isn't funny," Carrol said, then went quiet again. "No. Whoever this is, just stop." She spun and glared at Barry. He threw his hands up innocently, a smile tugging at the corner of his mouth. When his lawyer nudged him, giving him his own look of inquiry, he shrugged again and dropped his eyes to the paper in front of him.

Carrol stood and walked away from the table, keeping her back to them. "How?" she asked, then listened as she put more distance between them. "I'm going to ask you a question. Brandon would be able to answer without hesitation, so if you hesitate even for a second, I'll know this is a sick joke, and I'll have your ass." She spared a nervous look at the table and held up a shaky finger.

"Angelo has a best friend. What is his best friend's name?"

"Shiny Thing," Brandon answered on the other end of the line. "Because Angelo is a raccoon, and raccoons love shiny things."

Amy's brow furrowed as she looked at Brandon.

He nodded to her as a smile slid across his lips. "Okay. I'll be here." Brandon ended the call, tossing the phone aside.

"Is she coming?" Amy asked.

"She's coming," he answered, his face contorting with sadness.

"Oh, baby." Amy went to him, caressing his back. "I'm sorry it has to be like this."

"Me too."

"You know this is the only way. Don't you?"

Brandon shrugged. "I guess."

"Everything else is set up here." Amy danced her fingers along Brandon's shoulders. "We have a little time...."

Brandon pushed her hand away. "Go and make sure your mom is ready."

Amy stepped back, giving him a quizzical look. "Are you okay?"

"I've just called my mother to her certain death. You'll forgive me for not wanting a quick roll in the hay."

"I'm sorry. You're right, sweetheart."

Brandon nodded absently as she planted a quick kiss on his cheek and hurried out the door. He walked into the double window in the kitchenette and looked out at the pier, now bathed in the mid-afternoon sun. The old boards were weathered and uneven. The old pier looked ready to collapse and probably would have already if it were anywhere else. The thing stood only by the power of sheer will and, of course, the muck.

A smile slowly crept across his face as he stared into the dark water. As he watched, a clump of reeds began to shake. He couldn't hear them from here, but he knew the sound. The surface of the obsidian water around them erupted with tiny ripples that spread from one clump to the next, cascading across the field, setting all nine of the clumps into motion.

The muck was waking up. Again.

Brandon tore his eyes from the window, turning slowly to the phone that sat on the couch, now buzzing incessantly. His brow furrowed as he stared at it.

Crossing the room, he picked it up and looked at the caller ID before answering. "Mom? Is everything okay?" He nodded when she said that they needed to talk. "So you're still coming?"

His eyes grew wider as his mother talked. He listened patiently, adding an occasional "uh huh" or "okay" when he got the chance. His mother had a lot to say.

Carrol Stiver's metallic gray B.M.W. skidded on the grass, coming to a stop a few feet shy of the steps. She got out and closed the door, staring up at the river house that had been in the Stivers family for generations. Even in the afternoon sun, there was a pall over the house, like it held a dark secret.

When the door of the house opened, she ran up the steps, meeting Brandon on the porch. "My God, son. It's a miracle." She cradled his face in her hands, crying. "Tell me it isn't a dream."

Brandon smiled. "It's no dream, Mama."

Carrol clutched her throat as tears poured from her eyes. "Your voice is perfect for you."

"Thanks, I guess."

She threw her arms around her son, sobbing joyfully. "Thank you, Jesus."

"It wasn't Jesus, Mama." He nodded toward the pier and the field of muck that surrounded it. The reeds that had been clamoring all afternoon had gone silent moments before her arrival. "That's what did it."

"What?" she asked, looking back and forth between the muck and her son. "The river? I don't understand."

Brandon put an arm around her shoulders. "C'mon inside. I'll explain everything."

Carrol hesitated. "I probably shouldn't."

"It'll be okay. I promise." Brandon gently guided her toward the front door. "Everything will be okay."

Carrol froze as she entered the house. The 'old house' smell was prevalent in the air, but there was also something else, a light, flowery scent that she didn't recognize.

"I shouldn't be in here. My lawyer would have a fit, not to mention your father's."

"Don't worry about lawyers and all that stuff, Mama.

Can't you just be happy for me?"

Carrol visibly relaxed. "You're right." She touched his cheek. "My baby can finally talk." She smiled and hugged him again.

"Let me fix you a drink."

"Don't be silly. I should be fixing you one." She edged past Brandon, but he grabbed her elbow.

"No, let me do it. I want to." Brandon watched the surprise wash over her face and smiled. "You're going through a lot, Mama. I want to. You sit and relax."

Carrol let out a reluctant sigh and headed for the couch. "Just a soda will be fine. I'm going to have to drive back to town tonight." She paused, watching her son put ice in a glass. "I was hoping you'd be going with me." She watched him stiffen for a moment, then relax. "I've been thinking about just that, Mama."

"Good." She looked around the large room. "I see no one's been cleaning since I left."

"Boys will be boys," Brandon said with a chuckle as he dropped ice cubes into the glass on the counter. They landed softly on a layer of powder at the bottom of the glass. Shielding the glass from his mother with his body, he quickly opened a can of soda and poured it over the ice. He brought the glass to the coffee table and sat it down in front of Carrol.

"I just can't get over hearing your voice. You don't know how many times I've dreamed of this day."

"It's quite a shock to me too." Brandon laughed as he sat on the couch beside her. "I never realized what a pain in the ass I was."

"Stop," she said, slapping his arm playfully. "You were just you. I loved you as you were. You were perfect." She sipped the drink. "You know what they say about mothers; every old crow thinks her baby is the blackest."

Brandon laughed as he settled on the couch. "I guesso."

"Where's your father?"

Brandon shrugged. "He said he had a meeting in town. I haven't seen him since." He nudged the glass closer to his mother. "Aren't you thirsty?"

"I am. Thanks." She picked up the glass, hesitating just short of her lips as she stared at him. "I still can't believe this. Your voice sounds so natural. So, you. In a month, I won't remember what it sounded like to not hear it."

"It really is a miracle."

Carrol took a long swallow of the drink, allowing her eyes to wander to the window. Beyond the yard lay the muck, and beyond that, the river, but that wasn't what caught her attention. Her eyes traced the square, straight angles of the left side of the window, then shifted to the right. If the sun's angle hadn't been changing, she might have missed the faint partial silhouette of a face jutting out from the frame.

"That's good." She sat the glass down. "So, tell me about this girl who has stolen your heart away from your mother."

Brandon stiffened. "She's okay. Pretty."

"Just okay? That's all it took. I saw that she was pretty last week, remember?"

"I remember that you didn't like us hanging out together."

"I'm a mother. It's my job to be suspicious of every girl you like. Especially the first."

Brandon shrugged. "I like her. She's not like any other girl I've ever met."

"I'm sure that's true." Carrol sighed. "All I'm saying is to be careful. Sometimes the truth is hard to see, even if it is right in front of you." She lifted the drink and toasted her son. "But you're growing up. Sometimes I have to let you see things for yourself. I hope things work out for the best. I really do."

"Do you really?"

Carrol watched out of the corner of her eye as Brandon

began to wring his hands. When he was younger, he used it as a self-soothing technique but kicked it halfway through the fourth grade. She looked at him and smiled.

"You're my only child. My firstborn son. You'll more than likely — no — you will always be my only child. There's nothing I wouldn't do for you, Brandon."

Brandon wilted into the sofa. "Dad said you were trying to take everything in the divorce."

Carrol cleared her throat and picked up the glass. She cradled it in her hands, thumbing condensation from it. "When you were born, I saw you, and I thought you were perfect."

"What about later on?"

"You mean when you couldn't talk?" She shrugged. "I'm not going to say it didn't scare the hell out of me. You probably don't remember all the doctor visits." She shook her head and took a long drink. "For your fifth birthday party, you wanted a dinosaur theme. Not like the cartoon, but real dinos. You knew every damned dinosaur there was."

"I still have a lot of them in a box under my bed," he admitted with a smile, still wringing his hands.

"I know. You were always special. Not broken, but unique. You were completely different than what the world expected. To me, though, you were always wonderful, with big eyes. You made me see the world differently. You changed me in ways I can't even fathom."

"But I wasn't perfect."

"Perfection is an illusion, Brandon. Nobody's perfect." She put a hand on his knee. "But you're pretty darned close if you ask me."

"What does that have to do with the divorce and what Dad said."

Carrol nodded. "Oh yeah. Do you want to see the papers? You want to know what I asked for?"

Brandon clasped his hands together to keep them still. He started rocking slowly. "Yes. No." He took a deep breath. "I don't know. Just tell me."

Carrol took another drink and sat the glass down. She looked into his eyes and said, "You."

"What?" he asked, stilling himself.

"That's it. You. I asked for full custodial privileges."

"What does that mean?"

"It means that you live with me, and I say when and where your father can take you. I make the decisions." She watched him wipe a bead of sweat from his temple. "I did ask for enough money for us to live on. Your father was to get most of everything else."

"What about this place?"

Carrol laughed. "I wouldn't care if either one of us ever saw this place again."

Brandon nodded. "So you'd take me away from here, and I couldn't see Amy again?"

She nodded. "I'm sorry, but yes. You might not understand, but this is a bad place. It's for the best."

"For you, maybe."

"No," she shook her head. "No. It's the best thing for you."

Brandon shook his head. He clenched his jaw and closed his eyes. "No. I don't want that."

"I know you don't, and neither does your father."

"At least he cares about what I want."

Carrol rubbed her neck and cleared her throat. "He cares about what *he* wants." She stood, wavered, then sat back down. "Whoa. Must be all the excitement," she said, forcing a smile as she stared at Brandon.

She stood again slowly and straightened the suit jacket over her blouse. "I need to use the restroom. I'll explain everything when I get back. Okay?" She looked down at her son, now rocking nervously again. "Promise me you'll be here when I get back?"

Brandon nodded but didn't look up. The sound of his mother's footsteps echoed through the silent house as she walked away. Brandon ran his hands through his hair several times, then covered his face. He hated himself for doing this.

"Hey."

He looked up at the sound of the whisper and found Amy poking her head through the partially opened front door. "What are you doing here?" he asked.

Amy looked at the empty glass and smiled. "Did you put the stuff in?" When Brandon nodded, she opened the door and walked in wearing the same coral bikini top and cut-off jean shorts as the night they lay naked in Amy's special place.

Brandon's eyes washed over her, and for an instant forgot the situation. A deep longing welled within him, pushing everything else away. Desire consumed every pore of his body, and he began to shake.

A clinking sound came from the bathroom, snatching his back to reality. He shook his head to clear it, then looked at Amy again. Pushing himself off the couch, he went to her. "If she sees you, she'll be suspicious."

Amy put her arms around his neck and pulled him in for a quick kiss. "It doesn't matter now. If she drank all that, she'll be out like a light in a few minutes anyway."

"Still," Brandon insisted. "I thought you were with your mother."

"I've got her all set up downstairs. I figured she'd need to be close when we did this. She's fine." Amy looked at the window. The shadows were long on the yard. "She won't have to wait long now anyway. It's almost dark."

Brandon turned toward the sound of a toilet flushing. As he stared at the wall, the faucet in the bathroom came on with a creak. He listened to his mother wash her hands.

"You put it all in?"

"Yes. I'm not an idiot."

Amy pushed her body against his, caressing his face with her fingertips. "I know this is hard, but it's for us. I love you. Don't you love me?"

"You know I do. It's just that—" The sound of glass breaking snatched his attention from Amy.

She gently pulled his face to look at her. "That's just the drugs kicking in. She'll be asleep in a minute. I know it's hard, but it's almost over."

"But...."

"I promise, when this is over, we can do anything you want. You like that, don't you?" She rubbed her body against him. "Really, we can do it anytime you like when that bitch is out of our lives."

"She's my mom," Brandon whimpered, wiping a tear from his cheek. "I don't want her to suffer."

"I know, but my mom is suffering. Your mom wants to take you away from everything. Your dad, the waters...me."

"I know." Brandon turned from Amy, grabbing his hair in his fists as tears began to stream down his cheek. "But she's my mother too."

"Look," Amy began, her voice stern and cold. "It's done. If you don't go through with this, she's going to know that we drugged her, that you drugged her. She'll start to dig, and you, your dad, and me will all end up in prison, and my mother will die alone, sitting in her own shit in some state nursing home. We'll never see each other again. Ever."

"I know," Brandon cried.

"Your mother wants to keep us apart."

"Stop it!"

"Hey," she said, her voice softening as she touched his

cheek. "It's going to be okay. Everything is going to be okay. I promise. Just think about our future together. Don't think about what we have to do to get there."

Brandon nodded, then drew in a long slow breath to calm himself. "Do you think she's asleep yet?"

"Probably. If it helps, she probably just felt woozy for a few seconds, then passed out. It's like when you get drunk or high. You just drift off to sleep. You're happy, then you are asleep. She's not going to suffer at all."

"I've never been either of those things."

"Oh, me either. That's just what people say." She smiled at him. "She won't suffer at all."

"I might."

Amy puckered her lips, putting a hand on his cheek. "You're sweet. That's why I love you. Things will be better this way. I promise."

TWENTY-TWO

"Funny thing. That's going to be a hard promise to keep," Carrol said as she stepped into the doorway, clutching the broken pieces of a large, red gnome against her hip. A pair of bare plaster buttocks slipped from her fingers and shattered on the floor at her feet. "Oops," she said, sweeping the pieces aside with her foot.

"Mama?" Brandon looked between Carrol and Amy, his eyes wide with shock and indecision. "What...?"

"I thought you fixed her a drink," Amy snapped in a whisper.

Carrol smiled. "Oh, he did, little girl. He did just like you asked him to. It was a lot of hydrocodone. Enough to kill a grown man. Luckily, I know what pain meds Barry takes for his knee."

"But you...." Brandon trailed off.

"I brought some naloxone with me." Carrol shrugged, offering a thin smile. "It was a hunch. You see, it reverses the effects of opioid overdose. Paramedics use it all the time for junkies."

Amy stared at Carrol. A wry smile slipped across her lips. "You're still a little woozy. We could do this the hard way. I won't mind at all."

"I suppose you wouldn't." Carrol dropped the pieces of

porcelain into the recliner and dusted her skirt off. Reaching into her jacket, she produced a small pistol. "But that's up to you, Pricilla. Or do you still prefer to be called Sky?"

"Mom? What? What are you talking about?"

Carrol flicked the gun toward the couch. "I'll explain everything after you two have been secured. On the couch. Move it."

"But, Mom."

"Move it, kiddo. I'm saving your ass here." She ushered them toward the couch with the gun.

"You're still stoned. You probably can't hit the side of a barn."

Carrol laughed. "Pick a gnome, Brandon." She nodded to the window above the kitchen sink across the room.

"What?" he asked, confused.

"Pick one," she insisted.

"Okay. Okay. I don't know. The one with the red star on his hat."

Carrol raised the gun and squeezed the trigger. The report ripped through the house, and the three-inch gnome exploded, taking the window with it. She looked back at Amy with a grin.

"That good enough? Now sit your ass down before I start seeing red stars on your face."

"Mom!" Brandon exclaimed, shocked. "Stop."

"No. You stop it. I'm sure this little tramp looks good to you, Brandon. I don't guess anyone could blame you for picking low hanging fruit."

Amy laughed. "Please. Spare me the righteous indignation."

Carrol looked at Amy, and anger rose in her chest. She could end all of this right now. She could simply get rid of her and load Brandon up and drive home. She flexed her fingers around the trigger guard, letting them dance along the steel as a thought entered her mind. There *were* ways of disposing of the body.

Amy smiled at her. "I know what you're thinking," she said, almost singing the words.

Carrol shook her head. "I don't even think you're capable of knowing what I'm thinking." She turned to Brandon but kept the gun pointed at Amy. "There're some zip ties in the junk drawer. Get them and handcuff her to the couch."

"I won't do it," he said, pushing his chest out.

Amy laughed. "He sees how crazy you are. You've already lost."

Carrol crinkled her nose. "I don't think so, missy." She raised the gun, pointing it at Amy. "Brandon. You have ten seconds to get them from the drawer and tie her up, or I blow her stinking brains out and let you rot in jail for trying to kill your own mother."

"No, Mom. Stop. That's crazy."

"Drugging your own mother and tossing her into the stinking mud, isn't? Think about it, Brandon. All of this has been a ruse." She wagged the gun at Amy. "Your father and this tramp cooked it all up together."

"You're lying. I still won't do it."

"One. Two." She slid her finger against the trigger. "I'd really rather just do it this way anyhow. It's easier. Three. She certainly deserves it. Four."

"Mom."

"Five...."

Brandon begged her not to shoot as he ran to the drawer. He rifled through the assortment frantically until he found the ties. He grabbed a handful and ran back to the couch. Amy tried to talk him out of it, but when he didn't stop, she stood quickly, shoving him aside.

Carrol stepped forward and slapped her with the gun.

Amy fell back onto the couch, clutching the cut that had opened on her cheek.

"Stop!" Brandon cried.

"Six. Do it, Brandon, or I will shoot her right now."

Brandon cried as he did what he was told, apologizing to Amy as he secured her wrists to the wooden armrest of the couch.

"Now. You sit down beside her."

"She's gonna kill us both, sweetheart. Get her."

Carrol arched an eyebrow as she stared at Brandon. "What's it going to be?" Brandon dropped onto the couch, deflated. "Good. Now I don't have a ton of time, so if you'll excuse me. She took out her phone and dialed 911. "Yes, we have an adult female, average height and weight, who has overdosed on opioid painkillers at 1957 Darby Camp Road. She's had a dose of naloxone, but I suspect you'll be here before she could ever get to the hospital."

Carrol dropped the phone back into the pocket of her jacket and sidestepped back to the bathroom. "That noise you heard was me breaking Big Red," she called from the bathroom. "It took me a while to figure out which one it was in, but I got there."

She appeared in the doorway clutching a handful of papers and photographs. "You see, Brandon. I didn't hate your grandmother. Actually, I cared deeply for her, and she liked me. I guess mostly because we had one thing in common. We'd both had the unfortunate pleasure of marrying a Stivers man."

"She's crazy, Brandon," Amy shouted as she yanked at the zip ties. "It's all lies. Get her baby before she ruins everything."

"Everything for you?" Carrol asked as she wobbled across the floor to the kitchen table. She turned a chair out with her foot and sat down hard. "That is some strong medicine." She shook her head.

"What are you talking about?" Brandon stood abruptly.

Carrol pointed the gun at him. "I'll kill you myself before I leave you with that monster. Sit. Down."

"I told you she was crazy, Brandon." Amy laughed. "She's off her rocker."

"You see, we talked a lot," Carrol continued after Brandon complied. "Elvey and me. She was a hell of a woman." She rubbed her eyes with the back of the hand holding the gun. "She knew all about that shit out there, probably better than anybody. Certainly better than your little nitwit friend there. She hated it. She said it was evil and only brought evil."

"It made me able to talk."

Carrol nodded. "At what cost, son? What did you have to feed it? And besides, now you're hooked. It's like a drug, Brandon."

"She's crazy. See, I told you. Get. Her."

Carrol flicked the gun toward Amy. A shot rang out, and splinters rained down on the couch. She looked at the hole two feet over Amy's head. "Woah. I didn't even mean to do that. You'd better keep your stinking trap shut, or you might not be so lucky next time."

She dropped the contents of her hand on the table and rifled through them. "You see, Me Maw lived here all her life. For nearly eighty years, she watched that crap ruin people. Good people. People like your father and you, Brandon."

"It made me talk when nothing else could. I know I did some stuff, but ain't it worth it?"

Carrol sighed. "Maybe, maybe not. We still don't know what it'll take from you."

"It brought me Amy, and I love her. She loves me too."

Carrol laughed. "I hate to burst your bubble, kiddo, but she don't love you." She gathered three Polaroid pictures from the table and leaned forward, tossing them onto the coffee table in front of Brandon. "Have a look. The guy is your father. Pay close attention to the two girls."

Brandon picked up the picture closest to him. A teenage boy stood on a long wooden pier flanked by two girls in bikinis. He brought the picture closer, staring at the people. The man might have been his father, but the girl on his right was undeniably Amy. Her hair was shorter and blonde, but it was her. Even in the faded photo, she still looked the same.

He looked at his mother and shook his head. "No." He grabbed up another picture. The guy from the first picture was sitting on a motorcycle without a shirt. The other girl was leaning in to kiss him, but the one that looked like Amy was sitting behind him with her face pressed against his back. All three had their tongues sticking out. The boy and the short-haired girl had their fists in the air, with the index and pinky fingers extended.

"That's bullshit. Those are pics of my mom and her sister Brandon. She's trying to trick you."

"I wish I was." Carrol tossed a ratty newspaper clipping onto the table. "This is your mother, Priscilla. Melinda Drummond. You can read the whole thing if you want, but I can summarize it for you." Carrol laid the gun on the table and wiped her sweaty palms on her skirt. "When your father and your girl there and her sister were teenagers, it seems they were a bit of a wild bunch. They were into some pretty nasty stuff. Sex, drugs, rock and roll, and more sex." Carrol leveled her gaze at Brandon. "All three of them. Together."

Amy shrugged when Brandon looked at her. "You wouldn't believe me, so what's the point in defending myself. She's crazy. She's the one causing all the problems, Brandon. She's the one shooting at your girlfriend."

"It got so bad that Mrs. Drummond was getting ready to ship the two sisters off to reform school or something." Carrol picked up the gun again, waving it at the papers on the table. "Her obituary is in here somewhere. There was never a funeral because they never found a body. They just declared her dead after two years of being missing and emancipated the girls." Carrol leaned in, looking at Brandon. "Care to guess where their mother ended up?"

Brandon's brow furrowed as his mind struggled to put the puzzle together. His eyes darted to the window, then back to his mother. She nodded.

"Elvey couldn't do anything because Pawpaw was in it as deep as those three idiots. When he retired from the Foundry, someone gave him a puppy. Elvey said it was a prized coon hound, a big deal, I guess. He brought it home, walked out on that pier, and dropped it in. When she asked him what he wanted, he said that he wanted to fish every day until the day he died. Two weeks later, he was fishing upriver and had a massive heart attack. Elvey was sitting on the porch and saw his old boat drifting down around the bend. The current brought it home. When it nosed into that mud out there, it swelled beneath the boat on one side and tipped him right in. He was gone." She shook her head, sighing. "Some folks drug the river and even put up a net down the river, but they never found a body." She looked between the two people on the couch. "Nothing ever comes back, does it?"

"What about her?" Brandon asked. "What did she want?"

Carrol smiled. "She said she didn't know how it worked, exactly, but when PawPaw went in, she hoped that any other Stivers man would be spared its grasp."

"Boo-hoo," Amy quipped. "What a fucking load of crap."

"That's quite a mouth you got there, missy. For a teenage girl." Carrol shook her head. "In any event, I think what she really wanted, deep down, was for you two sluts to suffer."

"Screw you."

"Why did you act like you hated her then? MeMaw, I mean." Brandon asked.

"It was her idea. Carrol smiled. "She loved you so much,

Brandon. She really did. I've sent her hundreds of pictures of you through the years. Funny thing, when we got here, I didn't find one."

"What happened?"

Carrol shrugged. "Your father came down to get the place ready. My guess is that he burned them. You see, the plan was already in place, I suppose." Carrol rolled her head on her shoulders with a groan. "Elvey wanted me to keep you and your father away from this place. Especially you, Brandon."

"You really screwed the pooch on that one, Lady," Amy laughed.

Carrol shrugged. "This whole flu epidemic shit, or whatever it is, screwed everything up." She massaged her forehead. "To be honest, I didn't really believe all the stuff she said about this place. But once we got down here, it got you quick. You changed, Brandon."

"But how can this be Amy?" Brandon asked, tossing the picture back onto the coffee table. "It doesn't even make sense."

Carrol looked at Amy. "Do you wanna tell 'em, or should I?"

"It's your lie. You tell it any way you want. Bitch."

"If I had to guess, I'd say those two self-indulgent, extraneous sluts wanted nothing more than to stay young and live and drink and screw forever." She looked at Amy. "Is that about it?"

Amy shrugged one shoulder. "Whatever."

"So you're...." Brandon trailed off, doing the math in his head. "My dad's age?"

Amy smiled and shot him a wink as she arched her back. "Do these look like the tits of an old woman?"

Brandon shook his head and then looked at his mother. "What about her sister?"

"According to Elvey, she ended up going to prison

for trying to rob a gas station." Carrol dug through the faded newspaper clippings on the table and produced one. "Here's the article. I expect your father and this one here let her to take the rap. Probably bailed at the first sign of trouble. They got away. She didn't. Her sister got sent away for a long time because she already had a record. Maybe that broke the spell. I don't know. Maybe she never wished to be young forever." Carrol shrugged. "I don't know. Maybe she got another wish."

"But...." Brandon trailed off, staring at the one remaining picture in his hand. "Why does she have cancer and is old?"

"They say in the end, the muck always gets you."

"The catch," Brandon mumbled, nodding.

"Yeah, it's a real mess, but it's evil, so...." Carrol looked at Brandon. His face was contorted with anguish and indecision. "I'm sorry, Brandon. I hate this for you, but you need to know the truth. Besides, have you ever seen her sister? There's no telling what she looks like. Priscilla here lied about everything else. She might not even have cancer for all we know."

"She does have it, bitch. And I'm going to save her."

Carrol shook her head. "Never going to happen, little girl. Not at the expense of my son."

"We'll see." Amy held Carrol's stare, a smirk on her lips.

Carrol shrugged and checked the time on her phone. "I don't have a lot of time before the ambulance gets here or either the medicine wears off. Do you see what I've been saying, Brandon? They're evil. It's evil. It's all dark, dirty stuff that hurts everyone it touches."

"Like you never thought about using it," Amy snapped.

"Nope."

"Not even when your little baby boy here couldn't talk?"

"Not even then." She looked at Brandon. "I loved him just like he was." She offered Brandon a sad smile. "I still do."

"What about Dad? And the divorce?"

"Babe, your dad came back to this place of his own free will. He knew what it was. He wants to be here, probably with them. Or at least this one. It's had a hold of him his whole life. He wants it this way."

"But why? Why all this elaborate plan?"

"They've been talking all this time, Brandon. I didn't put it together, but your grandmother did. I kinda figured he was texting someone, you know, having an affair. When we came here, the pieces began to fall into place one by one." Carrol shook her head. "Priscilla here is still young and hot. I imagine your dad wanted to relive some of the good old days with her teenage body. Like I said, that crap out there feeds off our base instincts."

Brandon's shoulders fell as he realized both he and his father had been with the same girl. He sank into the couch when he realized that everything Amy had told him was a lie.

"You see, it's always about the same old things. Power, money, and sex. That's what it offers. Primal instinct stuff. It finds the worst in us and brings it out."

"But it let me talk," Brandon insisted. "That's not a bad thing."

"Yeah, and that only cost one old pervert," Amy laughed.

Carrol looked at Brandon, aghast. "You let her talk you into putting a person into the muck already? My God, son."

"Mister Simmons. He was really ugly and mean. He was a bad man." Brandon dropped his eyes, unable to face his mother.

"Dammit, Brandon." Carrol rubbed her forehead. The naloxone only lasted for an hour, ninety minutes tops. "What did you get out of it?" she asked Amy.

"Nothing I could tell 'cept a few good screwings from your little baby boy." Amy cackled. "After I taught him a few tricks, he did alright."

Carrol gritted her teeth as she leveled the gun at Amy, fighting the urge to pull the trigger. "That's really all you're good for, isn't it?" Carrol rubbed her left eye with the heel of her hand. "I should just kill you now."

Brandon looked at Amy with tears in his eyes. "Why? How could you do all those things?"

"What? The sex? Oh, grow up, for God's sake."

"You see, son. She's as evil as that crap out there."

"Look in the mirror. Check your wrinkles and your saggy tits. That's why your husband would rather screw me than you. You call it evil. I call it self-preservation."

"You'll have fun in prison. They'll like a young thing like you for a long time."

Amy shrugged but said nothing.

"Brandon, you got to get out of here. Run up the road and meet the ambulance. Something, anything. Explain what happened. I'm getting sleepy. I can't fight it much longer."

"I can't just leave you."

"You're in danger. Her sister's probably skulking around somewhere, and God knows who else she's screwed into helping her."

"What about Dad?"

"I suspect he's somewhere with a lot of witnesses. He doesn't have the guts to do this himself, so he puts his little whore up to it. They'd be rid of me, get everything, and be together. I'm sure eventually they'd get rid of you too, if not right now."

Brandon looked at Amy. The truth hurt in his chest like a knife, but a part of him still wanted to go to her and love her. "Amy or Priscilla. Whatever your name is. Was anything you said true?"

"Just go, for fuck's sake, kid. Get the hell out of my face already."

"If it matters, I really did care about you."

Amy rolled her eyes. "Just go. If I have to look into your sappy face anymore, I'll puke. Damn."

Brandon stopped by his mother long enough to give her a quick embrace. "I'm so sorry." He wiped tears from his face with the back of his hand and then looked back at Amy. "Be careful, Mom. Shoot her if you have to."

"Don't worry. The ambulance and the cops will be here soon. Meet them on the road and flag 'em down." She swept her arm through the air drunkenly. "Go, sweetheart. And don't say a word to the cops. Okay? I'll take care of everything."

She watched Brandon leave, then turned to Amy. "You really are a soulless bitch, aren't you?"

"Soul?" Amy laughed. "What the hell is that?"

"That's about what I thought." Carrol leaned back in the chair, resting the gun on her lap. "You just sit tight. It'll be over soon enough."

"You're more right than you know," Amy replied with a grin.

TWENTY-THREE

Brandon lumbered down the steps, digging his fists into his eyes to clear the tears. His heart ached, and his stomach knotted with shame. How could Amy have lied so much? How could she have fooled him so easily? He'd helped kill Mister Simmons for her. He'd even poisoned his own mother for her.

At the bottom of the steps, Brandon froze as the strength of the muck enveloped him like a fist. He wiped his eyes and looked toward the pier. Through the darkness, he could see the shapes. Once, he thought of them as "ladies," but now he knew they were anything but.

His eyes narrowed, and he shook his head. "No." He turned to leave, but the pull intensified. When he looked back to the muck, he saw a small light begin to glow. It began as a speck of color in a sea of darkness but quickly blossomed into a flower. He gasped as, one by one, the petals opened, curling back to reveal a ring of golden stamens.

The scent washed over him like a breeze, and he inhaled deeply. He smiled, every ounce of his body wanting to go to it, to pluck it from the dark mud and hold it in his hands.

"No." Brandon shook his head violently. "No!" Turning, he hadn't gone two steps when movement in the shadows beneath the house caught his attention. His heart leaped into his throat. Straining his eyes, he stared into the darkness but saw nothing else. Maybe it was just an optical illusion, he thought. Maybe it was his own shadow.

He stared into the darkness until he started seeing spots before his eyes, finding nothing. Shaking his head, he started toward the driveway. He didn't want to look again, but his head turned back to the pier. The flower was still there. The light from it illuminated the nine shapes that surrounded it, like campers around a fire. The faceless heads were all bent over the flower but looked up in unison. Though they had no eyes, he could feel their stares on him.

You can have anything you want.

Brandon shook his head, combating the thoughts slipping into his head in overlapping voices.

You can have Amy all to yourself.

You can make her do anything you want.

You can do the things you think about when you're alone, and no one can see.

Brandon drew in a deep breath. Turning from the flower. The windows of the house were lit with a dim, golden glow. His mother was up there. Amy was up there.

You can do things to her to punish her.

"No," he begged as tears began to roll down his cheeks again. He put his hands over his ears to silence the voices, but it didn't work.

Hurt her like you want to. Make her suffer like you're suffering now.

Struggling against the voices, Brandon didn't see the shadow moving behind him until it was too late. The small, frail form stepped from beneath the house. Clutched in her hands was the same hickory wood handle he'd hit Simmons with. Now, however, it was coated with mud. It slid through the air silently and landed hard across his shoulders.

"That kid of yours is really a simpleton, ain't he?" Amy asked with a grin.

"He's smarter than you'll ever be."

"Barry told me he was a retard, but damn. How do you stand him?"

"Shut your stinking mouth."

"I mean, really. You're acting the whole dutiful mother part really good. I have to give you props for that. But deep down, didn't you ever just want to be rid of him? I mean, shit."

Carrol shook her head and gave Amy a contemptible laugh. "You'd never understand."

"I can't argue with that. I'd have chunked his dumb ass in the muck when I first knew he was stupid."

"He's not stupid!" Carrol yelled. "He knows more about being a good person than you ever will."

"You're right about that, but he's still a fucking idiot. The dumbass don't even know the right way to put on a zip tie." Amy snatched her wrists, slipping the tails of the ties through the eyelets. Brandon had applied them backwards, preventing them from gripping.

Amy sprang from the couch and cleared the coffee table in one fluid motion. She lunged at Carrol, swinging a fist with an angry grunt.

Carrol raised the gun, but not in time to prevent the blow. The fist struck her right cheek, knocking her to the floor.

"I don't think I've ever been as glad to punch a bitch as you," Amy seethed as she bent over Carrol. "Guess I win after all. I'm going to have your husband and your precious little boy." Amy laughed. "Maybe at the same time."

She kicked Carrol in the ribs, then did it again. Smiling, she bent over and picked up the gun that had fallen to the floor.

"You fucking town people. You think you're so smart."

Brandon stumbled forward as pain exploded across the back of his shoulders. His hands clutched the damp grass as he fell to one knee. His mind groped for an explanation. At first, he thought that Amy had escaped, but he dismissed it. His mother would never have allowed that. There was a strange look in her eyes that he'd never seen before — desperation. He'd have heard gunshots.

When angry cursing drifted to his ears in a thin, raspy voice, he knew it wasn't Amy. It had to be her mother or sister. He spun and tried to stand but was met by a cold, claw-like hand. It fell on his face, shoving him back to the ground.

Panic rose in his chest as he scurried backward, putting distance between himself and his unseen attacker. His back struck something in the darkness. His hand flailed, then landed on the plank of the swing.

Pulling himself up by the rope, he scanned the yard. A shadow moved across his line of sight, then was gone again. He stood, silent and still, as he awaited the next attack.

He listened for movement in the grass but heard only the heart pounding in his ears. His breaths were coming in quick gasps as fear gripped him. She could be anywhere.

A shrill cry split the night. Brandon spun to his right as the old woman raced toward him with surprising agility. He grabbed the rope in one hand and strode backward. As the woman raised the hickory handle again, he whipped the swing toward her.

She howled as the wooden plank struck her in the chest. Her momentum carried her another step, and she fell, one arm entangled in the rope. The old woman released a torrent of curse words at him as she struggled to free herself.

Brandon sprang toward her, snatching the handle from her hand. He drew it back to hit her but paused as another voice filled his mind.

Yes. Kill the old hag. Bring her to us. You know she deserves it.

The anger that had risen in his chest subsided as he turned toward the pier. The shapes had surrounded it, looking like a group of vultures awaiting a meal. They wanted him to hit the old woman, to kill her. They wanted him to bring her to them so they could consume her the same way they'd consumed so many others.

The way they would have consumed his mother.

Brandon gasped at the thought. His shoulders slumped as the gravity of what he'd almost done sank in. He'd almost sacrificed his own mother to the muck, and for what?

"No," he said. "No more."

The sound of a thousand shrieks swept across the yard and washed over him in a wave, blowing the hair back from his forehead.

"You dunnit now, you little shit," the old woman croaked.

Brandon watched as the old woman freed herself from the swing and stood. She was petite like Amy but looked old enough to be her mother. She took a step toward him, and a ribbon of pale moonlight illuminated her silver hair.

"No!" Brandon screamed. He gripped the wooden handle at the end and flung it toward the pier, watching as it disappeared into the darkness. He didn't see where it landed.

"Now, whatcha going to do, dummy?"

Brandon gasped as two boney hands clutched the front of his shirt. She pulled herself up against him, her face looking up at him. A scent that he didn't recognize flooded his nostrils. It was faint and pungent, foul. When his mind told him it was the smell of death, he took a step back.

He gripped the old woman by her emaciated shoulders and shoved her to the ground hard. She crumpled at his feet like a wet bath towel and began to cry.

As he looked down at the woman, his eyes fell on the pier. The shapes had moved closer. In the darkness, he couldn't tell if they were still in the muck or if they were closer. Either way, it didn't matter. He was done.

Walking backward, his eyes shifting between the old woman and the dark shapes. The quiet squelch of mud came to him as they slithered across the grass.

"What about me?" the old woman cried, stretching one arm toward him as he backed further away.

"They can have you. You probably do deserve it anyway." Brandon took a few more steps back.

"So do you, you little shit. So do you."

Brandon shook his head as he stared at the old woman, knowing she was right. He turned his back on her pleading screams.

Behind him, shadows moved in the darkness. Unseen but not unfelt in their movements. The euphoric sense of revenge that washed over him and the pleading screams of an old woman told him that the "ladies" had her.

Brandon turned in time to watch feeble fingertips dig into the grass as the old woman tried to escape her fate. She cried out for help, but Brandon only shook his head. She began to slide backward toward the muck, cursing him for not helping her. When she disappeared into the darkness, Brandon turned and ran.

Amy's head jerked up as her sister's cries filled the night. "Dammit," she complained quietly, sparing a glance out the front windows. She'd hoped her sister could at least deal with the boy. The plan could still work. Now, there would be complications, but she could work them out. At least if her sister were dead, it would save her the trouble of doing it herself.

She grabbed a beer from the fridge and opened it. After taking a long drink, she crossed the room to where Carrol lay on the floor. Curled into a fetal position, her hands clutched her midsection.

"Tell me something," Amy said, squatting next to Carrol. The hand holding the gun rested on her right thigh as she clutched the neck of the beer bottle in the other. "How did you figure all this out?"

Carrol didn't respond until Amy poured beer in her face.

"Elvey knew." Carrol drew in a deep breath, grimacing as pain exploded in her ribs. "She knew what you were up to. She described you to a tee."

"Yeah, well," Amy replied with a laugh as she used the fingers around the bottle to rake hair from her face. "I've changed a bit since I was a teenager."

Carrol pushed herself into a sitting position, her arms clutching her sore ribcage. "Not really."

"I used to have short blond hair. Barry loved it short. He said long hair got in the way when I was…well, you know." Amy laughed and took another long drink of beer.

"Elvey wrote a letter a few days before she died. She said she had all the pictures and stuff hidden in the house."

Amy nodded. "I kinda figured that crabby ass old bitch was up to something. I searched the whole place when she died. I figured there was something, but I couldn't find it."

Carrol chuckled, wincing in pain. "She outsmarted all of y'all. You, Barry, the stinking mud out there. Everyone."

"Well, I wouldn't say that just now. You're probably still going to end up out there." Amy jerked her head toward the river. "Oh, I'm sure your dummy kid will complicate things, but we'll figure it out."

"Not a chance. She was always three steps ahead of all of us. The letter that she left me only had one sentence. It said, "I've already told you where to find the proof." Carrol coughed. "At first, I didn't know what she meant, then I remembered all the letters."

"Letters?"

"Yes," Carrol said, smiling. "You see, Elvey has been warning me about this place for years. Since Barry and I were married, really. That's what she meant. I'd always noticed the peculiar way she wrote. Sometimes she'd just say something that didn't make sense."

"Well, she was a crazy old bitch."

"I thought so, too, for a long time. You see, that's why I left so suddenly. I figured that I was the main target. Y'all needed me out of the way first. I went home and got the letters. When I knew I was looking for something, it all made sense. It took a little while to put it together, but I got it. I took it all to my lawyer. We were just about to come back with the Sherriff to get Brandon when he called me."

"Lotta good all that did you." Amy drank from the beer as she stood. "You're still going to end up with mud on your face." She laughed at her own cleverness.

"Wanna bet?" Carrol rolled onto her back, sweeping her legs at Amy's feet.

Caught off guard, Amy moved to avoid them but couldn't get clear. Carrol's legs struck hers, sending her tumbling to the floor. Grunting through the pain in her side, Carrol threw herself on top of Amy, grabbing the gun from her hand. A shockwave of pain exploded in her side as Amy punched her in the ribs. Carrol rolled off Amy and onto her back, pushing herself away with her feet.

"You damned bitch," Amy growled as she stood. "I'll kill you with my bare hands if I have to."

Carrol blinked her eyes to clear her vision, but it didn't help. Between the pain and the drugs, everything was a shifting mass of blurry light. Amy's voice filled the room. She was laughing. The sound was loud and came from every direction at once.

Carrol squinted her eyes against the overhead light. When a shadow of dark, frizzy hair moved over her, creating a shadow, she pulled the trigger. The gun kicked back, and she lost her grip. The shadow above her shrieked as it moved away.

Panting, Carrol forced herself to her feet. There was no way to tell how badly she'd hurt Amy or if she'd even hit her at all, but lying on the floor only made her an easy target.

Rubbing her eyes with the heels of her hands, she surveyed the room. Amy was crumpled on the floor in front of Elvey's old recliner. Carrol approached her cautiously, but when she got there, she found the girl unconscious.

Grabbing a handful of hair, she turned Amy's face toward her, grimacing. The bullet had torn through her left cheek, taking a lot of it with it when it left. Blood flowed from the gaping wound and ran down her bare skin, soaking into the bikini top.

Carrol laid two fingers along the clean side of her neck, checking for a pulse. There was one, but it was weak. If the ambulance came soon, she'd make it, but her days as a beauty queen were over.

As Carrol sat staring at the bloodied girl that had convinced her own son to drug her so they could toss her into the muck, one thing became clear. Elvey had warned her that you could never be free once connected to the muck, and now she believed her. Barry had been away for years but still succumbed to its call. Brandon was younger and less equipped to handle it. It would pull him back, there was no doubt.

Carrol released Amy's hair, shaking her head as she stood. Someone had to do something. She had to do something to break the spell it had on her son. It had to be stopped once and for all.

Carrol Stivers stepped onto the pier and stopped. Standing on the weathered planks, it occurred to her that she'd never once stepped foot on the pier before today. She'd never been this close to the muck.

She squinted her eyes tightly to clear her vision, then looked into the darkness before her. The area around the muck was darker and heavier than the rest of the yard, and for the first time, she began to feel its pull.

Barry is the cause of all of this.

The thought was clear and concise in her mind, but it wasn't her own.

It's them who ruined your son. They deserve to pay for what they did.

It was true. Barry and Amy had planned all of this. Brandon was just their fool. Carrol smiled. "You're right," she said in a whisper. "How can I make them pay?" She took a few more cautious steps onto the pier, stopping as the shadows began to move in the darkness.

They're evil, dirty people.
Amy did dirty things with your son.
We've seen them.

Carrol shook her head as the overlapping voices, each one sounding hollow and distant, echoed through her mind. She staggered a few more steps onto the pier, her hands wrapped around her midsection.

"Who are you?" she asked.

Multiple voices answered at once. *"We are the ones."*

"If I bring them to you, will you leave my son alone? Will you free him?"

A haunting laugh drifted across the muck.

Carrol walked to the end of the pier. "I haven't done anything. What if I gave myself to you too? Would you leave Brandon alone then?"

One by one, the clumps of reeds began to rattle. The chain reaction spread from left to right until the entire muck was alive with the sound of rustling leaves.

"An innocent sacrifice to save my only child." A quiet gasp escaped her as a shadow approached the pier. The shape, as tall as her and vaguely shaped like a bowling pin, stopped just shy of the end of the pier.

Other shapes moved closer, each one reaching into her mind with their hollow voices, each one completing the other's sentence.

"Why would you do that?"
"Don't you know the heart…?"
"Within him is poisoned…."
"With wickedness and hate?"
"He is as bad as they are."
"We didn't make them do anything…."
"That they didn't want to do…."
"Because of the lust already within?"

When their voices fell silent, Carrol found herself surrounded by nine shapes, nine spirits that were all pulling at her mind. She grimaced, moaning as their fingers searched her memory, looking for something to use.

"They both betrayed your trust…."
"Your love."
"They don't deserve to live."
"You can be free of them all."
"Free."
"Free."
"Free."

"I don't want to be free of my son," Carrol said, shaking her head. The spirits were tapping into her deepest secrets, finding the weight of the burden of caring for Brandon. Their slimy fingers dug into her frustrations, the momentary lapses when she resented the constant worry, the pain of having a son with a disability.

"There are...."
"No lies here."
"We know all about you...."
"Carrol."
She shook her head violently. "You don't know me at all."
"We know what you want."
"I know that you don't. because if you did, you'd know this." She reached inside her suit jacket and produced a bottle of lighter fluid in each hand. The caps were already removed, allowing her to immediately start dousing the reeds. She moved quickly, running up and down the pier, spraying the clumps on both sides.

The reeds began to rattle and shake, filling the muck with the sound of their anger. One of them moved back, and she hurried to it, moving to the end of the pier. She leaned over the edge, spraying it until the bottle in her hand was empty. She dropped it onto the muck and wrapped both hands around the remaining one.

"This is over," she said through clenched teeth. "You'll not get my son without a fight." She put her free hand into her jacket and withdrew a zippo lighter. Flipping the top open, her thumb found the striker wheel and hit it.

The voices inside her head began to shriek as the sight of the flame drove home her intentions. The shadows began to scatter, putting distance between themselves and the pier.

"You've got nowhere to go, damned you." Carrol squirted the remaining lighter fluid onto the surface of the much and tossed the lighter in after it.

The flame landed on the mud in a spot free of the lighter fluid. She'd missed. Her heart dropped as she watched the lighter begin to sink into the dark mud.

"No," she pleaded. Dropping to her knees, she stretched out over the edge of the pier. The mud reacted beneath her, swelling into a finger that stretched toward her hand.

"No!" she screamed as tears rolled down her cheeks. She snatched her hand back just before the mud reached her and collapsed onto the pier. Sobbing, she watched as the depression around the lighter widened, pulling it downward.

"No," she cried again, realizing that she'd failed.

The mud around the lighter opened slowly, unwilling to touch the flame. The lighter slipped into a concave depression, already an inch below the surface. Dark water began to move across the surface, collecting around the hole.

Carrol shook her head, staring at the lighter. The flame danced defiantly, lighting the surface with multi-colored reflections as fluid trickled into the hole. Coming from all angles, it filled quickly until it was just below the wick.

Her body ached from the fight with Amy, and she'd spent her last bit of energy emptying two full bottles of lighter fluid into the muck. All for nothing. Unwilling to watch her final defeat, she turned her head and hid her face in the crook of her arm.

The scent of the lighter fluid was strong on her clothes and in the air, reminding her of her carelessness. Rising to her knees with a grimace, she ran both hands through her hair, clutching the back of her head as she checked on the flame. The inky water had closed in around it but hadn't extinguished it completely.

Her eyes flew wide, and she gasped as an idea came to her. Moving with urgency, she ripped the front of her blouse open, sending buttons flying. She peeled her jacket off, dropping it to the pier, then her blouse.

Wadding the blouse into a ball, she left the arm saturated with lighter fluid free to act as a fuse. Reaching out over the pier again, she ignored the churning mud beneath her. The sleeve swayed back and forth above the flame as she struggled to steady herself on the weathered boards.

Finally, just as the water closed in around the flame,

it leaped onto the sleeve, igniting it with a sudden swoosh. Rejuvenated by one last chance, Carrol stood. The muck was as still and dark as death. There was no way to know where the shapes had gone, but she'd been right earlier. They could only go so far.

She looked at the flaming blouse in her hand, then at the darkness that surrounded her. She'd have to do something soon. The flame was already close to her hand.

Her head jerked in every direction, searching the pitch darkness. Flames moved up the sleeve, already hot on her hand. She moved to the end of the pier, feeding more blouse to the flame to spare her skin. She held the flame up, searching, but found nothing.

She sighed and shook her head. She was out of time. This would be her last chance.

"Please," she prayed and tossed the flaming blouse as far into the muck as she could. The flames lit up a path across the darkness as it flew in an arc above the muck. Her heart sank as it traveled, revealing none of the shapes. The ball of fire landed in the muck.

Carrol Stivers stared wide-eyed at the flame laying atop the dark mud in shock. She'd missed again.

"Son of a—" her words were cut short as a patch of the muck erupted in flames, quickly searing the foliage that grew there. She gasped as a line of flame raced across the muck, reaching the first clump of reeds. The dry leaves erupted in a fireball, lighting up the entire pier. Carrol took a step back, looking around as a woman's agonized shriek filled the air.

Finding no one behind her, she looked back in time to see another line of fire race in a different direction, doing the same thing to another clump of reeds. The fire spread quickly after that, racing in different directions to each of the clumps of reeds. As each caught fire, her screams fed into the collective, sweeping across the land like thunder.

Carrol stood on the pier, watching each one burn. The pain and anger of each one swept through her like a wave, sapping what little energy she had left. Inundated, her vision blurred, and she became unsteady.

The idea to get off the pier, away from the mud, came to her, and she turned to leave. The toe of her shoe struck the edge of an uneven board, and she was falling but helpless to stop it. She had time to turn her face before hitting the pier hard. She watched the flames dance on the muck until the darkness closed in around her, silencing their cries.

TWENTY-FOUR

The television mounted on the hospital room wall was muted, but the footage told Carrol that the news was out. The television crew had set up in Elvey Stiver's front yard, pointing the camera at the old house. The young blonde reporter said something, then turned and pointed at the house. The camera panned in slightly, bringing the rusted screen on the porch into focus for a moment, then moved back to the reporter.

Carrol sighed. Her life was never going to be the same again. Whether it would be better or worse, she didn't know yet. When a soft knock came at the door, she switched the set off and said, "Come in."

Conrad Shaw poked his head in the door and smiled, "You decent?"

"I'm dressed, but I don't look too good. Descent might be a lot to ask under the circumstances." She smiled as he walked in with a bouquet of flowers. "It's good to see a friendly face."

"I got you these." He shrugged. "Maybe brighten the place up."

"Thanks." She accepted the flowers, stealing a quick whiff before setting them aside. "You didn't have to."

Conrad shrugged. "Did you know the custom of bringing sick people flowers was originally intended to help mask the scent of death?"

"I did not know that. No." Carrol laughed, shaking her head.

"Me either. I just learned that from a show I watched last night."

"And they say the T.V. will make us all brainless idiots."

"I know, right?" Conrad sighed. "Anyway, I checked on Brandon this morning."

Carrol's eyes flew open wide. "How is he?"

"He's fine. I got him released to your parents. I talked to them a few hours ago. He was sleeping. He's upset, but he's okay. They gave him some medicine."

"Oh, thank God. I've been worried sick. Thank you. Are they charging him with anything?"

"They haven't yet, but they probably will." He held up his hands to calm the alarm on Carrol's face. "I'm already on it, though. Short of catching an overzealous DA, I'm sure my office can plead it down to some minor stuff, given his situation. Mentally, I mean."

"That's good," she sighed, relaxing into the pillows. She hated to play up Brandon's mental status, but if it spared him jail time, she would do it. He'd been used and tricked into trying to dope her. Her son would never do that on his own. It was Amy and the dark power in the muck, and his own father who was to blame.

"Carrol, there's something else. Your mother told me he hasn't spoken a word since he got there."

Carrol rubbed her eyes with her thumb and index finger several times before pinching the bridge of her nose. "I guess that's the catch," she muttered.

"Catch?"

"Oh, nothing." She pushed the hair from her face with both hands. "That's what Mrs. Stivers told me. The waters give you something, but there's always a catch. I guess in the end, it always comes down to what you're willing to give up."

"Don't tell me you really believe all that stuff about the mud? I mean, witches and dark spirits and all that. It all seems pretty far-fetched to me."

"I guess it would to any sane person. But it's as real as any other form of evil." Carrol sighed. "Honestly, I don't know what I believe, Conrad. All I know is that I watched my son change because of that place."

"Couldn't it just have been the girl seducing him?"

"I guess anything's possible, but there was more. The place is just dark, you know. I can't explain it." She looked at him and shrugged. "Sitting here, in a normal setting, it all sounds crazy. But if you were there and saw and heard the things I did...."

Conrad's eyes narrowed as he looked at Carrol. Her hair was a mess, and her skin was pale and splotchy. The light was gone from her eyes, replaced with a tired, haggard look. "Are you going to be okay?"

"I suppose. I'm recovering from an overdose. My husband tried to have me killed. My son gave me a handful of opioids. I shot another person in the face, apparently. But other than that, I'm just peachy."

"The important thing is that you'll make it through this. In six months' time, your life will be in order, and all of this will be a bad memory."

Carrol nodded toward the television. "I saw that we made the news."

"It's a big thing. A teenage girl was shot. Attempted murder, affairs, and an old woman's disappearance. Now they're looking to tie in a neighbor who went missing lately."

Simmons, her mind told her. That was the name Brandon admitted to tossing into the muck. Legally, she couldn't be compelled to testify against her own son, and she wouldn't.

Carrol shrugged. "I never laid eyes on the old woman. To be honest, I thought Amy was lying about her being sick. I figured it was just part of the scheme to get Brandon to do what he did."

"She existed alright. She was in her fifties and had stage four ovarian cancer. Nobody has seen her in days. That was easy enough. There have been some complications in positively identifying Priscilla. She's in her fifties as well, but damned sure don't look like it."

"Some fountain of youth, huh?"

"Some something. You should have seen the fingerprint analysis guy." Conrad let out a dry chuckle.

Carrol sighed and laid back in the bed. "What about Barry?"

"He denied everything."

"Of course, he did. Leave the whore and his son to take the fall."

Conrad shrugged. "His alibi checked out rock solid, but the girl got mad and started talking. The cops aren't buying all the stuff about the mud or muck, but the other parts check out. He's in some pretty hot water. They arrested him on your claim, but they're holding him on what Amy or Priscilla said. They'll both end up doing some time, I'm sure."

"How is she?"

Conrad's eyebrows went up. "She'll live, but they say it took one hell of a surgery to put the side of her face back together. She'll live but probably won't win any beauty contests anytime soon.

"And me?"

Conrad shrugged. "I'm working on it. I think self-defense will hold up just fine. I mean, they did lure you there to kill you, they drugged you, and the girl was physically attacking you. I wouldn't worry."

Carrol's hand went to the bruise on her cheek. "So, the bad guys lose, and the good guys win?"

"Isn't that the way it's supposed to go?"

"I guess." Carrol shook her head. "I don't feel like I've won anything."

"You and Brandon were victims of an elaborate plan to get rid of you so that Barry and his teenage lover could get all the money. That didn't happen. I'd call that a win."

"Sounds more suited for Hollywood than a sleepy river community."

"Bad people do bad things everywhere, Carrol. Unfortunately, this kind of stuff happens a lot."

She nodded. "I'll testify to that."

"And you'll have to, soon enough."

Carrol let out a long sigh. She hadn't thought about the trial. "Look, I want to spare Brandon as much of the court stuff as possible."

"I will try, but he'll almost certainly have to testify. It'll be part of the plea deal. He was a victim too in many ways."

Carrol seethed through gritted teeth. "What a piece of shit coward my husband turned out to be. I mean, I figured he was cheating on me. I've suspected it for years, you know. Just little things here and there. But to use his whore to seduce his own son to get rid of me."

"Makes you wonder what their plan was for him if they'd pulled all this off."

Carrol nodded. "You know, Barry never accepted Brandon's condition. I mean, he didn't neglect him or anything. He just never got over the fact that his son wouldn't follow in his footprints."

"In many ways, he did. Unfortunately."

Carrol shrugged. Conrad was right. Brandon had fallen for the same girl as his father, albeit many years later. He'd also fallen under the spell of the muck and done some terrible things to get what he wanted. In the end, however, she'd proven stronger than Elvey and had saved her son from the spell. Of course, without her help, she'd never been able to do it.

"Anyway." Conrad opened his suit coat and pulled out an envelope. "A courier hand delivered these to the office this morning. Well, actually, there were two. The one addressed to me just had an address and a check for five hundred dollars 'for my services of rendering you to the address.' This one was to you." He handed her the sealed envelope.

"Who is it from?" she asked, tearing the letter open. "My letter and the check were signed by Amelia Nightingale. I checked it out. The bank account and the address are both real. From what I was able to find out, she's very old and very wealthy."

Carrol's brow furrowed as she read the letter. "She wants me to come to see her. She said she could help me understand better what happened." She handed Conrad the letter after she read it. "Any idea who she is?"

He shook his head. "I researched her name. There isn't much. No birth certificate or driver's license that I could find. The address is local. I checked the map. It's not very far from your place down there. I think it's on the northern bank, though."

"It sounds like she knows about the place, the stuff in the waters."

"I'm at a loss, Carrol. It's all been a fantastic ride for me. My world is very concrete, you know. I have to admit, this voodoo stuff is knocking me for a loop."

"Join the crowd." Carrol rubbed her eye with a fist. "It's very odd that she'd reach out to me now. Why not before all this crap went down? What should I do?"

"That's up to you. If you want to meet her, I can take you. You probably shouldn't go alone, given the circumstances. If you just want to be done with all this and put it behind you, I'll draft a letter respectively declining."

Carrol sighed. "No. I think I should meet her. Maybe she can offer some sort of closure, some sense of why this happened."

"Okay. It's your decision. When you're up to it, I'll send word so they're expecting us." Conrad read the letter and shook his head. "You know, I run across all sorts of stuff in my line of work. I see some bad people who did some bad things, but I think this whole deal is just rotten."

"I think that whole place is rotten to the core. It's not just muck and water and weeds. It's a quagmire of evil. It sucks you in and never lets you go."

Conrad smiled, patting her foot beneath the covers. "Well, you made it."

Carrol covered her eyes with a hand as tears began to well in them. "Maybe I did," she whispered. "But at what cost?"

TWENTY-FIVE

"Is this it?" Conrad looked at the navigation screen and then back at the narrow track that would take them off county road 47. There was no mailbox, and the weeds in the driveway had grown tall. "They don't come and go much."

"Maybe she's a recluse," Carrol offered with a shrug. "Let's try it."

Conrad shook his head, reluctant to take his Mercedes off road. "Probably going to pick up a few scratches on this trip." He turned the wheel and pulled onto the drive.

The car wound its way through the trees, steadily climbing as they went. A long way through the dark woods finally brought them to the top of a mountain and an expansive estate.

"Holy cow," Conrad said, taking in the massive house. The white painted brick glowed in the afternoon sun. "I wonder if she needs a private attorney."

"From the looks of it, I wouldn't think she needs anything." Carrol got out of the car, her eyes washing over the immaculate grounds. "This chick might be the richest person in the county."

Conran agreed, sweeping his hand toward the wide stone steps leading to a set of towering oak doors. "Shall we go in?"

As soon as they mounted the top step, one of the doors opened, and a tall, thin black man appeared. What was left of his hair clung to the sides of his head and had all but turned gray. His eyes fell on them, and he smiled.

"Mrs. Stivers?" His voice was deep and comforting. His smile welcoming.

"Yes. This is Conrad Shaw, my attorney."

"Very well. Won't you come in?" He stepped aside and ushered them into the vaulted foyer. "I trust the directions were acceptable."

"Oh yes, thank you. We found it straight away."

"Good. Good." He led them deeper into the house, walking with a slow but purposeful gait. "We don't often have visitors."

"It's a shame. Such a beautiful place."

"Thank you. It is quite enjoyable, but my Mistress prefers her privacy and seclusion. Things being what they are."

Carrol shrugged at Conrad, giving him a wide grin as if to ask, "What in the hell have we gotten into?"

"Pardon the walk, but the mistress is in the solarium. She prefers the view from there this time of day."

"I'm sure from up here, there's quite a view."

"Yes," he glanced back over his shoulder. "The view is rather expansive." He stopped at a set of double glass doors and opened them. "You may go in. You are expected. I took the liberty to provide refreshments." He nodded his head to them, then turned and walked away.

Conrad swept his hand into the room. "After you."

The solarium was a hundred feet long and thirty feet wide. The afternoon sun slipped through the glass surrounding them, lighting and warming the room to a near uncomfortable level. A jungle of plants filled the room, basking in the light and soaking up the humidity.

Conrad hooked a finger behind his tie and loosened it. He raised his eyebrows at Carrol. "Warm," he whispered.

"Please pardon an old lady her indulgences."

They both looked around but saw no one.

"As the years have added themselves to my life, I've grown accustomed to the heat and humidity. The cold of the house pains my old bones sometimes."

Conrad stepped forward, peeping around a series of topiaries that had been trimmed to vaguely resemble the human form. He looked back at Carrol and motioned her forward.

Carrol joined him and found a frail, old woman sitting in a white wicker chair, looking out the bank of windows that comprised the entire outside wall. Her gaze followed the woman's, and her mouth fell open. Just outside the windows, a half dozen giant tortoises milled about on an expansive lawn. She tapped Conrad and pointed to them.

He nodded, his eyes wide with surprise.

"Won't you join me, please?"

Carrol made her way to the chairs but didn't sit down. The view was spectacular. Beyond the lawn, the mountain fell away quickly to the river. Her eyes followed it upriver. A massive gray boulder protruded from the forest, clinging to the edge of the water. Across a narrow slough from that, the river took a sharp turn to her left. Nestled in the crook, a dark patch of earth overgrown with reeds and wild grasses clung to the riverbank. Squinting, she found the rickety pier, and a shiver ran down her spine. Whoever this woman was, she could see the whole neighborhood from here, including their house.

Carrol looked down at the woman for the first time and took a step back, bumping into Conrad.

"My apologies for the freight. My years have far exceeded yours, and they haven't been kind to me, as you can tell."

Carrol cleared her throat, gathering herself. "That's not it at all." The old woman was hunched to one side, holding one shoulder much higher than the other. The bones in her shoulder pressed against the thin, black shawl that hung about her. The ghostly white hair that hung down her back was made more pronounced by her dark complexion. When she turned to look at Carrol, she revealed a tragically wrinkled face and piercing blue-gray eyes.

Carrol forced herself to sit, but she didn't settle in. There was a witchy air to this woman that she didn't trust or like. "You sent for me."

The old woman drew in a deep breath that rattled in her chest. "I did, and I suppose you're due an explanation for my intrusion."

"A good start would be telling us who you are and how you know us." Conrad stood behind Carrol with a hand on her shoulder.

"You're the Strivers woman." She sighed and shook her head, casting her eyes across the river to the pier. "You've been wronged by the darkness as much as any of us."

"I can't argue that."

The old woman turned back to the river as she began to talk. "We came here from the old country to make a life together. That's all we wanted. A better life and to be left alone." Her voice was a raspy whisper.

"Who is 'we?'" Carrol asked.

"Me and my sisters. There were ten of us. We bought some land upriver, around the bend there." She gave a slight nod toward the river. "We worked hard and built a home. We kept to ourselves and didn't bother nobody."

Carrol nodded. Barry's mother had told her a similar story, but she didn't believe it then. She did now.

"Things were fine for a long time. We were happy together." A hint of a smile tugged at the corners of her wrinkled mouth but faded as she continued. "Then the people in the little fishing community close by started getting curious. We avoided confrontation though we didn't have to. Mother wanted it that way. But they wouldn't quit. We told them we were nuns, but after a while, even that didn't satisfy them." She rubbed the thin skin on the back of her hand. "One night, a group of men came to the house. It was the Winter Solstice. We were in the middle of a ceremony when they set on us. Peace could be had no longer."

"What happened?" Conrad asked.

"The first man busted up into the circle. He was drunk enough to be brave." She pursed her lips and shook her head. "Mother told us all to run into the house, so we did. She was very beautiful, with long raven hair and green eyes like a jewel. I guess a few of 'em took notice. Before we knew what was happening, they had her on the ground, forcing themselves on her.

Mother didn't fight them at all. They were all whooping and hollering like a pack of mad dogs. When they finished, they turned their lustful eyes to the house. Mother just got up and fixed her dress like nothing had happened. Then she knocked 'em all down with a wave of her hand. They got up, and she did it again. When they got up, one of them came up from behind her and ran a pitchfork straight through her. He wedged the handle in the ground and left her standing there, bleeding."

"My God. That's horrible."

The old woman nodded in agreement. "With Mother taken care of, they came after us, but the doors and windows were all locked. A few of 'em took sticks of wood from our own fire and put 'em to the house. There was so much smoke. The flames." She shook her head solemnly. "We all ran out, but we were trapped by the men on one side and the river on the other. They came after us, so we all jumped in the cold water."

She paused to blot her cheeks with a tissue clutched in one boney hand. "The water was so cold, and the river was running from the rains. Most of us couldn't even swim. We didn't stand a chance. I heard my sisters crying out, but I couldn't see anything. It was so dark and cold. Something bumped into me, and I grabbed it. It was a dead log, but it floated. I was scared and alone for the first time in my life. I didn't know what else to do, so I held onto that log and closed my eyes until I washed ashore.

"The next morning, I looked for my sisters but couldn't find them. I climbed this hill you're on now so I could see, then I saw them. Their bodies had washed up in the bend yonder. They were caught in some deadfall, I suppose, or maybe just in the shallows."

A coughing fit racked her body. When it was over, she spat into the tissue in her hand and looked at it, grimacing. She shook her head and wadded the napkin around the black spittle.

"I was the only one. I could see all of them, even Mother. I sat out there on a crag and watched them for days. They lay there, bloating in the sun. Nobody came to bury them. I was so afraid, so I just sat out there. For days I watched them rot, watched them get picked over by crows and other scavengers. They sank one by one and disappeared into the mud."

"Is that why the place is like it is?" Carrol asked. "because of what happened to y'all?"

The woman nodded slowly. "Nine innocent souls were laid to waste on that shoal. They were lost. They couldn't pass over because of the evil set loose on them. They were angry."

"Rightfully so," Carrol said.

"I lived in a small cave down the hill a piece for years. I watched my sisters exact their revenge on anyone who drew close enough to be ensnared. Everything that went in, every living soul added, just strengthened the anger and hatred. All the greed, lust, and jealousy made it what it is today. My sisters just started by calling men into the mud, but each black heart added more darkness. Countless numbers of sacrifices, all in the name of greed and want."

"There's a lot of bad people in the world."

The old woman nodded slowly. "That there is."

"There's also innocent ones too."

The old woman looked at Carrol. "Like your little one?"

Carrol nodded. "Like Brandon."

"He was like us, innocent. Just wanted to live life his way. But that's not what y'all let him do, is it?"

"It was my husband."

"You know, most people would blame those men for what they did, and I suppose they deserve it. But how many of those men had wives who were whispering in their ears about those women living alone in the woods? Chattering about how we dressed? Our hair? How we disturbed their delicate Christian sensibilities?" She nodded. "Those men, like most," she glanced up at Conrad, then looked at Carrol, "are simple creatures. Easily led, easily persuaded by women."

"I tried to keep my son away from that place."

"But you didn't, did you?"

Carrol sighed, defeated by the truth in the woman's words. "No."

"I can't blame no one for what's been done to them. As far as I can tell, you mothered the child well enough."

"I did my best, and I think I did pretty good."

The old woman nodded. "But he was special, wasn't he?"

"I always knew there was something about him."

"He was a precious, innocent soul until the muck in that river got a taste of him. It wanted him the most because there's so few like him anymore."

"Will he be okay? We're never coming back here. Will that help?"

"It wouldn't matter where you went. He's connected. The muck will always call him. Darkness never faded, even in the light of day."

"He can fight it, though, can't he?"

"He can fight it, but he won't win. The darkness always

wins because people want it to win. It's the desire in hearts that turns the spirit black, the lust, the greed."

"I'm not going to let that place steal my son."

"I hope you don't. I really do. But even an innocent soul, once tainted, will always want to move toward the darkness."

"You were one of them. Can't you do anything?"

The old woman drew in a breath and exhaled slowly. "I can die."

"What does that mean?" Carrol asked.

"My sisters and I are all connected. My life spirit is keeping them close. It's allowing them to stay here."

Carrol shrank as the old woman looked at her. Her eyes stared at her for a long time. She smiled when Carrol looked away, unable to hold her gaze any longer.

"See?" she asked. "You want me to die so you can have what you want."

Carrol started to protest but didn't. The old woman was right. At that moment, she wanted the old woman to die so her son would be free. She dropped her gaze to the tiled floor, unable to look at the woman.

"We're all burdened with our own humanity, child. We're all lustful, greedy, and hungry for something. For me, it was revenge for my sisters and Mother. I wanted to make everyone pay for what happened."

The old woman fell back in the chair with a tired sigh. "But see, the thing is, I shouldn't look like this. If things happened different, I'd still be young and beautiful despite being so old. Every crushed soul, every time someone went into the waters, it twisted me. But I was so angry, sad, and vengeful that I kept going. A hundred years and everything that went in that water has turned me into a monster myself." She took her time, drawing in a few ragged breaths. "You asked if you could save your son. The answer is no, but he will be spared."

"How?"

"I'm tired. The bitterness has consumed who I was. Mother never intended for us to be this way. I see that now."

She looked through the windows, her eyes following the river.

"All we ever did was commune with nature. We never hurt anyone and caused no grief or pain. One thing Mother always told us was to carry seeds in our pocket." A smile wove its way through her wrinkles. "That way, she said, we'd always have new life with us. It just so happened that we'd all been down by the river that same day collecting bullrushes and such. I guess everyone had seeds from them in their pockets. We'd done it so much that it became a habit. I guess when they washed up there and sank in the mud, those things grew."

"But they were dried out and dead."

The old woman nodded. "Nothing good can grow out of hate and violence, dear."

Carrol nodded. She wasn't wrong.

"Anyways. The equinox will be upon us in a few months. I plan to spend my time trying to find the woman I used to be. On the equinox, I will equal things out and put things back in balance."

"How?"

"I will join my sisters, and all of us will finally be free." The wrinkles on the old woman's face shifted as she smiled. "Things will be balanced, and the curse will be over. Your son will be spared if you keep him away from here until then."

"Don't you worry about that."

"It won't be easy."

"I promise you."

The old woman smiled. "I hope you're right. He is a special soul. I knew it when I first saw his aura on the pier."

Carrol wiped a tear from her cheek and watched it

disappear as she rubbed it between her fingers. "I'm sorry for what happened to you and your sisters."

"I am too. Whenever evil is wrought upon the innocent, it's a tragedy."

"I'm sorry too for what you had to endure all these years."

The old woman shrugged. "I married a poor man who loved me dearly," A smile pulled at one side of her mouth. "I made him a rich man who loved me dearly. We had a good life. He's gone now. Old age. He went peacefully in his sleep last winter."

"I'm sorry."

"There has to be an end to every season, deary. My season of bitterness is drawing to a close. It's time. Well, past time, really."

Carrol stood. "How can I ever thank you?"

"I imagine you'd hate me for what it cost you."

"I haven't lost anything that was truly mine."

The old woman nodded. "That's true. You just go home and love that child and mind him good. Don't let the world get in him and dim his glow. He's a beautiful thing in an ugly world."

Carrol let the tears roll down her cheeks. "I'm going to do my very best to do just that."

TWENTY-SIX

"What 'cha doing?" Carrol asked as she sauntered through the open door to Brandon's room.

Brandon held a fist of crayons over his head.

"Oh? What are you drawing?" She peeped over his shoulder, and her smile faded slowly. She'd gotten used to the dark pictures he drew lately. They were disheartening, but her therapist said it was his way of working through what had happened, so she accepted them without saying anything.

He always drew from left to right on the paper, finishing top to bottom in one area before he moved on. Today there were tall, black trees leaning into the picture. Dark branches curled downward like claws.

She sighed and went to the window. The oak tree in their front yard was starting to show signs that summer was winding down. Fall was right around the corner. They'd navigated the trials and the divorce with less than expected trauma. Brandon had been spared the brunt of the trial but had performed admirably where he was required to participate.

He hadn't spoken since that night in the river house, but it was okay. She'd willingly give up the speech if it meant the place's hold on him was diminished. They'd both adjusted and were moving on. It would just take time.

She sighed as she turned from the window, lost in thought as she watched him bent over his desk, his hand furiously as he colored. Things will take time, she reminded herself. Patience, Carrol. Patience.

Brandon stopped coloring suddenly and sat up. He stared at the wall in front of him for a moment, then went back to work.

Carrol's brow furrowed; her interest piqued.

Pushing off the windowsill, she moved closer to her son. He'd gone back to coloring. She inched closer, staying as quiet as possible.

Leaning in, she peered over his right shoulder. Her eyes flew open, and her jaw dropped when she saw the picture. The color scene of the picture had changed suddenly around the middle of the page. The dark, foreboding image on the left had morphed into a bright, colorful scene on the right.

She smiled as tears welled in her eyes. The smartwatch on her wrist buzzed, alerting her of a message. She looked down at it and saw the calendar notification. She tapped the icon with her finger.

Carrol gasped when the calendar page popped up on the tiny screen of her watch. Tears began to stream down her face as she stared at the page:

Tuesday, Sept. 22
AUTUMNAL EQUINOX

Carrol threw her arms around her son and hugged him. They'd made it. It was finally over. The last of them were dead, and the power in the muck would begin to fade. The grip it had on Brandon was broken.

"Welcome back."

Brandon looked up at her, his brow furrowed. As he stared into his mother's smiling face, his own softened. He smiled back at her, then turned back to his drawing, picking up a bright yellow crayon.

John Ryland lives and writes in Northport, Alabama, with his wife and two sons. His previous works include the novels *Souls Harbor* and *Shatter*, the collection of short stories entitled *Southern Gothic*, and a poetry chapbook, *The Stranger, Poems from the Chair*. You can find his other works in publications such as *Bewildering Stories, The Eldritch Journal, The Writer's Magazine, Otherwise Engaged, The Birmingham Arts Journal, Subterranean Blue*, and others, as well as the online journal *The Chamber Magazine*. His novel *The Man with No Eyes* will be released in March 2022.

When not writing or attending various sporting events for his sons, he enjoys gardening, people-watching, and wondering what makes people do the things they do.

Made in the USA
Columbia, SC
17 July 2023